DIGGING IN THE DARK
A C.T. FERGUSON CRIME NOVEL

THE C.T. FERGUSON MYSTERIES
BOOK 18

TOM FOWLER

For Lisa and Isabel, who light the dark

CHAPTER 1

"WHERE ARE you going dressed like a mommy blogger?"

I asked this question of my wife Gloria. She was a beautiful woman who owned several closets' worth of clothes which would make many reality stars blush. No matter the occasion, she had numerous outfits and shoes for each, and she looked like a million bucks in all of them. This evening, she wore an oversized sweater which might have fit me atop a pair of yoga pants. I never objected to her wearing Spandex for obvious reasons, but it was a curious look.

Gloria glanced at me in the mirror while she pulled her chestnut hair into a high ponytail. She wore barely any makeup, and while she didn't need to, this was another unusual sign. "How many mommy blogs have you read?" she asked.

"One."

"And?"

"I saw no reason to read a second."

"Whose was it?"

"A girl I knew in college," I said. "She was a year or two ahead of me and couldn't wait to be married by the end."

Gloria's hazel eyes found me in the mirror again. If we were less confident in our marriage and relationship, she might have asked the question. *Did you sleep with her?* The answer would have been yes. I majored in computer science and minored in philosophy and bed-hopping. None of it mattered now, and it hadn't for years. My wife finished her hair and turned her head to inspect it from multiple angles. A single strand out of place would require a complete redo. Gloria left it alone, apparently satisfied. "A new season of *Harbor Homicides* drops tonight," she said.

"Sounds a bit grim for one of your home renovation shows."

Gloria chuckled. "It's a true crime podcast. You ever listen to it?"

"No," I said. "I live true crime. I don't need to immerse myself in it when I'm off the clock."

"That's fair."

"Can we get back to your attire?" I asked. "I'm not complaining about the yoga pants, but you almost never wear them out anywhere."

"A bunch of us are getting together to listen," Gloria said. She adjusted the sweater and left the bedroom. We were at her house in the tony Brooklandville area of Baltimore County. Down on the main level, Gloria opened her wine cabinet and chose a bottle of red. "We're going to have food and wine. It'll be a good night."

"If *Food and Wine* magazine ever needs to expand and include murder, I'll be sure to recommend you as an editor."

She set the wine down and kissed me. "You're always looking out for me."

"I look with a little extra enthusiasm when you're in Spandex," I admitted.

"You up to anything tonight?"

"Joey and I are going to meet up at a pub. When the cat is away . . ."

"Try not to pick up any strange mice," my wife said.

"I'll direct them all to Joey. I'm a hell of a wingman."

She picked up the bottle again and kissed me goodbye. "Don't wait up." As I watched her leave, I wondered how many people would be listening to the podcast. While I'd never tuned in, I knew it was one of the more popular ones in the country and especially in the Baltimore area. The show focused on older crimes in our city and cast the police and prosecutors in a negative light.

Even this, however, could not compel me to give it a listen.

———

"I think Cliff is going to be a no-show."

Joey chugged a large glass of beer. He looked around the room, and I did, too. We'd originally planned to go to the James Joyce Irish Pub, changed our plans when Cliff wanted to come, and now we sat in a mostly nameless Fells Point bar by ourselves. "What's his excuse?" I asked.

"Something about staying in with his wife." He shrugged his large shoulders. Joey was a black Sicilian of good humor and better appetite. I'd known him for ages, and he'd always been heavy. The weight hid a surprising amount of athleticism. I'd seen more than one frat bro underestimate Joey and end up flat on his back a moment later. "They're going to watch some murder show."

"You mean *Harbor Homicides*?"

"Yeah," Joey confirmed.

"It's a true crime podcast. Gloria is hanging out with a

bunch of her friends and listening tonight. The first two episodes are dropping."

"'Dropping.'" Joey chuckled. "Listen to you. You a junkie for this shit, too?"

I scoffed and gave him the same answer I did Gloria. "I can't imagine listening to one. Having checked the cops' work and found it lacking more than once, I don't want to hear some amateur with a murder fetish stumble through and get a lot wrong."

"Pool table's open," Joey said. We carried our beers over, setting them on a small table nearby. Joey fed quarters into the side while I chose a cue stick. In college, I loved using a red metal model someone left in the student union building. Here, I selected the one which bore the fewest pockmarks. You never knew when you'd need to use a cue as a weapon.

Joey racked the balls, and I waved a hand to tell him he could break. He'd never been very good at billiards, so I wasn't worried about him going on a run without me getting a shot. Joey placed the cue ball right of center behind the line, drew the stick back, and a loud clattering rang out when the balls collided. A colorful frenetic mess played out on the green felt, and a few seconds later, the 13 rolled into a corner pocket. "Looks like I got stripes," Joey said.

"When did you get mediocre at this game?"

"Maybe I was sandbagging in college."

I snorted as Joey walked around the table looking for his next shot. Two women watched us from the bar. I placed both in their late twenties, making them a little younger than Joey and me—he was thirty-five, and I would join him in a couple months. They were dressed like they wanted men to notice them. Mission accomplished. The brunette eyed me while her blonde friend sized Joey up just in time for him to miss the eleven in the side pocket.

"The pair at the bar are checking us out," I said as I surveyed the solid and striped carnage. Lacking a great shot, I called the five in the corner. It rolled in, but the cue followed more than I wanted, and now I lacked even a so-so option. Joey looked their way and smiled, causing the women to glance at each other and giggle like college freshmen. I tried the two in the side but didn't have a good angle, though I managed not to leave Joey a great look at anything.

"Christ," he muttered after checking out the suboptimal angles on a few potential shots. "When did *you* get mediocre at this game?"

"Grad school." With a little more time on my hands, I managed to learn I didn't need to hit the ball a hundred miles an hour every time. I'd always been good at math and geometry, so I used those to my advantage on bank shots. I'd never win a tournament or anything—and I carried a fair bit of rust into the bar tonight—but I did all right.

Joey whacked the cue ball, unleashing more chaos on the felt. Near the end, the twelve slowly rolled toward him and dropped into the pocket. "I'll take it."

"You didn't call it," I pointed out.

"We ain't in a league."

"All right. I didn't know we were playing Pennsylvania Avenue pool . . . but okay."

Joey's next attempt came for naught, and he left me a good look at the four. I went on a small run, sinking three in a row before petering out. "They're still looking at us," Joey said.

"Probably at me," I said.

Now it was Joey's turn to snort. "Whatever, stud. You're married."

"To the brunette's crushing disappointment, no doubt."

"It's all good. The blonde is a little prettier anyway."

"Go talk to them," I encouraged. "They've both eye-fucked you enough. Might as well see if one's interested in the real thing."

Joey downed the rest of his beer. Probably an infusion of liquid courage. "Maybe I will." He paused and frowned. "What if they're working girls?"

"In a joint like this?" I shook my head. "At a nicer place closer to the harbor or downtown, maybe. Not here."

His head bobbed. "Makes sense."

"Need a handsome but unavailable wingman?"

"I'll manage," he said, and he headed toward the bar. Both women greeted him with smiles. I couldn't hear the conversation, but it seemed to be going well. As Joey bought drinks for the three of them, I practiced my sleuthing skills by observing another table of women in short skirts and low-cut tops. They didn't appear to be carrying any concealed weapons. One can never be too vigilant.

After about ten minutes, I figured I would finish out the game, trying to go after the remaining balls in order and finishing with number eight. Some required more than one attempt, but I managed to sink them all. By this point, Joey had his arm around the blonde's waist. The brunette looked in my direction, and I held up my left hand to show her my platinum wedding band. A small smile played on her lips, and she raised her glass in my direction. I returned the favor and polished off my beer. As I headed toward the door, I gave Joey a nod.

———

I drove home from the bar and caught up on a science fiction series I watched by myself. Still no word from Gloria. I imagined the episodes were over by now, and she and her friends drank wine and talked about what they'd heard. Her red rocket-like Mercedes AMG coupe remained in the garage, so she'd had the good sense to take an Uber.

I got in bed just after eleven and tried in vain to avoid doomscrolling. A text from my assistant T.J. interrupted my reading. She rarely reached out at an hour like this unless it were something important.

> You up, boss?

> If I weren't, I'd be annoyed at your text.
> What's going on?

> I think I have a new case we can work tomorrow.

> Our workload is finally manageable again.
> Why add to it?

> I really think we should.

> We only have our intern one day a week now.

> You could always hire another investigator.

> The eyeroll emoji is insufficient right now.

> Can we at least talk about it tomorrow?

> Sure.

I let out an annoyed sigh and went back to my reading. A quiet chirp came from the house alarm, telling me a door opened somewhere. Eventually, a set of quiet footsteps moved through the lower level and approached the stairs. "Hey, handsome," Gloria called out.

"Hey, beautiful."

She appeared in the doorway a moment later, a cockeyed grin splayed on her face. Every time I saw her, the blood rushed through my veins a little faster. "How was the pub?"

"All right," I said. "Joey was there. One of our friends from college no-showed. I think he stayed in to listen to the podcast like you did."

"A sensible man," my wife said. "You pick up any loose women?"

"No, but I think Joey might have."

Gloria smiled and nodded. "Good for him."

"How was the podcast?"

"Interesting." She walked in and sat on the bed. "Two episodes dropped. Each was about an hour. Then, we had to stay and talk about them over wine."

"What's it about this season?"

"I think it's going to be different. Normally, Naomi . . . she's the host . . . has the whole investigation done. This time, she said it's evolving. Kind of a new situation. She said there might be delays between episodes as she has to look into things."

I rolled my eyes. "She's probably saying those things to drum up interest," Gloria frowned, but I continued. "Think about it. This Naomi might figure some things out, but she's also monetized her podcast. It's a business for her. There's a balance between investigating a case and getting downloads, sponsorships, and all."

Gloria shook her head. "I don't think she's doing this for the money."

"She's an idiot, then."

"She's the host of a popular national podcast. She must be doing something right."

"What's the case?" I wanted to know.

"A girl who got murdered in the city. There aren't a ton of details at the moment, but I think she was a hooker who got out of the life and went straight." I almost smiled at Gloria using terms she no doubt picked up from me. I wondered if this explained T.J.'s interest. My assistant probably saw something of herself in this season's victim. My face must have given something away because Gloria asked, "What?"

"T.J. was telling me about a case she wanted us to take on," I said. "Maybe it's this one."

"Probably hits pretty close to home for her."

"No doubt," I said. "I really don't need a bunch of publicity again. The serial killer back in the winter was enough."

"You'll be up to your neck in cases."

"And reporters. Pass." When I first started working as a PI, my parents' foundation funded my cases, and whoring myself out to the press was a necessary evil. Since I'd been on a more traditional business model for the last four years, I preferred keeping the press at arm's length most of the time.

"You have much to drink while you were out?" Gloria asked.

"Two beers."

"I think I had too much wine." She rolled over and situated herself atop me. "Pretty sure I'm tipsy."

"A lesser man might take advantage of the situation."

"Well . . . we can't have that, can we?"

She leaned down, gave me a Merlot-infused kiss, and I reveled in spending some time as a lesser man.

CHAPTER 2

A MORNING RUN in Brooklandville was a much different animal than heading out in Federal Hill.

Instead of the mean streets of Baltimore, my shoes pounded the posh pavements of Gloria's swanky neighborhood. Instead of a view across the harbor from Federal Hill Park, I saw an endless parade of manicured hedges and shrubs. It was a suburban paradise for those who could afford it, but I'd always been a city boy at heart. I missed the sights, sounds, and smells of Baltimore waking up and starting another day.

By the time I got back, Gloria was already awake. I showered, and she decided to join me, so we both took longer than we needed to. After throwing some clothes on, I headed downstairs to make breakfast. If I wanted to get to my office around nine—"around" often did some heavy lifting with respect to my arrival times—I would need to leave soon. I quickly assembled some sausage and egg breakfast sandwiches on toast, handing a foil-wrapped package to my wife. She smiled and accepted it. "Did we talk about the podcast last night?"

"A little," I said as I filled each of our to-go coffee cups.

"I think it'll be a good season. You should give it a try."

I shook my head. "Already too much true crime in my line of work."

"Maybe you and Naomi could team up," Gloria suggested, speaking as if the host of *Harbor Homicides* were an old friend from high school.

To avoid sounding cross before we each left, I said, "Maybe. You're not working from home today?" Her outfit was the main giveaway. When she worked from home—either her house or mine—Gloria usually wore a professional shirt or top over something like shorts or yoga pants. Business up top, party down below. When she ventured out, she wore a dress, shirt and skirt, or pantsuit.

"Looking at a new site," she said. "Could be a recurring event. Once a year . . . maybe twice."

I offered an appreciative nod. Gloria had built a fundraising company from scratch, going from occasional involvement five or six years ago to getting her firm up and running about two years prior. She'd already been featured in the *Baltimore Sun*, and more writeups were sure to follow. "Sounds great."

We kissed goodbye. Her AMG coupe roared to life. My Audi S4 made a more muted but still satisfying noise when its V6 turned over. As an owner of the car's previous generation, I enjoyed a rare model which still came with a manual transmission. Looking at my phone for music to accompany my morning drive, I stared at the podcast app. Though I'd never listened, the popular *Harbor Homicides* showed a new season.

"Why the hell not?" I said to the empty interior as I tapped on the icon.

———

A sound effect like waves lapping onto a beach yielded to midtempo elevator music. If the host had monetized her podcast, she should have been able to afford something better. Thirty seconds in, and we were already off to a subpar start. "Welcome to *Harbor Homicides*," a pleasing female voice said. "I'm your host, Naomi Chambers. Eight years ago, in the early hours of March twelfth, the body of thirty-two-year-old Alyssa Winters was discovered in room one-fourteen of the Water View Motel, a budget establishment on the outskirts of downtown Baltimore.

"The room told a familiar story to investigators . . . drug paraphernalia on the nightstand, a half-empty bottle of vodka, and the deceased wearing clothing typically associated with sex work. The narrative wrote itself. A former prostitute who'd fallen back into old habits. A drug overdose that turned fatal. A john who fled the scene and was never heard from again. A sad but ultimately unsurprising end to a troubled life.

"Within three weeks, Baltimore Police arrested Darrell Wilson, a man with prior drug convictions who witnesses placed at or near the motel that night. Case closed." More music played, and if it were possible for a tune to sound inquisitive or even skeptical, the one Naomi chose did.

"But what if that entire narrative was carefully constructed? What if Alyssa Winters wasn't just another statistic but a woman who had uncovered something dangerous enough to get her killed?" Naomi paused, building suspense. It worked. As I sat at a red light a few minutes from the office, I wanted to hear more.

"For the next seven episodes . . . maybe more if I need to go beyond eight . . . I'm going to take you deep into the life and death of Alyssa Winters and the disturbing questions surrounding her murder. Because make no mistake . . . Alyssa

Winters was murdered. The official cause of death was strangulation, not overdose, though that detail was oddly minimized in media coverage.

"Let's start with who Alyssa really was. By all accounts, Alyssa had successfully left sex work behind at least three years before her death. After escaping an abusive pimp, she had not only rebuilt her life but dedicated herself to helping others do the same. She founded a small nonprofit based in Annapolis called Second Tide that helped women exit sex trafficking and find stable housing and employment."

I thought this sounded a lot like my friend Melinda Davenport. A few years ago—not long after Alyssa made her major change—I got Melinda off the streets, where she worked as Ruby, and she underwent a similar transformation. Melinda now ran the Nightlight Foundation dedicated to helping girls who felt as trapped as she once did. My assistant was its first such graduate. I wondered if either T.J. or Melinda knew Alyssa. A different woman's voice spoke next, probably a clip from an interview.

"Alyssa saved my life. She knew exactly what we were going through because she'd lived it. Been through the worst of it, y'know? She wouldn't take no for an answer when it came to helping girls like us."

Naomi resumed her narrative. I was two blocks from the office and would need to drive around because I wanted to hear how the episode ended before talking to T.J. "Alyssa had secured grant funding. She had an office in downtown Annapolis. She had testified before state legislators about human trafficking. She had been clean for over three years, confirmed by regular drug testing required by her probation, which had ended a full year before her death. So why was a woman who had transformed her life found dead in a motel room staged to look like she had relapsed?" The music swelled with urgency.

"The Baltimore Police Department, from officers to detectives, and up to the lieutenant who ultimately signed off on everything, quickly focused their investigation on Darrell Wilson."

"Shit," I muttered as I turned past the office. Even without knowing any of the names involved, this case touched all levels of the BPD. The cops would insist they got things right—after all, a lieutenant approved the investigation. Now, I definitely wanted no part of this mess.

"Witness statements placed Wilson near the motel," Naomi continued. "His prior drug convictions made him an easy target. The case moved with unusual speed through the system. But my investigation has uncovered troubling inconsistencies.

"First, the timeline. Security footage from a gas station two miles from the motel shows Wilson purchasing cigarettes at eleven-forty-two PM, when other witnesses claimed he was already at the motel with Alyssa. Second, multiple witnesses from Alyssa's nonprofit reported that she had been acting nervous in the weeks before her death. She told one colleague she was 'sitting on a bombshell' that could 'bring down powerful people.' Third, and perhaps most disturbing, key evidence appears to have been overlooked or actively dismissed during the original investigation.

"I have obtained portions of Alyssa's journal through a confidential source. In them, she makes repeated references to what she calls 'harbor parties.' I don't know exactly what those were yet, but I will. I'm sure you're imagining some possibilities. I did, too. We know Alyssa was a prostitute in her past, and the term 'party' in that trade tends to mean sex. The harbor introduces more possibilities, and none of them are good."

My stomach turned as Naomi kept the sordid tale going. "Alyssa made more references to these parties." The music intensified briefly before softening again. "In the weeks before her death, Alyssa confided in a friend that she had photographic evidence that would 'end careers' and 'maybe finally get justice for these girls.' This meant powerful people must have been involved. Why else would she be so nervous before her death. What else could the 'bombshell' mean? It's all tied to what she'd worked on compiling.

"That evidence was never found. Her apartment had been thoroughly searched before police arrived, according to the building manager who discovered her door ajar the morning after her murder. The drug paraphernalia in the motel room? No fingerprints. Not even Alyssa's. None found in her home, either, by the way. The alcohol in her system? Alyssa was allergic to alcohol according to her medical records and multiple people who'd known her for years . . . a fact never mentioned in the police report. The clothing she was found in? Two sizes too large, according to the medical examiner's measurements.

"Someone wanted Alyssa Winters silenced, and they wanted her credibility destroyed in the process. Over the course of this season, we'll follow Alyssa's final months as she built her case against . . . we don't know what or who, unfortunately. I don't want to speculate, so once I know more, you will, too. We'll examine how the police investigation was potentially compromised from the start. We'll hear from witnesses who were never called to testify." After driving around the block twice, I pulled into the lot to listen to the rest, easing the S4 to a stop next to T.J.'s gray Mustang, a vehicle she'd recently bought used.

"And we'll ask the crucial question: If Darrell Wilson didn't kill Alyssa Winters, who did? And why was there such a rush to close this case? Eight years is a long time for justice to be delayed. It's even longer for an innocent man to sit in prison. But it's not too late for the truth. Alyssa Winters dedicated her life to saving others. It's time someone fought to save her legacy. I'm Naomi Chambers . . . and this is the fourth season of *Harbor Homicides.*"

"Jesus," I said as I killed the engine. Part of me understood why Gloria and her friends liked this show so much, and why it had earned its national popularity. I didn't need to be a regular listener, but on some level, I got it. I also got why T.J. might want us to involve ourselves. I wasn't looking forward to the inevitable conversation with my assistant as I climbed out of the car.

———

"You're late," T.J. said as I let the heavy door close behind me.

"I have a good excuse."

She wrinkled her nose. "Morning sex with Gloria again?"

"Okay, a different good excuse this time," I said.

I set my bag and now-empty travel mug on my desk. T.J. crossed her arms and leaned back in her chair. She was twenty-two, tall, blonde, pretty, and smart. Every day, I wondered when she'd find a better job, but she seemed genuinely happy to do what she did, and I wanted to avoid going back to the days when I didn't have an assistant. "Let's hear it."

"You first. What did you want to tell me?" I headed to the table where we'd set up a small kitchenette. A mini-fridge squatted under it, and a microwave and coffee maker sat on its wooden veneer surface. It was frat house chic, but it worked in the space we had. We occupied the second floor above the administrative area of a car repair shop in Fells Point. Thanks to recent renovations, we'd gained two feet along the back wall. The rent went up in proportion, but the extra square footage made the space feel a little more open. I filled my mug with fresh java and carried it back to my desk.

"The podcast," T.J, said once I'd taken my seat. "*Harbor Homicides.*"

"You been talking to Gloria?"

"No . . . why?"

"She went to a friend's house for the premiere last night," I said. "They had a listening party and discussion over food and wine. Mostly wine."

"I listened, too."

"I'm surprised."

"Why?" T.J. wondered.

"I've never bothered with these podcasts because true crime has basically been my life for seven years. I don't need to hear some amateur stepping through an investigation while trying to avoid the landmines."

Her brows furrowed, and she nodded, apparently accepting my reasoning. "This season is different. It hits kinda close to home."

"I understand," I said.

"You do?"

"It's the reason I was late. Gloria was talking about the damn thing last night and this morning, you were dropping hints, there was a lot of overlap there . . . I finally bit the bullet and listened to the first episode."

T.J, smiled. "What did you think?"

"It was oddly compelling. I didn't like the elevator music at first, but the rest of her choices and cues were really good. I can see how this season's topic is of particular interest to you."

"I was wondering if we could get involved," T.J. said. "You heard Naomi." Like Gloria, T.J, referred to the host as if they'd been friends for years. This overfamiliarity was an odd part of the culture I didn't think I could ever adopt.

"I did."

"And?"

"And she can hire us if she needs us," I said. "Considering the host has a few seasons under her belt already, I can't imagine she's running out to local PIs all the time."

"Maybe she will this time," my assistant said. Her tone carried a degree of certainty I didn't like. She tried a sweet smile. "You never know."

I had the distinct feeling T.J. did in fact know something.

CHAPTER 3

WE'D both gotten lucky picking cases recently.

Last winter, a serial killer terrorized pretty women, managing to kill three while leaving no trace of his presence. T.J. wanted us to work on it early. I told her someone needed to hire us, and the first victim's family did. More recently, I'd been out for a run when an explosion rocked Federal Hill. A few more followed, and thanks to getting involved so early, I wanted to take the case. This time, I needed to remind myself of how the agency worked, and fortune smiled upon us again when another family asked us to investigate.

Now, I thought T.J. burned to work this one. I sympathized. "We can't just look into whatever we want," I reminded her.

"I know." She put on a voice where she tried to sound like me but came up far short of imitating my dulcet tones. "Someone needs to hire us to investigate. I'm a stodgy rule-follower when I want to be."

"I'm not stodgy," I said. "I prefer to think of it as selectively pedantic."

"You select it pretty often," T.J. pointed out.

"There are times I have to. I don't mind doing some *pro*

bono work, but for the most part, someone has to come in and hire us. They need to sign the contract you developed."

"And agree to the rate schedule I refined. Where would you be without me?"

"Here in the office not arguing about some true crime podcast," I said.

"You're not just arguing with me, though, are you?" T.J. tugged at her ponytail, redoing the scrunchie holding it together. "Gloria talked to you, too."

"She did," I admitted even though I had a good idea where this was going.

"Did she want you to look into this?"

I shook my head. "I think she was too tipsy to put in a request."

"Well, if you didn't hear it from her . . ." T.J. took out her phone and dialed a number. She placed the call on speaker as the sound of ringing filled the space.

"Hello?" Melinda Davenport said.

"Hi," T.J. replied in a sing-song voice which filled the office. "We were just talking about the podcast."

"Do you listen to things like this, C.T.?"

"Not normally," I said, "but the two women I see most often were both going on about it, so I gave it a try. I listened to the premiere episode this morning."

"What did you think?" Melinda wanted to know. She modulated her tone so I could tell she was interested in my thoughts without pressing me for them. It was a subtlety my assistant hadn't yet mastered.

"I understand how it hits close to home for you and T.J."

"But?"

"We don't just go off and investigate whatever case we

want. Legally, we're supposed to be hired by someone and do the work on their behalf."

"So you need a client," Melinda said. Now, her tone carried the definite hint of a setup I'd wandered into.

"Yes," I said, internally wincing for what might follow.

"You're in luck, then," T.J. said. "While you were in the parking lot listening to the episode, Melinda and I reached out to Naomi. She's already said this season might be slower in terms of how quickly the episodes drop because there's a lot to comb through and try to get right. We made the case that a detective agency which has been in the news a lot recently could help her out."

I rubbed my temples and wondered when a business with my name on it fell out of my control. "In exchange for what?"

"She'll pay us. The individual rate, not the corporate one."

"She's also agreed to credit your agency on her show," Melinda added. "It'll be a lot of publicity."

"Just what we need," I groused.

"I told you he was stodgy," T.J. said.

I didn't object because I knew it would play right into her comment. Instead, I went with, "When is she coming?"

"This afternoon," my assistant said.

"She's made sure her publicist is also—" Melinda started.

"No," I broke in. "We'll meet with her and her alone." T.J. crossed her arms. "I'll talk to her about her investigation because it means so much to the two of you. I'm not dealing with a spin doctor, though. How this case affects her downloads, Q score, or other bullshit isn't my problem to solve."

"She always brings her publicist to interviews," T.J. said.

"This isn't an interview. We're not reporters. She comes alone or not at all."

Melinda sighed over the speaker. "All right."

"Can I call you stodgy now?" T.J. wondered.

"I'll allow it," I said.

———

I needed to review relevant details before Naomi arrived.

T.J. wanted to help. I told her the best way she could was to pick up lunch, and then she could look over things with me when she got back. She grumbled about it, but at the appointed hour, she left without a complaint but with a threat to spit in my fries. I chalked it up as the cost of being stodgy.

Wherever the political ramifications of Alyssa Winters' murder played out, her body was discovered in Baltimore, which gave our local police jurisdiction for investigating the crime. During my first case, my cousin Rich—now a homicide lieutenant but then a uniformed sergeant—committed the cardinal sin of leaving me alone at his computer. Within a minute, I had the data I needed, and ever since, I've been able to pass off one of my virtual machines as an official BPD resource. The cops didn't always share case files with people in my profession willingly. All I did was cut out the middleman.

Alyssa Winters died far too young at only 32. It didn't take me long to see this would be a shitshow. The presence of drug paraphernalia, a bottle of booze, and a victim dressed like a sex worker led police to the obvious conclusion. Notes confirmed they'd checked out Alyssa's past and figured she'd relapsed into both drugs and turning tricks. Without being able to contact a next of kin, the BPD and the medical examiner decided against an autopsy. They had their answer about cause of death, and the only remaining factor was determining if anyone had been responsible. So far, Naomi's investigation had been accurate.

Even when the ME's regular exam concluded Alyssa died

of strangulation rather than anything related to what was on the nightstand, the order of no autopsy remained. A hooker went back to her old ways, celebrated with drugs and pills, and someone strangled her to cap off the evening. The same exam revealed no sexual contact at all. The fact no one ordered an autopsy in the face of all these reasons to do it angered me. I clenched and unclenched my hand into fists before continuing to scroll.

T.J. returned with chicken pitas and fries from a nearby Greek restaurant. I checked my food for loogies and found none. "I didn't spit in it," she confirmed.

"I should hope not. Me not wanting someone's publicist here is perfectly reasonable."

"Yeah. I decided you had a good point on the drive over."

"I'm checking out the case file," I said. "Not too far into it. Pull up your chair."

T.J. wheeled her chair close. I had the largest desk in the room, but both of us spreading out to eat strained the space. As I unwrapped my sandwich, I noticed it had a lot more onions crammed inside the pita than T.J.'s did. Perhaps pungent breath would be the price I paid for my prior stodginess. I scrolled back to the top and let her catch up as I ate.

"No autopsy?" she said. "What bullshit."

"I agree. Her death was way too suspicious. Even if you don't think someone staged the scene to tell a story, she was murdered. Anyone who died by force should get a full autopsy."

"I thought they were supposed to."

I shrugged. "Maybe. I confess I'm not up on the latest edition of the police handbook."

"You haven't read it yet?"

"I'm waiting for the movie."

T.J. munched a fry and frowned. "The podcast mentions Alyssa knew a lot, and we can presume her knowledge could bring down some powerful people. You think one of them threw his weight around and convinced the cops to ignore procedure?"

"It's possible." We kept reading. The rest of the investigation seemed fine if cursory. Darrell Wilson landed on their radar quickly, though the exact means of putting him into the suspect pool were missing. This made me wonder if the same mover and shaker who benefitted from Alyssa's death also provided a fall guy. Darrell Wilson's checkered past—including his prior solicitation of women like Alyssa—and the testimony of an eyewitness ensured the case continued building. Naomi mentioned footage of Wilson at a gas station miles away around the time of the murder. The file made no mention of it. I didn't even know if police were aware of it. Eight years ago was recent enough for security cameras to be part of a proper investigation.

"Seems like she picked a good case," T.J. said.

"There are definitely some holes and inconsistencies," I agreed.

We read to the end. A few officers and detectives' names appeared for their contribution. Two names drew my eyes. The lead investigator: Sergeant Richard Ferguson—my cousin. The lieutenant who signed off on the whole matter: Leon Sharpe, who got a promotion to captain soon afterward.

"Shit," I muttered.

"Yeah," T.J. said. "This one is going to suck in every conceivable way."

CHAPTER 4

"MIGHT AS WELL KEEP the suckitude going," I said, picking up my phone.

"You're going to call Rich?"

"The BPD's investigation is going to come out eventually." I shrugged. "If he really was the lead on it, I think he'd rather talk to us than Naomi or get hounded by the press."

"I doubt he'll tell you very much," she said. I agreed, but I needed to make the effort anyway. While T.J. chomped on her sandwich, I called Rich's cell. He picked up, and I put the call on speaker.

"To what do I owe the pleasure?" he said.

"I'm not sure this is going to be a pleasurable call."

"What else is new today?" He sighed, and it sounded like a snake hissed on my desk. "All right, lay it on me."

"Remember a case from eight years ago? The vic's name was Alyssa Winters."

"Working girl found in a no-tell motel room?"

"*Former* working girl," T.J. said. "She'd been out of the life and clean for three years."

"We didn't find much evidence of her being clean in the room," Rich pointed out.

"Because no one in history has staged a crime scene to try and trick the police." T.J.'s face was going red as she talked. I moved my hands up and down in an effort to get her to dial it back. She pursed her lips but offered a single nod.

"We think of these things, too, you know," my cousin said. "I was still a sergeant at the time. Wouldn't really start working homicides exclusively for another year. Back then, I was on loan to the squad here and there because Captain Sharpe . . . he was Lieutenant Sharpe then . . . saw potential in me. This was the first messy one I handled."

"So you investigated Alyssa's murder?" I said.

"I wasn't the only one, obviously, but yes. My name is in the report."

"There was no autopsy," I pointed out while inwardly cursing. If Rich and the cops got this one wrong—and Naomi sniffing around gave the possibility decent odds—I didn't want the backdraft to consume him.

"True. I thought we needed one for all suspicious deaths, but a couple days in, the ME said there wouldn't be one. No known family to give the results to, pretty obvious circumstances." I could practically hear him shrugging at his desk. "I rolled with it."

"It's irregular, though."

"Yes," he admitted.

"Do you remember the doctor involved?" I said.

"Not offhand, but I'm pretty sure he left a few years back."

"Convenient," T.J. muttered.

Rich didn't take the bait, so I pressed on. "You think Sharpe might have asked to skip the full exam?"

"I don't see why."

"He's not exactly known for being a strict rule follower."

"He wasn't then, either," Rich said. "If he exerted any influence there, I don't know anything about it."

"Let's talk about the guy you arrested, then."

"Hang on. Why are you two grilling me over an eight-year-old matter we put to bed within a few days?"

"You ever hear of *Harbor Homicides*?" I asked.

Rich snorted. "I *live* harbor homicides every goddamn day of the week. Am I supposed to know what you mean?"

"It's a true crime podcast," T.J. said.

"Christ Almighty."

"It's popular. People all over the country listen to it. Last night, the first two episodes came out, and the focus for this season is the Alyssa Winters murder."

"Great," Rich said, and enough sarcasm dripped from his voice to wet the floor in his office.

"I figured you'd rather talk to us than a podcaster," I offered.

"True, but I would just punt her questions to the public relations folks. Look, nothing jumps out at me. I think it was a good investigation. We had a suspect, followed the evidence, arrested him, and he's in jail for the rest of his life. Put a check mark in the box for the good guys."

"I guess we'll see," T.J. said. Before I could warn Rich we were about to meet with the podcaster in question, he broke the connection. "That went well."

"I suppose it could have gone worse," I said.

"You believe him?"

"I believe he thinks he did things right."

"Is looking into one of his old cases going to be a problem?"

I spread my hands. "Not for us."

———

About a half-hour after Rich hung up on us, footsteps rang on metal rungs.

The steps were set just off the main entrance to the shop. Walking through the primary door and heading right brought you to the staircase. It made us impossible to sneak up on. Thanks to a few goons walking in and trying to intimidate us in the past, we keep the door locked and monitor who approaches via security camera. I recently installed an electronic lock any of us could open from our computers, and T.J. buzzed our potential new client in.

Naomi Chambers stood about five-five. Long blonde hair spilled down her back. She had a classic hourglass figure, and her sweater worked extra hard to keep her neckline modest while still extending past the waist of her jeans. Naomi wore large oval glasses. In high school and college, my friends and I would have called her "librarian hot." I'd expected someone older and frumpier.

T.J. introduced herself as a fan of the podcast, and then Naomi and I shook hands. She had a strong grip and showed a ready smile. "Nice to meet you," she said. Her voice worked well as a media host. "Thanks for meeting with me today."

"Sure," I said. She took one of my guest seats, and T.J. wheeled her more comfortable chair into the space. If we ever got the carpet replaced, she might need a new tactic.

"This is an unusual inquiry for me," Naomi began without waiting to be prompted. "I normally have everything I need before I even start recording the first episode. In the past, I've covered older cases. Colder, if you prefer. You'd think something newer would get more people to talk, but it's been the opposite."

"Why do you think that is?" T.J. asked. I didn't plan to pursue this line of inquiry. Naomi was already here and willing to hire us.

"My guess is someone is threatened. I don't know who yet. There are rumors about most aspects of Alyssa's murder."

"What do you have so far?" I said.

Naomi chuckled. "Another episode to record and not enough material for it. I keep running into walls. My hope is you can get over or around them."

"What about FOIA requests?" Journalists and even private citizens used the Freedom of Information Act to get the answers they sought from government agencies reluctant to part with them. There were limits, however.

"Denied," she said. "Every time. If anything, they've gotten creative at coming up with reasons."

"They can't just keep telling you no," T.J. protested.

"I wish you were right."

"We can't necessarily get everything," I said. "Our office has a good relationship with the BPD. If we need to get info from Annapolis, though, no guarantees. Cops love not sharing with private eyes. It might be their favorite thing to do."

"I think you'll be able to uncover more than I can," Naomi said. A small smile played on her lips. "I've heard that you . . . don't always use conventional methods."

"I don't think clients come to people like me looking for the conventional." Naomi nodded. T.J. seemed content. An elephant remained in the room, however, and I needed to get it out in the open. "Let's talk coverage. Presuming we're able to get actionable information, what are you going to do with it?"

Naomi arched a brow. "Present it to my listeners."

"Obviously. My question is how?"

"Have you listened to my show, Mister Ferguson?"

"Call me C.T. Before today, no." Now, her brows knitted. "It's nothing personal. Investigating crimes is what I do. When I'm off the clock, I'd rather do literally anything else."

"I think I present events and arguments fairly," Naomi said. "You could probably say I'm biased toward the victims. The police would . . . and have. Something tells me you are, too, though."

"We want to see everyone get justice," T.J. said.

"We do," I added, "but only one of us in this room is concerned about downloads, views, subscribers, and advertisers."

"That's not fair," Naomi protested.

"It's very fair. This is serious. A woman was murdered, and there's a chance the wrong man paid for the crime. It means the real killer is still out there. I know your show needs to entertain people as well as intrigue them. I guess I want to know how you balance it."

"As well as I can. In an ideal world, I wouldn't need to care about any of the things you mentioned. This is how I pay my bills. I take all my investigations seriously. Anyone who presents this material to the public needs to think about entertainment. If *Dateline* were just a recount of murder details for sixty minutes, no one would watch it."

"I'm not sure anyone does watch it."

"You get my point, though. Entertainment has to be a part of it. People will tune in to anything if it's compelling enough."

"True. Millions of folks watch others play video games."

"Christ, you sound old," T.J. said.

She had a point, so I steered us back to the topic at hand. Before I could say two words, Naomi broke in. "Look, I'll play it fair. My focus will be on Alyssa and telling her story. It's what my listeners have come to expect. Entertainment means more interest in the case, which can put more pressure on police departments, cities, and mayors. It's not all about monetization."

I bobbed my head. "Fair enough. There's one more thing. If we do this, I don't want to hear you mention someone T.J. and I talked to or how we obtained a particular piece of information."

"I protect sources and methods."

"No offense," I said, knowing my next words would likely offend Naomi, "but most people who make the claim have decades of institutional history standing behind them. You're not a journalist."

"I'm not," she allowed, and she hid any annoyance well. "You can trust me, Mist . . . C.T."

"I hope so." I turned toward T.J. "Draft a contract."

She clapped her hands together. "We're really going to work with Naomi?"

"Against a few of my reservations, yes. While you're getting the paperwork sorted out, I'll be over here day drinking and wondering if Mensa is going to knock me down a rung." For her part, Naomi beamed, my rung on the ladder of the intelligentsia not her concern.

Naomi and T.J. adjourned to the latter's desk. My assistant prepared an electronic contract for digital signature. I didn't have any booze stashed in a drawer at the moment, so I couldn't drink. Instead, while they reviewed the terms and the appropriate digital signatures got added, I spent a few minutes wondering what the hell I'd just signed up for.

By the time the workday wound down, T.J. and I knew we needed to talk to someone else about what we'd just agreed to do. We drove separately to the Nightlight Foundation. The foundation's office recently moved to be closer to City Hall. I wondered if this was because Mayor Vincent Davenport wanted to keep an eye on his daughter. Or maybe he wanted easier access to her. Despite the fraught political nature of her past, Melinda had been helping her father with his re-election campaign, and numbers indicated voters found her authentic.

It was almost enough to compel me to head to a polling station myself in a couple months.

Melinda sat behind a large desk in her office. She didn't stuff it with the usual accoutrements people did to look important. No bookshelf full of dusty old tomes designed to look good to visitors. The only other furniture was a small round meeting table with four chairs around it. Melinda stood as we walked in. She was a couple inches shorter than T.J., with fiery red hair, and she looked terrific in a sweater and jeans. She embraced us each in turn. "I think I know why you're here," our hostess said once T.J. and I both sat.

"Not for the view," I said. The window behind Melinda showed a street from one story up. It wasn't terrible, but her office didn't look out onto the harbor or anything scenic. Such were the drawbacks of being a short walk from City Hall.

"We're in," T.J. said. "We're going to work with Naomi on her investigation."

Melinda let out a sigh of relief. Between her, Gloria, and T.J., the three women I talked to the most wanted me to solve this conundrum. Maybe I needed to poll my mother on the drive home. "I'm glad to hear it. Alyssa was a friend, and I wanted her to succeed for . . . obvious reasons. When I got out of the life, she was my inspiration to start the foundation."

"We'll find the guy who killed her," my assistant promised.

I didn't relish being a wet blanket, but we needed several

metric tons more information before we could hope to have a resolution. "Whatever you can tell us would be important," I said. "I know your life was a lot different eight years ago."

"It was." Melinda's brows furrowed slightly. I knew her well enough to see a pall of sadness cover her face. "We weren't so different. She was a little older and had her shit together more. It helped her get out and really start something."

"Did you talk much back then?"

"Here and there. We worked different areas most of the time, and we never had the same pimp. Still, girls looked out for one another."

"Just like me and Amy," T.J. added. Amy—who worked in the world's oldest profession under the *nom de rue* of Velvet, exited the life more recently than T.J. and received training in social media management by Melinda's foundation. I'd heard she got a job somewhere but couldn't remember the company.

"Does the term 'harbor parties' mean anything to you?" I asked.

"No." Melinda shook her head. "I can't imagine it's anything good, though. A 'party' is always code for sex."

"Alyssa's notes seemed to make them a big deal. Something else to look into."

"I know her memory is in good hands."

I appreciated the sentiment, but I struggled to match my assistant's enthusiasm.

CHAPTER 5

AFTER C.T. LEFT, T.J. stayed behind at Melinda's invitation.

"I'm worried about you," the older woman said.

"You're always worried about me."

"And I always will be." Melinda crossed her arms. Her charcoal gray sweater looked great on her. Once T.J. got off the streets, Melinda made sure her new ward had access to medical care and food. "I needed to regain about fifteen pounds," the redhead had said. "So do you. No one will hire you if you still look like a hooker." It took a while—and plenty of fatty foods she now ate in moderation—but T.J. got there, too.

"You don't need to," T.J. protested.

"Really?" The corner of Melinda's mouth turned up. "You've worked a ton of cases where a former working girl made good was the victim?"

"No."

"That's my point. This hits close to home for you. It does for me, too."

"Alyssa was dead before I even started," T.J. said.

"Doesn't matter. You'll see yourself in her . . . now and with every new detail you uncover." When T.J. remained silent,

Melinda added, "I know because it happened to me. She and I were different in a variety of ways, but everything I've learned about her these last couple days might as well hold a mirror up to my soul."

T.J.'s head bobbed slowly. "I get it. When C.T. and I worked that priest murder, and Amy was involved, it was tough for me. She and I walked the same streets, and we looked out for each other, so there was personal involvement. Still . . ."

"I've listened to the podcast," Melinda said. "Naomi might be kicking a hornet's nest."

"What do you mean?"

"She's basically said the man in jail didn't do it. One of the people she's pointed a finger at is the mayor of Annapolis. I've met him a couple times. Once was at a fundraiser for the foundation, and the other time was with my dad." Melinda's expression remained difficult to read. T.J. couldn't even tell what the woman thought of her own father. Melinda could have a future in politics or consulting if she wanted it. "He seems all right. His chief of staff is a shark, though. Always vigilant when it comes to his boss."

T.J. shrugged. "Isn't that what a chief of staff is supposed to be like?"

"Sure," Melinda admitted. "It wouldn't surprise me to learn he's taken some . . . extra measures behind his boss's back, though. Just be careful around him if they come up in your investigation."

"We will."

"Will you? C.T. is something of a risk taker, and I fear you're cut from the same cloth in that respect."

T.J. grinned even in the face of what sounded a little like an accusation. "Guilty as charged."

"This guy might be, too. I don't know. I just want you to be aware."

"You're always looking out for me. Between you and C.T., you're like the older siblings I never had."

Melinda chuckled. "I'm not sure how to take that. I'm going to presume it's meant as a compliment."

"Most of the time," T.J. said.

———

The next morning, T.J. got up early to hit the gym in her building.

She felt a pang of disappointment because the cute guy she often saw was absent today. They smiled at each other at every opportunity, but neither had worked their way up to breaking the ice with an actual conversation. Maybe he was shy. T.J. never used to be, but the years in her old life skewed her relationships with men—not permanently, she hoped. She and her boss got along well, and it remained the only consistent male relationship in her life.

For now, at least.

In her first few months under Melinda's care, T.J. filled out and regained most of the pounds she'd lost living hard. Now, she was in a good place, carrying a healthy weight for her tall frame and working on building muscle two days a week. Today, she focused on cardio, listening to an up-tempo playlist as she put herself through the paces on an elliptical machine.

When her thirty-five minutes were up, T.J. strapped on MMA gloves and beat on a heavy bag. She'd been taking kickboxing classes for a while now, and while circumstances had never forced her to put her training into action, she wanted to remain sharp. After twenty minutes of abusing the bag with fists, elbows, knees, and feet, she drank water and did some stretches to cool down.

Back in her apartment, she showered and put on fresh clothes. While T.J. waited for her oatmeal to heat up, she looked out her kitchen window onto the parking lot. The 501 was a great place to live. It stretched her budget but was convenient to so many things in the city, and many of her fellow residents were age peers. Her gently used gray Mustang sat in its parking spot. It replaced a similar car blown up by the criminals in the last major case she and C.T. worked. T.J. had been worried the building management would hold her responsible, but they'd been surprisingly cool about everything. The positive press the agency received for catching the Vox Populi killers might have helped.

As T.J. ate breakfast and read the local news, publicity leapt to the front of her mind again. She came across an article she hadn't wanted to see—not for a while at least.

PODCASTER PARTNERS WITH LOCAL DETECTIVE AGENCY

By Helen Benjamin, Staff Writer

Baltimore, MD—Naomi Chambers, host of the nationally popular Harbor Homicides podcast, announced she is working with the Ferguson Detective Agency on her latest investigation.

The agency, headed by licensed PI C.T. Ferguson, has been in the news of late for catching serial killer Adrian Brown and the Vox Populi bombers. Ferguson did not return a request for comment.

Chambers' current investigation is into the murder of Alyssa Winters, a reformed prostitute who was murdered in Baltimore eight years ago. While police arrested a suspect, Chambers thinks the real killer remains at large.

The first two episodes of Harbor Homicides are now available to stream on all major podcast platforms. More will be coming, though Chambers said the release schedule may be irregular "depending on the cadence of the investigation."

"Shit," T.J. muttered, setting her phone atop the table. While publicity generally helped the business, T.J. had also seen how press coverage could get out of hand quickly. She didn't want reporters hounding her on the way into work and trying to follow her and C.T. around. She knew he would feel the same.

CHAPTER 6

"FUCKING HELL," I said as I saw a throng of reporters perched on the sidewalks outside our office.

News vans dotted the curbs. One even pulled into the lot and took a spot. In the past, I referenced encroaching journalists to Manny, who was happy to tell them to get the hell off his property. They'd smartened up since. Even the building owner couldn't evict them from the sidewalk. I kept going and made a left at the next street.

The plan was to scan headlines as I waited at red lights, and Baltimore traffic did not let me down. The *Baltimore Sun* knew about Naomi's arrangement with our office. Fine. Even in the face of dwindling subscribers and changing ownership, they were a major paper. I kept checking.

The Baltimore *Banner* proclaimed, PODCASTER AND *PI TEAM UP*. The term made me feel a bit like a lesser-known superhero who got to cross over into a Spider-Man comic. The *City Paper* went the lascivious route with, *LOCAL PODCASTER and PI IN BED TOGETHER ON CASE*. Gloria didn't read this rag—few people did anymore—but I made a mental note to push the editor responsible into traffic if I ever learned their identity.

By the time I circumnavigated the block, my sleuthing powers told me the whole city knew Naomi hired us. The story even picked up some regional attention. National papers and cable news would pick it up next. I pulled into the lot, ignoring the clamor as a dozen people fired questions at me. The volume increased when I got out of the S4, but the reporters talked over each other so much I couldn't have picked out a question even if I were inclined to answer one.

"We need to talk to our client," I said as I shut the door behind me. "This might be the shortest engagement in history."

"I've already turned down several requests for comment," T.J. said. "It's gotten to the point that I'm not answering the phone. If it's legit, whoever's calling will leave a message."

After preparing a cup of coffee, I sat at my desk and ran a hand through my dark brown locks. "I wonder if I should get a trim."

"Why?"

"If I'm going to appear on CNN, I need to have better hair than Anderson Cooper."

"Pretty sure that's impossible," my assistant said.

"You're fired."

"Your hair is fine. I have a small bottle of spray in my bag if you really need something."

"What I need is to talk to Naomi," I said. T.J. dialed the woman's number and put the call on speaker.

"You have something already?" Naomi asked.

"Yeah," I said. "A burning desire to kick you to the curb."

"What? Why?"

"Maybe we should have talked about the balance between

doing a job unimpeded versus having a gaggle of reporters waiting for us."

"Oh." She had the audacity to giggle. I took a sip of coffee to avoid going on a profane tirade. "It's fine. I'm used to the press by now. They're harmless. Besides, this will raise your agency's profile even more."

"I'm not concerned about raising my profile. It's been plenty high for a year. I want to catch a killer, and I thought you did, too."

"I do," she insisted.

"No more bullshit like this, then. If you want the press to chase after you, fine. It's your life. I don't like being followed and interrogated."

"Noted. By the way, I requested the full police file." Before I could say I'd already found it online, Naomi added, "The one they uploaded may be incomplete. It happens with cold cases . . . anything older than six years or so, really. After that, every-thing went digital, but there's a window of about four or five years where things are a hodge-podge."

"Do they tend to honor your requests?" I asked.

"The blowback if they say no generally compels them to. I know how to use the media, C.T. If you want me to try and keep them away from you, I will, but I'll also turn them against the BPD if they try to stonewall me."

"I like your style, girl," T.J. said.

"Thanks. We'll talk soon."

After Naomi hung up, I said, "'I like your style, girl'?"

"What?"

"Really?"

"Hashtag girlboss," T.J. said.

"Don't make me fire you again."

A few minutes later, Naomi texted and said the police

would be dropping off the file later, and she would love to come by and review it with us. I figured it might be a multi-day endeavor. The police were likely to practice malicious compliance and include any record which might be two percent relevant to Alyssa. It was like a big law firm sending a ton of papers to the small one to bury them in discovery.

I hoped this wouldn't end up being the way things shook out, but my job rarely gave me cause for optimism.

By lunchtime, we didn't have anything from the BPD, but we did have a delivery.

Gloria was in the area to check out a site and talk to a potential client, so she stopped by with lunch. A white bag made mostly translucent from grease sat inside a plastic one. They held three pit beef sandwiches and three large cups of fries. "Hard at work?" My wife asked as we all got plates and started spreading our food out.

"In a holding pattern now," I said. "Our client went and ran to the press, so there are a lot of eyes on everyone now. The cops are supposed to drop off a full report later." I paused, looking for a couple items. "Did you—?"

"Right here," Gloria said, producing small cups of horse-radish and sliced onion from a small bag hiding under her sand-wich wrapper. "I know what my man likes."

I eschewed the obvious lascivious reply, but T.J. must have seen a twinkle in my eye because she said, "Gross. Get a room . . . and not this one."

After a few minutes of quiet eating, my wife posed a ques-tion to my assistant. "Do you listen to true crime?"

T.J. smiled. "Definitely. I wouldn't say I'm a junkie or

anything, but I have a few I like. I've even found listening parties for some of the big ones."

"For *Harbor Homicides?*"

"No."

"You should tune in with my friends and me. We get a group together, hang out, drink wine, and talk about the show."

"I don't know," T.J. said. "We're working on this one. It feels a little weird." I understood, and I was glad she spoke up. From what I knew of T.J.'s life, she needed a few more friends, but there were other ways of finding them.

"If you change your mind," Gloria said, "we'd love to have you."

"Thanks."

Gloria's hazel eyes turned to me. "I know there's considerable publicity around this one, but are you excited to work it?"

"Right now, I'm excited to eat a pit beef sandwich." The added horseradish and onion made a difference. The meat was smoky and flavorful, and the great char filled my nostrils every time I picked it up. Most places selling this kind of food would stop once the weather got cold in six weeks or so. A few such establishments had burned down over the years trying to move their operation indoors for the winter.

"I'll take that as a no," she said.

"The case is definitely one we'd like to work," I said. "I could live without the media presence. Are they still on the sidewalk?"

"A couple."

"There were a dozen here this morning. I know we've worked a couple high-profile cases in the past year, but it feels a little more stifling this time. Naomi attracts press attention no matter what. I would have preferred she kept it to herself."

"You think it'll be a problem?"

"We'll get it done. It'll just be fifty percent more annoying along the way."

"Fifty percent?" Gloria grinned. "You already know how much?"

"It's an initial estimate. I reserve the right to adjust upwards."

"I'm not worried," T.J. said. "Adrian Brown was a member of the press. As long as none of these folks are closet serial killers, it can't be worse."

I took another bite of my pit beef. I liked it a lot better than the thought of being hounded by reporters every step of the investigation.

———

The boxes arrived about an hour after Gloria left.

I looked out the window. Two police vans idled near the main entrance. At least they didn't bring a tractor trailer. I didn't envy the officers carrying everything up the stairs. When it became obvious I had no plans to help, a brawny young cop asked me, "You gonna give us a hand?"

"Nope."

"Why not?"

"Hurt my back," I said.

"How?" he demanded.

"Carrying your department to respectable conviction numbers."

T.J. chortled, the cop suggested I perform a biologically impossible action, and he left to fetch more boxes. By the time the four-man crew was done, our ability to eat lunch at the table and move around the office had been severely compromised. I signed for everything, smiled when the salty uniform

I'd spoken to earlier glared at me, and blew out a deep breath when the BPD contingent left.

"Where do we even begin?" T.J. wondered.

"No idea. They've dumped all this on us in the hopes we won't find anything to counter the official story. You ever watch lawyer shows?" She nodded. "This is their version of burying us in discovery."

"How's your speed reading?"

"I go pretty quickly," I said. "Always have. I don't need Evelyn Wood to teach velocity at the expense of retention."

"Who?"

"Never mind."

Footsteps came up the metal stairs. The clangs were light, suggesting either a woman or a small man. The door remained locked, so when I heard a key working the tumblers, I knew who it was. Our intern Lexi Tyler walked in a moment later. Her eyes widened when she took in the sight. "How the hell are we supposed to work around a thousand boxes?"

"To be determined," I said. "In the meantime, I think we can get in some killer games of hide and seek."

"Where do we even begin?" she wondered, echoing T.J.'s question from a few minutes ago.

"How'd you know we had all this work to do?" I asked.

"I texted her," my assistant said.

"I don't listen to the show," Lexi said, "but I've heard of it. I'm sure you're not happy with all the press coverage so far."

"Not especially. I'd rather talk to them once we've wrapped things up. Then, we can say how brilliant we were."

Her eyes swept the room again. Her father was retired Green Beret John Tyler, a man I knew and didn't get along with too well. I imagined he did the same as he hunted for exits and adversaries. Today, his daughter was probably counting containers and pondering the enormity of the task before us. "This is insane."

"It is." I checked out some of the boxes. Each had a number, date range, and quick summary of the contents written in marker on both ends. Everything was out of order, of course— probably a tactic to make things harder for us. "The first thing we need to do is organize this chaos." I pointed toward the entrance. "Let's start to the left of the door with number one." Most of the stacks were five high. "Let's go five boxes per pile. They don't have to be in strict order, but let's keep one to five together, six through ten, and so on. It'll make things easier once we need something. We'll stage on the table and our desks."

We got to work. Considering the disarray with which the cops left everything, it took a while to even get started, and our desks strained under the added weight of a million pieces of paper and folders. After about an hour of careful arrangement, we started making real progress. It took another hour, but we got all the boxes grouped roughly by number. After a communal water break, T.J. asked, "We starting with the first?"

"Might as well." Both young women sighed. "I get it. As tedious as it seems, mistakes are most common early. Bad assumptions, contradictory witness statements, and all. Let's each start in a different spot, though."

"I'll take the initial stuff," Lexi volunteered.

"All right," I said. "T.J., you start with number eleven. I'll start with twenty-one. Let's all just write down things we find on paper, and we'll compare once we all knock out a stack."

"I'm almost impressed at how organized this is for you," T.J. said.

"I guess your systems are rubbing off on me."

We all got to work. The normal end of the day came and

went. Cartons got hefted, set down, and arranged again. Papers spilled out of overstuffed folders, and a squad of scurvy-laden sailors would have applauded our strings of curses each time. After a while, I ordered pizza for delivery, even overpaying for sodas to accompany them. The first fifteen total file boxes gave us a few notes and some things to keep track of but nothing major. The delivery driver came and left with a nice tip. "Where's Naomi in all this?" T.J. wondered as we paused to eat. "I thought she was going to do the review with us."

"Maybe she's too busy getting ready for an interview," I said.

"She *did* hire us," Lexi pointed out.

I nodded. "True. If she comes by, though, she doesn't get any pizza."

Everyone agreed this was fair, and we resumed working a few minutes later. The evening teetered on the border between dusk and dark by the time we finished another stack each. This time, we'd all compiled more notes. Lexi jotted down a few poor witness interviews. "The Lincoln Lawyer would tear them apart on the stand," she said.

"Great," I said. "Someone call Netflix."

T.J. added some investigative shortcuts. For me, the big thing was Darrell getting gas when he was supposedly killing Alyssa. Buried deep in box eighteen were witness statements. One man attested he'd seen Darrell at the station, and the attendant confirmed this. There was no receipt, photos, or screen caps from a video, and the odds of getting these things years after the fact were basically nil.

Still, the sum of what we'd uncovered so far didn't bode well for the BPD. "I think Rich got it wrong," T.J. said, finally putting into words what I'd been thinking.

"Yeah," I concurred. "I think he did."

CHAPTER 7

DARRELL WILSON WAS NOT A SAINT, but was he a killer?

This was the crux of Naomi's podcast and—for the moment —our investigation. While the tons of evidence provided by the BPD did not explicitly finger a killer, it did a good job making the case for Darrell Wilson's innocence. The only thing tying him to the scene of the crime was eyewitness testimony, and a bunch of other evidence suggested he wasn't at the motel when Alyssa met her violent end.

It should have been simple for a lawyer to get the case against Wilson thrown out. Everything the state presented screamed reasonable doubt. However, Wilson went down for the murder and remained behind bars, though intermittent news stories about men who proclaimed their innocence included him. His attorney had been a longtime public defender who retired about six months after the case. I knew the office got overwhelmed with cases, and most good lawyers left for private practice.

"The witness," I said. "We need to dig into the woman. Her testimony may be the only thing standing between Darrell Wilson and a possible release from prison." The ladies agreed with this avenue of attack, so we dove in. A few minutes later, we'd already learned enough to make the whole case even shakier. Renee McGee, then fifty-one, allegedly booked a room at the same motel. The only record of it, however, was a hand-written entry in the guest log. No credit card or other transaction proved she'd been there.

Her claim consisted of identifying Darrell Wilson, attesting she saw him go into another room, and further attesting he left the other room a short time later. Conveniently, this was the exact location and timeline of Alyssa's murder. No other guest in the motel—for whom more proof of their stays existed—offered any corroborating statements. The closest came from another guest who saw someone go into and out of Alyssa's room, but the description he offered could have fit a quarter of the men in Maryland.

"It's hinky," Lexi said.

"I can't believe they sent a man to prison based on one woman's testimony," T.J. added.

"A white woman testifying against a black man and holding him up as a liar," I said. "To a jury with nine white folks on it. I'm not trying to stoke the fires, but I think they're smoldering on their own."

"Eight years ago, too," our intern said. "We need to prove this McGee woman lied."

"There's plenty of evidence suggesting she at least got it wrong." I shrugged. "It didn't matter then. We need something else besides gas station footage no one can find."

"What if she got paid?"

I thought about it and nodded. "It's possible. We don't even know for sure she was a guest on the night in question."

"How do we get into her accounts?" My assistant wondered.

Lexi already sat with her fingers hovering on the keys like ten little snakes ready to strike. "Work together," I said. "See if you can find her in data breach records and the like."

"On it," Lexi said. T.J. wheeled her chair over—taking a less direct route thanks to the boxes—and Lexi talked her through the process. Many people were victims of data breaches, and thanks to lax reporting laws, a good percentage of them had no idea. An enterprising security specialist can comb through records on the public internet and the dark web to find names, emails, and passwords. If someone didn't know they got wrecked, they'd be unlikely to change their login.

About fifteen minutes later, Lexi said, "I might have something. I see her email and two common passwords. They look to be the only ones she uses."

"Spray them against the bank sites," I said. "Start local. Less odds of top-flight security."

The clacking of keys filled the space. Lexi frowned in apparent concentration, while T.J. grinned like a kid whose parents finally said she could ride the Ferris wheel. She was eager to learn the cyber dark arts and had the aptitude to do well. "Bingo," Lexi exclaimed a short while later. "Rosedale Federal."

"I guess we're looking for suspicious transactions around the time of Alyssa's murder?" T.J. wanted to know.

"We are," I confirmed. Stepping around a couple piles of boxes, I joined my assistant and our intern. Lexi navigated to prior years' statements. The system wouldn't display them on screen but allowed for a PDF download. Once we had the file, confirmation was easy. Renee McGee received four wire transfers totaling $20,000 dollars around the time of the trial. Based on the dates, she got half up front and the rest after taking the stand. Nice work if you can get it.

"The transfers don't go anywhere," Lexi said, pointing at another browser tab. "Looks like a short-lived LLC."

"Registered where?" I asked.

"Baltimore. No ownership or management records."

"It did its job."

"Are we talking to Renee McGee?" T.J. said.

"I'd rather do it in person. She can lie and hang up on us if we call."

"What's the plan for the meantime?"

"We're on a hot streak," I said. "Might as well keep shooting."

———

"If we're sure Darrell didn't do it," Lexi said, "then it stands to reason we need to figure out who did."

"Yes," I said.

"What about Darrell?" T.J. wanted to know. "An investigation could take a while. If he's innocent, he should get released from jail."

Darrell Wilson was not our client, but I sympathized with my assistant's interest in getting him out of prison. "He'll need a real lawyer," I said. "His was a buffoon, and the guy retired. I don't know all the legal loopholes, but if we can impugn the witness's testimony, it should open up some options for him at the very least. Finding out who actually killed Alyssa . . . and proving it . . . are the best things we can do for everyone." I thought about Liz Fleming, a former public defender I'd worked with before. She hung her own shingle a few years ago, and most lawyers took the occasional *pro bono* case because it made them seem a little less like bloodsuckers.

"We have any suspects?" Lexi asked.

I shrugged. "The police never seriously considered anyone else. I don't think we'll glean much from their investigation. I think we listen to Naomi's two episodes and start digging on our own."

"So we'll need to compile our own list."

"Yes." Both women frowned. "I don't know if it'll be a big effort or not. At the risk of sounding indelicate, Alyssa was a hooker who got out of the life. Who would want her dead?"

"Her old pimp," T.J. offered with an immediacy which forced me to wonder whether hers ever tried to reach out to her. She offered a quick head shake to my inquisitive look.

"Former clients," Lexi said. "Especially high profile ones. They might have feared some kind of backlash after she went straight."

We played the first episode of Harbor Homicides at double speed as the three of us got to work. About fifteen minutes in, T.J. paused the podcast. "I found her old pimp." She sent his picture to the TV mounted on the back wall. "Meet Sam Wannick . . . street name Warlock." A bald black man with a mean expression stared back at us. A scar ran from under his left eye down his cheek. It certainly helped him look unpleasant. "Several priors for the usual stuff, including a bunch for assault. His social posts around the time suggest he might have been obsessed with Alyssa."

T.J. displayed results from the social media scraping script I developed and updated periodically. Warlock made no effort to obfuscate his interests. *Alyssa, you got away. Ima get you back, bitch.*

I beat your ass once when you didn't have the money. How big a whooping you think you got coming now, A?

Ain't no street walking pussy gonna get away from me.

"I almost hope he did it," I said. "I'd love to see him resist arrest and get clobbered for it."

"Should we put him on the cops' radar?" Lexi sounded hopeful.

"I can't establish where he was on the night Alyssa was murdered," T.J. said. "He's a fucking prick, but he might be innocent of this."

"Let's keep going, then," I said.

I used the scraper to dig into Alyssa. She'd been active on social media thanks to her advocacy work. Even in the years prior, she maintained a sporadic presence. I snagged the profiles of a few women whose profile pictures at the time suggested they were also sex workers. Maybe they could fill in some gaps for us.

It took many insipid posts, but I finally found some references to parties. AW was obviously Alyssa. Others involved also received the initials treatment. Without a fair number of context clues, deciphering their identities would be challenging.

The podcast kept playing. "Multiple witnesses from Alyssa's nonprofit reported that she had been acting nervous in the weeks before her death. She told one colleague she was 'sitting on a bombshell' that could 'bring down powerful people.'" There were many ways in which a person could amass power. Politics. Money. Church. Alyssa lived and worked in Annapolis, a city I enjoyed visiting but whose heavy hitters remained unknown. Still, I had a collection of initials and great Googling skills.

Before long, I said, "I might have something." Lexi and T.J. navigated the cramped office and appeared at my desk with speeds suggesting I'd promised raises and free pizza. I went into a brief speech about the app, the initials, and the connections I made—tenuous though they may be.

"Yeah, yeah," Lexi said. "What's the scoop?"

"RH and MD."

She shrugged. "And they are . . . ?"

"I'm not a hundred percent sure," I said. "We'll still need to verify this. The current mayor of Annapolis is named Robert Hargrove. He would have been a candidate eight years ago when he was a real estate developer. His current chief of staff used to work for him even back then. Marcus Dunning."

"If you're right," T.J. said, "this just got much, much bigger."

If I were right represented the big variable. I'd found social posts, blogs, and the like which all stated Hargrove had an affinity for ladies of the evening. This was before he suddenly found religion and committed to his then-girlfriend (now wife) a short while before the election, of course. Phony or not, his conversion worked with fifty-four percent of Annapolis voters. "We need to get Naomi in here. Tell her to cancel with her publicist or whatever she's doing. If she wants this info, she can come here and listen to us make our case."

My assistant nodded. "I'll call her."

Loud footfalls coming up the metal stairs announced Naomi's arrival. She wore jeans and a sweater, and her heels clacked a little even on the carpeted floor inside our office. "Sorry," she said with a smile akin to a cat who'd just plucked a fish from the aquarium, "I wanted to be here earlier. My publicist lined up way more appearances than I'd planned for, and they just took a while."

T.J. shot me a meaningful look before she answered. "We're glad you could come in." Her response was more charitable than mine would have been.

"What do we have?" Naomi looked around at the stacks of boxes, running a hand over a couple before making her way to my desk.

"Serious doubts about Darrell Wilson's guilt," I said.

Our client spread her hands and smiled. Despite my annoyance with her late arrival, I would admit she had a great smile. "I can pick good cases."

"I'm not sure our criteria are always going to line up, but they do here."

"Lay it on me."

Lexi and T.J. joined me, and we spent about twenty minutes setting everything out there. Naomi already knew some of it, since we used what she revealed in her initial episodes as a jumping-off point. The alternative suspects were both new, and her eyes lit up in a way I didn't like when we mentioned the Annapolis mayor and his chief of staff.

"I knew there were powerful people behind all this," she said.

"I hate when people say 'allegedly' when someone is obviously guilty," I said, "but we're not certain here. There's a whiff he's involved in some way. It could simply be he was a past client of Alyssa's. The former pimp is probably the better suspect, and we haven't established where he was yet. It's all still early. These things take time."

"I know how to run an investigation, C.T."

"You know how to do research and tell a good story. There's more to it."

"Do you mansplain the job to all your clients?" Naomi demanded.

"Only the ones who might run off and put a bunch of speculation out into the world. It might be your show, but you've gone public with our arrangement. If you start talking shit about the mayor of Annapolis, it's going to blow back on us, too."

"I'm used to releasing on a schedule. My listeners expect it."

Before I could ask a pointed question or two about her listeners' expectations, T.J. said, "We just need to keep pursuing these leads. I think there's enough for you to present to your audience without naming any sensitive names."

"You mean like the mayor?"

"Yes."

Naomi shrugged. "He's a public figure. Courts have ruled that public figures are hard to defame."

"But not impossible," I said. "There's a clause in the contract you signed with us. Pretty standard stuff. Basically, if you do something which brings legal action, we drop you as a client, and you're on the hook for our legal expenses."

Naomi blew out a short breath and shook her head. "Let me guess . . . he's expensive."

"His silver Lexus matches his hair," I said. "You know his retainer is insane." Thankfully, James Snyder—a longtime friend of my parents—never gouged me for the infrequent legal work I asked him to do, but Naomi didn't need to know this.

"Fine." Naomi put up her hands. "I won't name names until you get more details. You're going to send me what you have so far?"

"It'll be in your inbox tomorrow," Lexi said. An optimistic promise but a reasonable one.

"Okay. I'll wait for your email, then." She stood and fixed me with her gaze. "You're coming on the podcast at some point.

Maybe when this is all done, and we've found out what really happened to Alyssa, but I'm getting you in front of a mic."

"I have an outrageous appearance fee," I said, "not to mention the riders in my contract."

"A bowl of green M&Ms?"

I grinned. "Blue, actually. I'd hate to be accused of copying Van Halen."

"You got it. Thanks, everyone. This is going to be the best season of the podcast yet." She headed for the exit. The door swung shut and locked behind her, and her noisy footsteps retreated.

"This is going to be the best season of the podcast yet," I said in a catty voice. T.J. and Lexi both rolled their eyes. "What? I'm already guilty of mansplaining. Might as well add to my charges."

"You don't like her," T.J. said, and she didn't phrase it in the form of a question. What would Ken Jennings think?

"I don't like her priorities. She was ready to run out of here and tell everyone the goddamn mayor of Annapolis might have strangled a former hooker he used to patronize eight years ago. Maybe he did. We have no idea at this point, and I'm not going to have the agency's name attached to something irresponsible."

"At least you read the contract," Lexi said.

"More than most of our clients do." I stretched and stifled a yawn. "We've been at it a while. Let's pick it up in the morning."

"Maybe you'll be less salty then," T.J. said.

"Maybe," I allowed. "But I balance less salt with more acid."

CHAPTER 8

T.J. SIGHED as she kicked her apartment door shut. It had been a long day at the office. Productive, but getting home after nine wasn't normal. If it were, she'd make her requests for raises and bonuses even more frequent. In all the activity of the evening, they'd never gotten dinner. It was already late, and T.J. was way too hungry to order something and wait for delivery. She found half a cheeseburger from a few nights ago in the fridge, found it free of mold or slime, and heated it up. She put it on a plate with some potato chips.

"Another glamorous dinner," she said to her empty apartment. Thankfully, it never passed judgment on her.

When she'd finished, she stopped trying to find something to watch and checked email on her phone. A new message popped up.

TJ,

I know you're working the Alyssa case. I knew her back in the day and might have a couple things to tell you. I'll be in the city for a few days, so I want to do it in person.

Come alone. Just you. Your boss is probably trustworthy, but he doesn't understand the life we led.

Reply to this email, and I'll tell you when and where I can meet you.

-B.

"That's fishy." Again, her apartment offered no opinion. The address was Proton Mail, so whoever it was took their privacy seriously. The sender might be another former street walker, or it could be someone who heard about the investigation thanks to Naomi and now wanted to silence T.J. Services like Proton got their reputations by valuing privacy and protecting identities—even when scammers and others with bad intentions used them.

"You can't go," Melinda Davenport said when T.J. called her. "This might be the most obvious trap I've heard about in a while."

"What if it's not?"

"I think the odds are slim."

"Slim isn't zero," T.J. said.

"Neither is the risk," Melinda said. "I'd say it's pretty high. You might meet some woman who did the same work we used to, or it might be some big meathead who punches you in the face and throws your unconscious body into the harbor."

"Jesus." T.J. rubbed her jaw. She'd taken a few blows to the face in her former life. "Maybe give the true crime a break over the weekend."

"You know I'm right."

"I know those are both possibilities," T.J. said. "The risk is mine to take."

"C.T. is rubbing off on you."

"It's mutual. He cares about organization now, and I take more chances when it makes sense. Maybe we both won."

"They're not the same," Melinda grumbled, "and you know it. I'm coming with you."

"No, you're not."

"Don't go alone."

"Fine," T.J. said. "I'll even bring the rape whistle."

"I hope you're not making a mistake."

"This could be a break in the case."

"Text me when you're back home . . . or when you wake up in the hospital. I don't care how late it is."

Melinda was a more risk-averse person than T.J. in general, especially now with a foundation and other girls depending on her. Still, she was like the overprotective big sister T.J. never had and could have definitely used in her early teen years. "I will. Gotta go."

———

Once she got off the call with Melinda, T.J. tapped out a reply.

B,

I'm in. Tell me when and where.

-T.J.

She wanted to tell C.T., but then he would share Melinda's opinion about the likelihood of a trap and insist on coming. When she refused, he'd somehow find a way to track her phone or find her car on traffic cameras and show up anyway. If Melinda was the big sister she'd never had, C.T. was T.J.'s older brother . . . the kind who would lift weights or polish his shotgun when her date arrived to pick her up. She could have used one of those back in the day, too, but at least she had people who cared about her now.

A new message flashed at the top of her inbox.

Fells Point square, midnight. The bench in front of the hot dog stand.

T.J. knew the location. It was a pretty easy walk from the

office, and she'd gotten hot dogs and soft pretzels for lunch on several occasions. The stand would be closed this time of night —the owner shut it down once the dinner rush ended even on weekends—and Fells Point would be crowded. It was a pleasant Thursday night in the fall, and revelers had their choice of about a hundred bars and pubs.

She definitely couldn't go alone.

"Obvi, I'm in," Lexi said when T.J. called and asked her.

"You sure? Didn't you already drive back to College Park?"

"It's fine. I don't mind. Besides, I might get to kick some drunk frat bro in the face."

"Always a perk," T.J. said.

"I'll be packing just in case."

"I hope you don't need to use it." She and Lexi arranged to meet near the destination a half-hour early. She didn't know who would be waiting for them. To use Melinda's scenario, it could be more than one large meathead waiting to punch both women in the face. Lexi's pistol would be a huge help. T.J. put on a fresh shirt and redid her ponytail. She listened to the first episode of *Harbor Homicides* again before heading to her car.

———

The pubs, bars, and restaurants were pretty crowded, and plenty of people strolled up and down the sidewalks. Still, finding Lexi near the square was easy. At five-eight, she was taller than most of the other girls, and none had quite the same shade of auburn hair she did. Tonight, she wore it in pigtails rather than the usual high pony. A loose windbreaker covered her shirt and hung over the waist of her jeans. T.J. figured the gun was holstered at the back.

"I haven't seen anyone lingering in the area," Lexi said.

"Let's not stand around and make ourselves too obvious." She headed up Broadway from Thames Street, and Lexi fell in stride beside her.

"I brought a couple earbuds." Lexi passed one to T.J as they went along. After a few minutes of scanning the crowd, they headed back down the other side of the street. Brick Oven Pizza—a lunchtime favorite at the office—teemed with late-night diners in varying stages of sobriety. When she worked the streets, T.J. plied her trade near John Hopkins University. It wasn't that far, but it seemed many more miles away from an area like this.

Each woman slipped an earbud in, and T.J. understood why Lexi wore pigtails. She paused outside a shop and took her hair out of its ponytail, letting it hang free. It came past her shoulders and hid the bud in her right ear. A quick call later, and they had a communications channel established. "It feels like we're on an op," T.J. said, unable to keep herself from giggling at the thought.

"My dad uses the same tech," Lexi said.

With ten minutes to spare, T.J. took a spot on the bench. No one else occupied it. People milled about. A guy around her age who had clearly stayed an hour too long at whatever bar he left ambled to her. His brows knitted, and he turned around when T.J. glowered at him.

"You didn't give me a chance to shoot him," Lexi whispered through the earpiece.

"Maybe next time." T.J. didn't know where her friend went, but buildings cast plenty of shadows in the artificial lights. Even on a busy night in a popular area, one person could disappear.

Three minutes after the appointed time, a woman walked

behind T.J. and sat on the opposite side of the bench. She had stringy hair the color of wet sand, and her clothes were a size too big. T.J. guessed her for late twenties, though years of hard living made her appear older. Idiots like the guy she'd dismissed a short while ago would probably think the newcomer a cougar.

"B?" T.J. asked. A single nod came as the only reply. "Nice to meet you?"

"You alone?"

"Yes?"

"No boss?" B demanded.

"He doesn't even know I'm here," T.J. said. "You have a name other than a letter?"

"You can call me Bree."

T.J. didn't ask if it were the woman's real name. The ones they used on the streets always had some basis in reality or desire. "Why did you want to talk to me tonight, Bree?"

"I knew Alyssa," she said in a small voice. It was hard to hear her over the din. "She helped me."

"Get out of the life?"

Bree again offered a lone bob of her head. "It didn't take. I . . . fell back into old ways. I'm good now, though. I have an Only Fans, but that's all I do. I'm clean."

"I'm glad to hear it," T.J. said. When Bree made no reply, T.J. offered, "A local woman helped me make the same transition about three years ago."

A wan smile played on Bree's face but failed to light it. "I heard the podcast. You work for the investigator who's on the case."

It wasn't a question. "I do." T.J.'s employment wasn't public knowledge, and C.T. had been careful to keep her out of the limelight. Still, someone could figure it out.

"Alyssa knew a ton," Bree said. "She was popular. Lots of men came to see her. Some of them were powerful . . . are powerful."

"You mean the mayor?" T.J. asked.

"He wasn't bad. Pretty nice guy. He partied with me a few times. Everyone knew he was into whores back in the day. How he got people to forget about or stop mentioning it . . . I don't know. Something to do with Marcus."

"The chief of staff?"

"Watch him. He's a snake." She glanced around and sighed. "Look. I don't know for sure if either one is involved. But I know there was an election going on then, and Marcus didn't want some random hookers blowing it for his meal ticket. The mayor recommitted to his religion and proposed to his girl-friend." She snorted. "That bitch needs some self-respect. Marcus made sure the path was clear."

"How?" T.J. wanted to know.

"By getting rid of people like Alyssa," Bree said. "She'd already helped me get out. I wasn't in Maryland at the time."

"I mean how did he do it? The cops arrested someone. There was no indication they even had another suspect."

"I told you . . . he's a snake." Her head moved left and right like she expected someone to jump out from the shadows at any second. "I gotta go."

T.J. put a hand on Bree's arm before she could leave. "How can I reach you if we need something else? You have a phone?"

She glanced down at T.J.'s hand. "Use my email. It's safe." Bree pulled her arm free, got up, and blended in with a crowd of men and women headed toward the water. T.J. watched her go. When she turned back around, Lexi stood nearby.

"That was weird," Lexi said.

"Yeah." T.J. let out a slow breath. "She seems to think it's the mayor and his fixer."

"Maybe it is."

"Maybe it is," T.J. said in agreement.

CHAPTER 9

I ARRIVED at the office Friday morning and didn't see T.J.'s car in the lot.

This was unusual. She almost always made it in before I did. My goal was 9:00, but I accepted 9:15 as more realistic and could live with 9:20. T.J. typically rolled in by 8:30 and set coffee to brew—a very important part of the morning. Considering I was flexible with my own arrival time, I'd never been an ogre about hers. If she needed a little more sleep, she should get it. I unlocked the door, set my bag down, and worked the coffee machine.

When I sipped fresh java as the clock struck 9:25, I sent a text. *You coming in late today?* On Fridays, Lexi the intern joined us, though she usually got here around ten. During the fall and spring semesters, she put in just the single day per week. I sent her a similar message, also, knowing she and T.J. had become friends and talked outside the bounds of the office.

About ten minutes later, both their cars pulled into the lot. Once they'd each settled in with their own mugs of coffee, I said, "I'm not sure how to take you two arriving at the same time." Both arched eyebrows at my comment. "It's either a good thing or one of the seven seals."

"Someone reached out to me last night," my assistant said. "She told me she could tell me something about Alyssa, but I needed to come alone."

"I'm going to guess you stuck to the spirit of her request but not the letter."

"Right. No offense, but she didn't want to involve you. She wanted to meet late at night. I asked Lexi to go along, and she did." For her part, our intern patted her hip where she normally wore a holstered pistol.

"At least you had backup," I said. "You learn anything new?"

"Sort of," T.J. said. "Bree basically told us we should be considering the Annapolis mayor and his chief of staff. Called Dunning a snake."

"We were going to look into them anyway."

"They should jump the line," Lexi said. "Ahead of the former pimp."

"I imagine it's harder to get onto the mayor's calendar once the weekend rolls around," I said. "Let's make sure we can talk to him today."

"You think he'll see us?" T.J. wanted to know.

"I think the alternative is him getting painted as a person of interest on a national podcast." I shrugged. "I've never been a politician, but it seems like a big part of the job is controlling the narrative. Even if a negative story is out there, clever people can spin it. I think 'Annapolis mayor who used to hire hookers stonewalls investigators in Alyssa Winters case' is difficult to reframe."

"We're not taking Naomi with us, are we?" Lexi said.

"God, no. We might need the circus she brings later, but for now, this should be a normal meeting with the mayor and his chief lapdog."

"Snake," T.J. pointed out.

"Whatever. Let's get our ducks in a row before we drive there. We want to ask good questions, so we need to dig into both men. Marcus should be hissing at us."

My assistant grinned. "Embracing the metaphor?"

"For now," I said. "Ultimately, the best thing to do with most snakes is cut off their heads."

Going after political figures always represented a major challenge.

Anyone with resources can come after you. A rich asshole can hire enforcers, goons, and even professional shooters to solve problems. I'd learned this lesson after getting shot twice and nearly dying in the harbor. A mayor, however, could bring official resources to bear. The good thing was Annapolis cops couldn't conduct their duties in Baltimore.

Still, some unscrupulous types might want off-the-books overtime, and if Marcus Dunning was really a well-connected snake, we would need to be careful.

For now, we carried on with our research. I directed T.J. and Lexi to do background work on the mayor and his fixer-in-chief. I looked for more recent avenues of questioning. Before becoming mayor, Robert Hargrove was a real estate developer with a mixed business reputation and known predilections for booze and ladies of the evening. When a political opening appeared, he suddenly recommitted himself to religion and proposed to his girlfriend of three years. I wondered how much she knew and what she accepted to become a mayor's wife.

More than any other job in America, politicians tend to fail upwards.

Since assuming office—and now well into his second term—Hargrove generally got good press. America is far too polarized for any politician to be universally popular, but Hargrove's margin of victory the second time was larger than the first, and polling showed him with an approval rating of 60%.

This meant two out of every five people didn't like him, of course, and their perspectives could prove more useful. I found a column talking about Hargrove's big initiative. It avoided the glowing conclusion similar pieces came to.

Progress at What Price? Hargrove's Vision for Annapolis Comes with Hidden Costs

By Jessica Laurent, Opinion Columnist

Mayor Robert Hargrove calls it "Annapolis Renewed." Historic preservationists call it vandalism. The truth about our mayor's aggressive redevelopment program likely falls somewhere in between—though increasingly, the scales are tipping against City Hall's bulldozer-friendly policies.

The debate over Hargrove's initiative to ease historic building restrictions has dominated our city for the past six years. On its surface, the mayor's argument appears compelling: Annapolis needs modernization to remain competitive, historic preservation codes create prohibitive maintenance costs, and new developments will expand our tax base while creating more housing options.

"We can't live in a museum," Hargrove declared at last month's Chamber of Commerce luncheon. "History is great, but Annapolis must evolve or stagnate."

The mayor's supporters point to genuine concerns. Our housing costs have risen 37% over five years, pricing out middle-class families. Historic building codes do make renovations more expensive, and certain structures have deteriorated beyond reasonable repair. Every Annapolitan wants economic vitality and affordability.

Yet examining the actual outcomes of the "Annapolis Renewed" program reveals troubling patterns deserving closer scrutiny.

First, despite promises of affordable housing, virtually none has materialized in completed projects. The Shipyard Commons development, which replaced three 19th century warehouses, offers condominiums starting at $750,000. The promised "workforce housing" units were quietly reduced from 20% to 5% of the building through a series of amendments to the original agreement.

Second, the "dangerous condition" designations that fast-track demolition have been applied inconsistently at best, suspiciously at worst. The Banning House, suddenly declared "structurally unsound" after standing for 204 years, was demolished just weeks before engineering reports commissioned by preservation groups could be completed. The property's new owner? Tidewater Development — a significant contributor to the mayor's campaigns.

Third, the economic benefits have largely flowed to a small circle of developers—a profession which included Mayor Hargrove before his election—rather than the broader community. Of the eleven major projects approved under relaxed historic guidelines, seven went to companies with direct connections to Hargrove's administration or campaign.

Most concerning is what we're losing: Annapolis's identity. Our city's historic character isn't merely aesthetic – it's economic. Tourism generates $400 million annually, with historic appeal our primary draw. Each building lost represents not just history but a piece of our economic foundation.

The compromise position the mayor publicly champions – preserving historic facades while modernizing interiors – sounds reasonable. But in practice, these "preserved" elements often amount to a stone entrance or decorative fragment incorporated into otherwise generic structures.

Even development advocates should question the process. Multiple projects have received expedited approvals after mysterious structural "emergencies," bypassing public review. The pattern of convenient collapses, fires of "undetermined origin," and sudden structural condemnations stretches coincidence to the breaking point.

What Annapolis needs isn't an either/or approach but thoughtful, transparent redevelopment with genuine community input. We can modernize while preserving our heritage through adaptive reuse, targeted tax incentives for restoration, and development focused on genuinely underutilized areas.

Mayor Hargrove claims to be creating Annapolis's future. But a future built on demolished history, broken promises of affordability, and insider dealing should concern citizens across the political spectrum. Our city *deserves development that honors both its past and its people – not just its developers.*

While we need economic growth and more housing options, the current path sacrifices too much of what makes Annapolis special for benefits that seem increasingly reserved for a select few. Renewal shouldn't require erasure, and progress shouldn't demand amnesia about either our history or the questionable patterns emerging in how these decisions are made.

I liked it and shared it with my assistant and our intern. "He's shady," Lexi said when she finished reading it.

"Doesn't make him a killer," I pointed out.

"No, he farms out the dirty work to his chief of staff," T.J. said. "Dunning is former military. Got a convenient medical discharge after an 'incident' with some prisoners. Now, he's started the Harbor Patrol. It's a way to employ people who have his background and moral flexibility."

I checked it out. The Harbor Patrol—officially created by the mayor—offered increased enforcement of the waterways around the city. Legally, they were on par with the Annapolis police, though social media posts and Reddit comments suggested a frosty relationship between the two. "Goons on a boat," as one commenter put it. "We don't often encounter official resistance," I said. "We might on this one."

"Don't you know a good lawyer?" T.J. asked.

"More than one. You're presuming we'd be in a situation where legal representation matters."

"Are we going to visit these pricks?" Lexi wanted to know. She frowned at a stack of boxes which infringed on her space. "The sooner we get rid of all this shit, the better."

"Let's see if we can get on the mayor's calendar." I called his office. A secretary answered quickly. Her voice reminded me of the woman who worked the front desk at my high school. She had a sweet, professional voice for parents and administrators, but she sounded like an angry mother eager to levy a draconian punishment when talking to most students. I explained who I was and why we needed a half-hour of Hargrove's time."

"This doesn't sound like something the mayor needs to get involved in," she said. "He doesn't have time for this."

"Maybe he can make time for all the reporters who will be flooding your office," I said. "Not to mention the city council. Maybe even the governor. I wonder if he could find a half-hour for them."

"What are you saying, sir?" Her voice veered toward punishing mother territory.

"I'm saying the mayor can ignore me but not my client. She has a large national platform, and I'm sure she would interpret his failure to cooperate uncharitably."

"Like everyone else, Mayor Hargrove is presumed innocent."

"Sure," I said, "because it's nineteen ninety-three, and those old norms still apply."

The secretary sighed and put me on an unannounced hold. When she came back a moment later, she offered us a 5:00 PM slot. I knew she did it to put us in maximum traffic, but I accepted anyway. As soon as I did, she offered a curt good-bye and hung up right away.

"She must be fun at parties," I said.

"Were you even alive in 'ninety-three?"

"I turned four in December."

"Christ, you're old." She and T.J. enjoyed a chuckle at my

expense.

"Then, you won't mind indulging an old man and leaving early to beat the traffic." When she grimaced, I added, "The secretary is smart. She knows there's still some traffic going to the Eastern Shore and Ocean City. If we turn up at five-oh-one, she's going to give us a saccharine smile and apologize, but the mayor is busy now."

"Fine. You're probably right."

"With age comes wisdom," I said.

———

Annapolis's City Hall was the kind of building the column about the mayor complained about.

It looked historic from the outside. I could imagine men with muskets fighting off the Redcoats almost 250 years ago. Inside, however, everything was new, glitzy, and modern. A museum full of status must have died to provide all the marble in the building. Exposed brick, beams, and pipes combined with a stark color scheme to complete the modern motif.

We found the mayor's office—pro tip: important people love to take the top floor—and walked through its ornate double doors five minutes before our appointment. I felt like I'd wandered into a palace during the height of the Roman Empire's decadence. Hopefully, no one would try to feed the three of us to lions.

When I announced who we were to the secretary, she visibly deflated. I gave her a nice smile anyway. "The mayor will be with you shortly," she announced with all the enthusiasm of someone staring down a day full of dental surgery. Lexi, T.J., and I sat side by side on three cloth chairs. The whole setup felt very much like being in the principal's office. I went to some nice private schools, but none could have afforded anything like this.

Another thing important people have in common is a love of keeping everyone waiting. It validates their ego and serves as an obvious power play. We weren't in a position to storm out, so we sat in our chairs like bad little students and waited for an interior door to open. At ten after, it finally did.

"The mayor will see you now," the secretary said, confirming a very obvious fact.

Past another fancy door, two men waited. I recognized the one behind the desk from a trove of photos. Robert Hargrove wore a tailored navy suit with a subtle pinstripe. Even at the end of the workday, his brown hair remained perfect. The other man looked shorter sitting down. He was black with a shaved head, and his tailored gray suit looked as good as his boss's. "Marcus Dunning," he said, not offering to shake anyone's hand, "chief of staff. This is Mayor Hargrove."

"Thanks for meeting us on short notice," I said.

Dunning snorted. He moved from a chair at the side of the room and perched on the corner of the mayor's desk. T.J., Lexi, and I dropped onto a trio of guest seats. "Didn't sound like you were giving us much choice. Before we begin this farce, I want to see your ID." I showed him my PI license. "I could get this suspended."

"It's issued by the state," I said, "and I'm in compliance. Good luck."

"You don't think I could?"

"I think the state police are used to dealing with petty demands from self-important people." I tried to be nice. Really, I did.

"Listen here, you smug prick—"

"Marcus." The mayor held up a hand. "There's no need to

threaten a man's livelihood over a simple inquiry." Marcus let out a very noisy breath but remained silent for now. "This is about Alyssa Winters, right?"

"It is," I said.

"I knew her," Hargrove said. "There are some parts of my past I'm not proud of today. I knew other women like Alyssa, too."

"We're pretty sure the man who's in jail for her murder didn't do it."

"And you think the mayor of Annapolis did?" Dunning demanded.

"Maybe an overzealous member of his staff. The kind of guy who might start yelling for no reason. Know anyone who fits the bill, Marcus?"

Dunning didn't take the bait, but his boss didn't give him much of a chance to. "You're aware I used to . . . party with the ladies?" Hargrove asked, and we all nodded. "It's not a chapter I look back on with pride, but I've accepted it. Now, I have faith and family to get me through everything." I managed to avoid rolling my eyes, but the effort was almost Herculean. "What happened to Alyssa is a shame. She'd really turned her life around, and I think she could have helped other women do the same."

Since the mayor used a particular word, I inquired about it. "Do either of you know the term 'harbor party'?" Dunning's face darkened for an instant, but he recovered and shook his head. Hargrove made the identical gesture. "We've found references to it in some pages from Alyssa's journal."

"She had a journal?" Dunning wanted to know.

"As far as we can tell. We're still trying to find the whole thing, but the term intrigued me. Neither of you know it?" Both men indicated they didn't. I wasn't sure I believed either.

"In the context of women in Alyssa's profession," T.J. said, "a party usually refers to sex."

"I'm familiar with the term," the mayor said.

"The harbor's a big place," I said. "Once you're on the water, you can more or less go anywhere. The harbor takes you to the Chesapeake Bay, which feeds into the Atlantic Ocean, and from there, you could take a boat all up and down the coast. It'd be easy to pick up someone from another state."

Dunning put up a hand. "Hold on. What are you saying?"

"I'm trying to figure out what the term means." I shrugged. "Lot of possibilities. Some of them are innocent. Others are federal crimes. Maybe while you're calling the state police, I'll dial the FBI."

"I think we're done here," the chief of staff barked.

"So neither of you can help us figure out what happened to Alyssa?" Lexi asked before we got the boot.

"Drugs, wasn't it?"

"Someone wanted the police to think so."

Dunning spread his hands. "I didn't know her well. Only saw her with the mayor a few times. She seemed like a nice girl."

"She'd been out of the life for three years," T.J. added.

"People relapse," Dunning said. "It happens."

"I hope you find out the truth," Hargrove said.

"I think we will," I said.

Before I could leave, Dunning grabbed my arm. He had a strong grip. "I think this is a shame," he said, "but it's not a story. Famous podcaster or not, there's nothing here. There's certainly nothing involving the mayor of the greatest city in Maryland."

I jerked my arm free. "Save the slogans for your posters." We left.

As we walked back to my car, Lexi said, "Dunning really wants this to go away."

"Yep."

"He threatened us, right?" T.J. said.

"Yep," I repeated. "Not explicitly, but he did.

"Prick," Lexi muttered. "He's obviously used to getting his way. I look forward to disappointing him."

"You think he did it?" T.J. asked.

"I don't know," I said, "but he's a much better suspect than Darrell Wilson."

CHAPTER 10

MY LEAST FAVORITE way to wake up was via text or phone call.

So of course, my phone vibrated and buzzed on the nightstand. We were at Gloria's house, where the table configuration was different, and it took me longer than normal to find my mobile. Opening my eyes would have helped, but I was determined to remain asleep as long as possible. Naturally, this presented a problem when reading the text, forcing me to concede to the inevitable. Rich sent a message. *Let's meet for breakfast. Double T in an hour.* It was just after 8:30 on a Saturday morning. I didn't want to be awake, but I might learn something from talking to Rich, so I said I would meet him there.

As I dressed after getting out of the shower, Gloria stirred. "Headed out early?" she asked. Sleepiness made her voice even more alluring. I needed to leave the room before my knees buckled.

"Rich wants to meet for breakfast." I leaned down and kissed her. "I'll put coffee on before I go."

"Thanks," she murmured. After a quick stretch, my wife

drifted off to sleep again. I headed downstairs, started the promised pot of magic morning juice, and headed for my car. The Double T Diner was a local chain with a bunch of locations in the Baltimore metro area. Rich didn't specify a location, but I knew which one he meant. It was on Belair Road, maybe a mile from the Beltway. I remembered it as a Denny's even a few years ago and didn't know when it had made the transition.

I pulled into the lot five minutes late. Among the assembled vehicles was Rich's familiar blue Camaro. I walked inside. Warring smells of coffee and sizzling meat welcomed me as forks scraping on plates provided a screechy soundtrack. Rich waved from a two-top table near the back. The restaurant was about half full, but Rich—like most cops—somehow had the power to keep the tables around him empty. Maybe some of it would rub off on me over breakfast.

A moment after I sat, a middle-aged waitress with her hair in a bun approached. I ordered coffee, promised to need frequent refills, and looked at the menu. Like most diners, it read like a novella. Page after page of options presented themselves, and if I were stumbling in drunk in the wee hours of the morning, I might have faced a difficult choice. As it was, when the waitress returned with my coffee, I ordered a spinach and cheese omelet with toast and sausage. Rich told her he would have the same, and we handed in our menus.

"You have any room to move around your office?" he asked after sipping his coffee.

Unlike Rich, I added some cream to mine. "There's not enough space to play baseball anymore," I said, "but we have some great walls for Nerf gun battles."

Rich's frown suggested he didn't know whether he should take me seriously. Little did he know all three of us kept Nerf guns in our desks—for Lexi and me, these were in addition to the less colorful versions which fired actual bullets. "Find anything?"

"Despite the BPD trying to bury us in discovery, yes. We're making progress."

Rich chuckled. "Listen to you. Someone's been watching *Perry Mason*."

I scoffed. "I couldn't get into the new one. Too much backstory."

"There are plenty of old episodes."

"Sure," I said. "When I'm ready for a nightly glass of prune juice, I'll look them up."

Our food arrived. I added a little salt and a healthy amount of pepper to the omelet. It was the perfect shade of eggy yellow with a little browning at the edges. Green hunks of spinach broke the surface in a few spots. Our server topped off our mugs before departing again. Rich and I both ate for a few moments before he resumed the conversation. "What do you think of the podcaster?"

"I don't know her very well yet. Seems like she's done good work in the past."

He shook his head. "She's an amateur."

"So are the people who went back and solved actual cases the police got wrong."

"You're going to see this through?" he asked.

"Yes," I said. "We're already sure the guy you arrested isn't the killer." In this case, since Rich was the lead investigator, I didn't mean the royal "you" I often used to refer to the work of the BPD as a whole. Rich was smart enough to understand this.

"Great. Two people who don't know what they're doing are digging in the dark and looking for answers."

"I'm pretty sure I've established my bona fides plenty of times." I sipped some coffee and used those few seconds to avoid an angry rant. "Should we go over all the cases I've helped the BPD solve or get right? Maybe we can start in the recent past with Adrian Brown. How did the homeless guy you arrested work out?"

"Fine." Rich put up a hand. "You've done good work. I shouldn't have painted both of you with the same brush. I don't trust the podcaster."

"Naomi."

"Whatever," Rich said. "She's an entertainer. They all are. Clicks and downloads matter more than justice."

"I expressed similar concerns when she wanted to hire us," I said.

"And?"

"And if Naomi's goals were as you described, I would have sent her packing."

Rich finished his omelet and spread grape jelly on his toast. Not being a philistine, I opted for the far superior strawberry. "There are other effects," my cousin said. "*Serial* might have done some good things, but at least one witness in the case got harassed nonstop."

"I don't think Naomi will do those things," I said. "I certainly won't." I ate my sausage patties while Rich's brows knitted in thought.

"You come up with a suspect?"

"Working on it. We have a couple people we like."

"Be careful," Rich said. "The BPD still considers the case solved, so I don't know how much help you'll get."

"We'll be all right."

"Anything I can unofficially do?"

"Get Darrell Wilson released."

Rich snorted. "How about something realistic?"

"Be ready to make arrests," I said. "We're going to figure it out."

———

"Are you bringing me anything?" Gloria asked.

She was awake now, and based on the clarity and tone of her voice, I guessed her to be halfway through her second cup of coffee. "An omelet and bacon."

"I love you."

"With good reason," I said.

"What did Rich want?"

I kept an eye on the rearview mirror. Shortly after I pulled out of the Double T's parking lot, a gray Chevy SUV exited behind me. It merged onto the Beltway behind me, and mirrored my lane changes while hanging two or three cars back. Its tinted windshield made it easy to spot. I've never been accused of keen observation, so if I spotted a tail, the drivers either weren't very good, or they wanted me to know they were on my six.

"You there?" my wife asked.

"Yeah. I'm not sure what he wanted, really. It was an odd mix of telling me amateurs can't crack the case and pledging his support when I need it."

"Weird."

"Yeah," I said. "It's like he needs to give me the official company line but also remembered I've helped him close quite a few cases."

Gloria chuckled. "Which I'm sure you pointed out."

"Moi? Do I seem like the type to tell Rich he needs to invite me to his next commendation ceremony? Or how he should get a comfortable chair if he's going to ride my coattails?"

"Never," Gloria said.

"Right. I'm way too polite to be such a jerk." I peeked at my mirror. The gray SUV was still back there. I moved to the left lane to get around a slower car. Of course it was a Prius. Several seconds later, my followers did the same. I'd been planning to return to Gloria's, but I wouldn't lead this asshole to her doorstep. "I'm gonna make a stop before I come to your house."

"Everything all right?" she wondered.

"It's fine." We said our adieus. If I'd been driving to my home in Federal Hill, I would have gone a different direction. My pursuers may not have known my destination, however. I wanted them to remain ignorant of the fact I'd sussed them out. When the exit for I-83 South neared, I got into the right lane and took the ramp. The SUV needed to speed up to make the same merge.

I headed down 83, settling in at 65 miles per hour. It was slower than I normally drove, but I still wanted to maintain the illusion. Going to my office would be easier from here, so I stayed on President Street when the highway ended and drove into Fells Point. I pulled into the lot, took my usual spot, grabbed my pistol from the glove box, and waited.

The Blazer drove up a few seconds later. A generic badge logo was painted on the driver's door. The window was down, and the two guys inside stared at me as they moved past. They were both white with short hair and goatees, and sunglasses hid their eyes.

I waited a few minutes to see if they would circle back. When it became apparent they were gone, I texted my assistant and our intern.

We must be on the right track. Two guys in a government-looking Blazer just tailed me and gave me the stare down.

T.J.: Did you shoot them?

Lexi: I was going to ask that!

No. Let's be vigilant as we keep working, though.

T.J.: You got it, boss.

———

Gloria and I spent the day enjoying the good weather in Baltimore. She dragged me into a bunch of shops, we ate a large and excellent lunch, and her smile was the best thing I saw all week. Before dinner—and ahead of dusk and darkness—I told her I wanted to head back to Annapolis. "Something bothers me about the mayor and his chief of staff," I said. "Several somethings, really."

"You think they did it?"

"I don't know, but I'm certain they're better suspects than the guy currently in prison."

"Be careful," Gloria said. "My husband being a podcast hero is only cool if I can show you off."

I chuckled. "I'll be fine." We were staying at my house after our day in the city, so I grabbed an actual camera and headed out. My father bought it for a photography class he took years ago. Not long after, he decided he'd rather be the sort of man who talked about taking a class at parties than snapping a bunch of pictures—an outcome I'd predicted when he enrolled —so he gave me the camera. It took much better photos than my phone, and the additional lenses offered superior zoom capabilities. I wasn't the kind of PI who lurked in the trees and waited for the right moment to take a picture, so I didn't get to use it often.

Tonight seemed like a good time.

The mayor had two locations in Annapolis—his desk at city hall and a campaign office. City law limited Hargrove to two terms if elected consecutively, so whatever campaign he and his staff prepared was for something bigger. This could be added motivation for him and for Marcus Dunning, a man who made his career clearing a path for whatever Hargrove wanted, both in the real estate arena and now in city politics.

City Hall was a bigger building, well guarded, and potentially hard to see someone moving around in. I drove by, didn't see any lights on the top floor, and kept going. It was a Saturday evening, and the weather remained warm, so people were coming to the city. The older parts of Annapolis were filled with pubs and eateries similar to downtown Baltimore. I lucked into a parking spot about a hundred yards from the campaign office. It was a large house with only a small sign indicating its purpose, and it stood on a block with no bars or restaurants.

Lights shone through curtains on the second floor. I took this as a good sign and settled in. I had a bag of peanuts and a bottle of water in case my mini-stakeout took a while. After about twenty minutes, I saw a figure walk past one of the windows. It was the right size and shape to be Dunning, but I couldn't see anything other than his outline. It made sense he would be here. His job defined him. He'd built his professional life around the ascension of Hargrove, and it worked out. Dunning wasn't married, and I surmised his job bled over into whatever passed for his personal life.

The same figure moved back and forth a couple times. I got a photo of one, but after reviewing it on the camera's screen, I knew it was useless. No editing software in the world would let me see through the thick yellow curtain. The front door opened, and a young man walked out. He must have been a staffer or volunteer. Judging by his age, he may not have made it to high school when Alyssa died. I took the photo anyway. You never know who thinks the boss is a jerk and wants to flip on him.

Not much else happened for about an hour. Any remaining parking spots on the block got sniped by people walking to nearby destinations. I sat low in the S4 driver's seat, and the deepening dusk probably made me hard to see for anyone walking by the car. A loud engine heralded the presence of a large vehicle. A gray late-model GMC Yukon cruised down the street. There was no parking, but something told me whoever drove the SUV wasn't looking for a space. The rear plate identified the vehicle as belonging to the city of Baltimore.

I held my camera at the ready. The two upstairs lights in the campaign office winked out. A moment later, Marcus Dunning emerged from the front door. He locked up and waited. The Yukon had its flashers on, and the intermittent amber light was both bright and annoying. The right rear door opened, and I made sure to get a good angle on whoever stepped out.

It was Captain Leon Sharpe.

"Shit," I muttered as I snapped two pictures. Sharpe was tall, probably six-six, and built like he could lift the Yukon if a kid's ball rolled under it. His bald black head gleamed in a nearby streetlight. If Sharpe wasn't distinct enough already, he wore his official uniform. I held out hope he would walk up to the house, punch Dunning in the face, and drag his unconscious body into the GMC.

Instead, Dunning met him in front of the house, and the two shook hands like old friends.

"Shit," I said again as I took the photos.

CHAPTER 11

I SNAPPED A FEW MORE PICTURES. Neither man faced me, so I couldn't hear or see what they were saying. Even if I took a video, I wouldn't have a shot of their faces. I was far enough away they didn't notice me. After a second handshake, Captain Sharpe got back into his SUV and left. Dunning checked the door and headed away from the house. He got in a car whose make and model I couldn't discern and drove away.

When they both left, I also headed out of the city and called Rich. "I just saw something you should know about."

"What is it" he asked.

"Before I tell you, I just want you to know I'm trying to avoid saying 'I told you so.'"

Rich sighed. "Let me guess. It's about this case, isn't it?"

"Yes," I said. "I just saw Captain Sharpe shaking hands with Marcus Dunning in Annapolis."

My cousin didn't say anything for a few seconds. "So?" He finally asked.

"Really?" I said "I drop this on you, and your response is 'so'?"

"What do you want me to say?" he demanded.

"I don't know. How about, 'You were right, C.T.,' or, 'I should never doubt you, C.T.,' or, 'It's unfair someone so handsome is also so brilliant.' Something like those."

"You don't even know what they were doing there."

"You're right. I don't. But don't you think it's a little suspicious?"

"Not really. Dunning is ex-military, right? They could know each other from the service."

"Dunning knows we're at least looking into him," I said. "We went to talk to him and the mayor, and he tried to shut us down right away. Threatened my license. Now, he meets with your boss, the lieutenant who signed off on the case eight years ago, and you don't think it's at least a little weird?"

"He's not my boss, "Rich said.

"Right. Because chain of command is the *obvious* takeaway there."

"Like I told you, you don't know what they were meeting about. It could be something totally innocent."

"If Dunning is involved, I don't think there's anything innocent about it." When Rich offered no response, I asked, "How much was Sharpe involved in the original investigation?"

"I don't know."

I understood Rich wanted to get to the truth and make sure the right person ended up in prison, but his staunch loyalty to the police department frustrated me at times. "How did you get to Darrell Wilson as a suspect?"

It took Rich a couple seconds to answer. "Sharpe mentioned him as a possibility."

"Jesus Christ."

"It might have been legit."

"You think so after what I told you I saw tonight?" I pressed. "I have pictures I can show you if you don't believe me."

"I believe you," Rich said in a quiet voice.

"You're a lieutenant today. How often do you present suspects to the cops working under you?"

"Almost never." He breathed a couple times. "All right, I'll admit this doesn't look good. You don't know what they were talking about, though."

"You're right," I said. "I couldn't hear them, and I was trying to stay out of sight. I'm going to focus on the 'doesn't look good' part of it."

"Sharpe's a survivor," Rich said. "I can't imagine he'd be involved in something so shady."

Rich was right. Sharpe was an old-school cop who still managed to keep his job and rank in a world which looked more and more unfavorably at the methods he used for years. Even when the Justice Department slapped the city around in the aftermath of Freddie Gray's death in police custody, Sharpe kept going. He was a door-knocker and a head-kicker operating in an era of online investigations and de-escalation techniques. I liked Leon Sharpe, but I also wondered how he'd survived this long. Knowing a reputed fixer like Marcus Dunning could help. "Maybe he's not," I allowed. "I need to run this down, though. Darrell Wilson probably needs a new lawyer."

"If he didn't do it, he shouldn't be in jail."

"Still think I'm some amateur who's digging in the dark?" Rich hung up on me. "I'm taking this as a no," I said to the dead connection.

———

The next morning, I woke up before Gloria. While I usually did, today, I got up earlier than normal for a Sunday. It was just after eight, and I remained agitated from the events of the prior evening. My sleep hadn't been great, and I knew lying here and trying to doze off again would be futile.

I changed into running attire and hit the mean streets of Baltimore. The city woke up later on Sundays. Even with the archdiocese consolidating houses of worship, church was the priority for many people. Fewer cars navigated the roads, and the pleasing smells which normally accompanied my morning constitutionals during the week were largely absent. I walked at a brisk pace to Federal Hill Park, and once I felt warmed up, I broke into a run.

Even though it was a nice morning, not many people ran the circuit with me. I looked across the harbor as the reflected sunlight roiled in the waves. A few people ran on the opposite side, past the defunct pavilions and approaching the Maryland Science Center. The Ravens were on the road today, so traffic remained light on the other side of the water, too.

I thought about why Sharpe might have been meeting with Marcus Dunning. They could have known each other from the military. Still, why not go to a bar and catch up over beers or whiskey? Meeting at the mayor's campaign office was a choice both men made. They must have expected to be alone—or at least not be seen by anyone who knew who they were. Just two guys shaking hands and chatting on the street. Happened every Saturday in a city the size of Annapolis.

Thirty-odd minutes later, I walked back up Riverside Avenue, breathing heavily and sweating. My agitation made me run harder and faster than I normally did. It made for a good workout even if it didn't provide me any epiphanies. I slipped inside my house and headed to the basement. The ceiling's height prevented me from standing straight unless I put my head between the beams. Even with this limitation, I added some weights and equipment a couple years ago to supplement my cardio routine.

After twenty minutes of dumbbell and kettlebell work, I headed upstairs for a much-needed shower. Gloria stirred when I emerged fully dressed. She mumbled something I couldn't understand. "I'm making coffee and breakfast," I said. She mumbled again. I took it to mean acknowledgement. Sure enough, she headed downstairs when the java finished brewing. "Perfect timing," I said.

She planted a minty kiss on me. "You were up early."

"Rough night."

Gloria squeezed my butt as she grabbed a clean mug. "I could have made it nicer for you." I smiled. "What's going on?"

I told her over breakfast—scrambled eggs, turkey bacon, and sourdough toast. "I'm not sure what to think," I said in conclusion. "Sharpe's one of those guys who always walks the line, but I've never seen him cross it. Rich keeps telling me I don't know what they were talking about, and he's right. The whole thing doesn't sit right with me."

"I like Captain Sharpe," Gloria said.

"Me, too."

"You're right, though . . . it doesn't look good. He put Rich onto the man who's been in jail, and now he's shaking hands with someone you're looking into?" She frowned. "Do you think Sharpe knows you're investigating?"

"Yes," I said. "I doubt he listens to *Harbor Homicides*, but he probably knows people who do. Any one of them could have tipped him off. Marcus Dunning had plenty of time to call him and say we'd harassed the mayor."

"It could be nothing."

"Maybe."

"This is going to gnaw at you all day, isn't it?" Gloria asked.

"Probably."

———

The case definitely gnawed at me.

I watched the Ravens game—a victory against Cleveland—minus some of the joy and absent instances of shouting at the TV when the team played badly or when the officials made one of their many bad calls. We never had lunch, so Gloria used her turn on dinner to order delivery. This was far better than the alternative. I loved my wife, and she had many virtues, but aptitude in the kitchen would never be counted among them.

She chose a Japanese restaurant I'd never heard of. Our vegetable tempura remained crisp thanks to holes in the container allowing the steam to vent. We shared the two entrees—one steak, the other chicken and shrimp—as we watched the early edition of the local news following the game. After I put the leftovers into containers, I rejoined Gloria on the couch.

"Why don't you go to the office?" she said a few minutes later, apparently sensing my mood.

"It's Sunday. We just had a nice dinner."

"It's fine." She smiled. "You're working a big case, and you can't let something go. I'd rather you try and figure it out than sit here and stew in silence."

"I don't think I was stewing," I said.

"You were."

"More of a light simmer."

"Whatever you want to call it," Gloria said, "I know you

want to run something down. Go ahead. Meet me at my house when you're done."

"Have I told you recently how awesome you are?"

Gloria kissed me. "No . . . but you can show me later." I smiled, and she jerked her head toward the door. "Go." I went. Manny's was closed on Sundays, but I had a key to the main entrance and the code to disable the security system—which I'd basically set up for him. I unlocked the upstairs office and shook my head at the stacks of boxes. I wanted to keep looking, but now, the enormity of the task stared back at me in the guise of cardboard cases.

"You wanted to come here," I reminded myself.

I couldn't just grab a box at random, leaf through it, and hope for a breakthrough. This required a more methodical approach. I considered calling T.J. or Lexi to help. They'd probably both be willing, but they also deserved to have the day off. I needed to handle my mini-obsession alone. We'd already been through some of the evidence, mostly the early parts of the investigation. Reviewing them again would serve no purpose.

No matter what was in here, I didn't expect a smoking gun. There would be no investigative note stating *Lieutenant Sharpe talked to Marcus Dunning and told us we should investigate Darrell Wilson.* Even if Sharpe were on the up-and-up in all this, no direct attribution would exist in writing. The later boxes would be the police building the case—such as it was—against Wilson.

I started around the middle, grabbing a case and carrying it to the table. It held little of interest. Nothing about Darrell or Marcus Dunning. The notes were mostly about Alyssa's life as a prostitute. The cops interviewed a bunch of people—many of them women in the same profession—who knew her back then. I set the box to the side and kept going.

It took four to find something of real interest.

It was most of a handwritten note. The top part of the paper had been torn away, so I didn't know the addressee's identity. Even eight years ago, I wondered how many people wrote notes versus sending emails or texts. Before I saw the name at the bottom, the neat handwriting convinced me whoever wrote it was a woman.

> on the boats.
>
> The harbor parties continue. They go on for hours. The boat is fast enough to make it to Virginia or the Carolinas and turn back around. No one knows who gets on. The guys and girls always come back to Maryland. I don't know what happens from there.
>
> Be careful. If anyone asks you about working one of these, say no. If you're being pressured, come find me. I don't want you anywhere near these.
>
> Alyssa

I blew out a deep breath. This didn't fill in all the gaps about the harbor parties, but now, it was clear men and women hopped onto the boat at different ports of call. I inferred the women didn't necessarily come of their own free will, which represented trafficking. If the origins were Virginia or anywhere outside of Maryland, it became interstate trafficking and a federal crime. I wondered if Marcus Dunning somehow made Darrell Wilson into a fall guy, presented him to Sharpe, and watched him go down for Alyssa's murder to head off the FBI.

Regardless, there was no evidence entry of this note, and I found no indication any officer or detective—or sergeant—ever followed up on it. "Shit," I said to the empty office.

CHAPTER 12

MONDAY MORNING, both T.J. and hot coffee were waiting for me in the office.

I poured a mug and carried it to my desk. My assistant stood staring at the assembled boxes, hands on her hips. "Were you here over the weekend?" she asked.

"Guilty as charged."

"What were you doing?"

"Looking for something," I said. I hadn't filled her in on my adventurous Saturday evening or the resultant chat with Rich, so I spent a few minutes catching her up. "Basically, Leon Sharpe may or may not be dirty in all this, Dunning definitely seems like a snake, and Rich is going to walk the blue line until we come up with something he can't ignore."

"Someone had a busy weekend."

"I did."

"You could have called me," T.J. said.

"I wanted you to have a couple days off."

"*You* didn't."

"My name is on the door," I said. "It doesn't only matter when I'm fighting off goons or putting myself in danger."

"Let me see the note you found."

"It's in the top box in the third stack. First file folder."

T.J. got the cardboard case down, took out the folder, and read the note. She frowned and held it up. "This gives us a little more on harbor parties but not everything."

"I know."

"It's worth looking into. I want to run a couple things down."

"All right," I said. While T.J. busied herself with her phone, I wanted to know more about Darrell Wilson. The BPD's investigation into him seemed perfunctory. Once he appeared on their radar as a suspect—via some combination of Marcus Dunning and Leon Sharpe—the cops assembled enough of a background to make him plausible, took their case to the DA, and got a conviction thanks to circumstantial evidence and an overworked public defender's office.

Before I forgot, I dashed off a text to Liz Fleming, a lawyer I knew. She used to serve in the public defender's office. I met her on one of my first cases, and we worked together a few times. She struck out on her own a few years ago and had since made a name for herself as a capable but principled defense attorney. *I might have a case for you. Someone wrongly imprisoned 8 years ago. Had a PD the first time around. We're trying to prove he didn't do it.*

It was the right time for court to be in session, so I went back to my research. T.J. turned away and talked in a low tone. I couldn't hear her, and she seemed to want it this way, so I didn't try. Maybe it was the coffee, but another realization hit me . . . the harbor parties needed to begin and end somewhere. A port. A marina. Considering the possible involvement of Hargrove and/or Dunning, Annapolis presented itself as a likely beginning and end of the boat rides. The city did not lack for possibilities.

I looked at them on a map when T.J. turned back around. "I might have something."

"Do tell."

"Bree is willing to meet with us," she said. "With you this time."

"This is the girl you and Lexi talked to in Fells Point?" I asked.

"Yeah. She didn't want to talk to you before. I think she doesn't trust men very easily."

"I understand." I'd dealt with this the first few months T.J. worked for me. We'd met nearly two years prior on an earlier case, but the life she led saw her come into contact with men who wanted one thing from her and cared about nothing else. It took her a little time to warm up to me, but we'd enjoyed a very good working relationship since then.

"She's willing to come by," my assistant said. "She told me she can fill in some gaps about Alyssa."

"Good. We have a few chasms in the case. When's she coming?"

"Ten-thirty."

I glanced at my watch. We had almost an hour. "Okay. We don't know the last time she had a good meal. Let's make sure she has breakfast and fresh coffee."

T.J. smiled. "I'll run out and get something. You can be on java detail."

"I'll manage," I said.

———

Bree was a few minutes late, but she stopped by as promised.

Even wearing a sweater and jacket, she was noticeably thin. I remembered thinking Melinda and T.J. needed a steady diet of cheeseburgers when I first met them. This young woman did, too. Her hair was a dull brown, and I didn't know if it's general lifelessness was the cause or symptom of its lack of styling. Her age was impossible to guess. Based on the timeline involved, she must have been at least twenty-five, but any number under fifty wouldn't have surprised me.

Our guest smiled at T.J. but frowned at me. I gestured toward our small round table. "There's breakfast if you want it, and the coffee is fresh."

She glanced between my assistant and me a few times. Eventually, T.J. nodded, and Bree took a seat. A breakfast burrito—wrapped in foil to stay hot—sat on a plate. Bree tore a swath of the wrapper off and took a massive bite. Steam flittered up, but if the heat bothered her, she gave no indication.

After a few ravenous bites, she said, "Thanks. I need to eat."

"No problem," I said. She kept eating. "May we join you?"

Her eyes took us both in again before she bobbed her head. I let T.J. sit closer to her and took a chair across the table. Bree obviously didn't trust me, and I figured this stemmed from the way she'd been treated by countless men over the years. "I'm glad someone is looking into Alyssa," she said after finishing the massive burrito. I'd always struggled to put one away in a single sitting, and even if I could, it took me half again as long as it did her. "I never believed the guy they arrested really did it."

"We don't, either," T.J. said.

"Proving it is harder," I added. "We want to get Darrell a real lawyer to try and get him out, but we also need to have a better suspect."

"Darrell was basically a nobody," Bree said. "Whoever

killed Alyssa had something to lose. She knew too much about too many powerful people."

"Harbor parties," I said.

"You know about them?"

"In general terms. We need more specifics."

Bree reached into the pocket of her jacket. She pulled out a plastic zipper bag full of folded papers. "Alyssa wrote things down," she said. "I took some pages when I thought she might be in real trouble."

"From whom?" I asked.

"Someone with a lot to hide."

"Did she keep anything else?" T.J. wanted to know. "An online journal?"

"I know she had some digital stuff," Bree said. "Like a flash drive. Maybe CDs since it was so long ago."

"Do you know where?"

Bree shook her head. Her hair barely moved when she did. "No. I don't think anyone knew."

"Do you think the mayor might have been involved?" I asked.

"It's possible," Bree said. "He was still running for office, and even then, most people knew he loved the ladies." She snorted. "He's a bad lay and a worse tipper."

"Probably not a slogan he'll use in his next campaign."

Our guest smiled. "I suppose not."

"You ever go to a harbor party?"

"A few."

"What do you remember?" T.J. nudged, her tone gentle.

"Being on the boat." Bree's eyes took on a faraway look. "They used more than one. I think one of them was called . . . *The Wayward Woman?* Something like that. The weather was always great. A good mix of guys and girls to start, but always more guys. Then, I'd have a drink or two, and the rest is always . . . hazy."

"Someone roofied you," I said.

"Not just me."

"Jesus," T.J. whispered. "They're lucky no one fell overboard."

"Somebody could've," Bree said. "It's not like any of us would remember."

I wondered if it ever happened. Even with no mention of a harbor party, a body found at sea would make the news. "Anything else you can tell us?" T.J. prompted again.

Her brows knitted. "I don't think so."

"Thanks for coming in." I patted the small stack of folded papers. "We'll put these to good use."

"You're not bad," she said, "for a guy."

"You definitely need to work on your slogan writing."

"I'll walk you out," T.J. offered. The two headed through the door together. A few minutes later, a single set of footsteps returned. "I think she helped."

"Yes," I said. "We really need to crack these harbor parties. I think it's a major detail."

"Let's figure out a way, then," T.J. said.

———

"I might have a way to get more info on the harbor parties," I said.

T.J., who had been busy fiddling with her ponytail, stopped. "How?"

"Marinas." She frowned but didn't say anything, so I elaborated. "Whoever's involved isn't going to say anything. The vulnerability is the takeoff and docking. Employees there won't be paid as well, and their silence may not be for sale if they know what's really been happening."

My assistant nodded. "True. We'd ideally need to find people who worked at these places eight years ago and are still on staff."

"I had the same idea," I said. "I'm already looking at the possibilities." Annapolis was a city on the water, but we didn't need to presume boats would leave and arrive within its limits. I stuck to the surrounding area, and the number of marinas which could accommodate a boat large enough to traffick out-of-state women for discreet sex parties was manageable. Six in total.

"How are you going to get their staff rosters?" T.J. asked.

"I'll need a few minutes."

"Want me to start calling around?"

"No," I said. "We don't want to draw any suspicion." The best ways to get employee lists were from the HR departments or payroll providers. A few minutes of intelligent Googling told me all six used the same local company to process their biweekly checks. A quick scan of the firm's website showed an unpatched vulnerability I could exploit.

A couple minutes later, I was in. I jerked my head, and T.J. moved her chair next to mine. The stacks of boxes prevented her usual method of pushing off and wheeling it across the floor. "Not bad," she said. "How'd you do it?"

I realized I should have shown her and included her from the beginning. It was another reminder how she made a better student than I did a teacher. "Scanned their web server," I said. "There's a weakness they haven't patched yet. It's exploitable." I went into a few more details, making sure to stick to things I knew she'd done or practiced before, and she understood.

"Remind me next time, and I'll make sure you're side-saddling me while I do it."

"It's fine. What do we have?"

"Two places have employees we might be able to lean on. Both are men who've been at their jobs about ten years each."

"They might have seen a number of these harbor parties, then."

"It's likely." I pulled up reviews of each location and scrutinized the pictures.

"That one," T.J. said, pointing to the fancier of the two. "We should start there."

I nodded. "We can't go in and pepper someone with questions. We need a cover story . . . like we want to put on one of these damn things."

"Reporters?" I shook my head. "Two people looking for their sister?"

"They'll shut us down in either case. We want to ask questions, but we can't make our real purpose there obvious."

T.J. pursed her lips. After a moment, she clued me in to her latest idea. "We're married. You're the *much* older man, and I'm your trophy wife."

I chuckled. "Not dressed in jeans and a sweatshirt."

She swatted my shoulder. "I clean up nice. What's your story?"

"I'm a handsome and vital man of forty," I said, running with her idea even though it weirded me out a little. "Retired, wealthy, and idle. We're looking for good times on the water and don't mind paying for discretion."

She shrugged. "It'll probably work. Like you mentioned, though, we need to look the part more."

"And I need to change my appearance a little," I said. "Too

much publicity recently. One image search, and our jig would be up.”

“Let’s meet back here, then. How much time do you need?”

“Two hours?” When I required a disguise before, Joey set me up with an associate. I hoped she could squeeze me in again today.

T.J. glanced at her watch. “Let’s make it two o’clock.” It gave us an extra twenty minutes.

“All right,” I said. “See you back here.”

CHAPTER 13

I MET Joey and his "appearance lady" at her place in the Greektown neighborhood of Baltimore.

He wanted lunch out of the deal. I insisted on a rain check because T.J. and I needed to get to the marina before the second shift began. Joey agreed to postpone his injury of my wallet for the good of the investigation. As its name suggested, Greektown was home to quite a few restaurants, and I could have thrown a heavy rock to Ikaros. It was also a short drive down Eastern Avenue from the office. If we had more time, I might have walked.

Joey's contact was Cynthia, a woman who'd worked in makeup and costuming for both TV and the theatre for decades. She lent a hand when he needed to alter someone's appearance as part of making them disappear. She'd done similar work for me about three years ago when I last went undercover as a long-haired, blond, and slightly portly database administrator in Frederick. Hopefully, today's adventure would be one-and-done for my disguise.

As before, the back area of Cynthia's shop was a mess of cardboard boxes and clothes hanging from long racks. I wouldn't want my worst enemy to be found dead in most of what she kept on hand. Cynthia emerged through the curtains a moment later. She was tall and thin with a mop of dark curls and a pencil always tucked behind her ear. A ring light in the room reflected on her glasses, and she moved them to her forehead. "Look who's back."

"It's been a while," I said.

"I remember you."

"I'm sure the best-looking clients are hard to forget." Joey snorted despite the obvious truth of my statement.

"No comment," our hostess said.

"Like before, I need to look a little less handsome. I know it's going to be a steep challenge."

"Steep like a one-degree hill," Joey remarked.

"Christ, you two are still at it," Cynthia said. "Like Statler and Waldorf, just twice as young and half as funny."

"I think we're a little better than half," Joey said.

"One of us is," I said. "I'm here at seventy-five percent dragging your unfunny ass around." He chuckled and shook his head. "Dibs on Statler, by the way. He's the better looking of the pair.'

"Which one's Waldorf?"

"He has the darker hair, and his chin looks like someone glued a Muppet butt to his face."

Cynthia stopped what she was doing and chortled. "You're right, you know."

"I'm used to it," I said.

She sat me in one her chairs and mussed my hair. "What do we need this time?"

"Something short term. I hope I only have to use it once. I want to look like I retired before forty, and I'm rich and successful enough to have a trophy wife."

"Gloria?" Joey wondered.

"Not this time. T.J."

"You sure using her is a good idea?"

"She's like my weird and occasionally annoying little sister. I can admit she's pretty, but it goes no further."

"You want a little gray in the hair?" Cynthia asked, focusing us back on the task at hand.

"Maybe," I said. "What's the threshold to refer to myself as a silver fox?"

"At least half."

I frowned. "Too much. I just want a little. Unfortunately, I'm only adding a little over five years."

"All right." Cynthia put her glasses back on her nose, looked around the space, and disappeared behind a rack of tacky garments. In addition to the table where I sat, she had dressers scattered about the room.

"How's T.J. feel about being your trophy wife?" Joey wanted to know.

"She suggested it," I said. "We need to be people who can ask a few questions but not have it seem like it's our job."

He pursed his lips but eventually nodded. "I'm still dating Sasha."

"Who?"

"The girl from the bar."

"Just give me plenty of notice for picking out a tux," I said. "I'd need to evaluate what's in my closet before I considered a rental."

"We're pretty far away from walking down the aisle."

Cynthia swept back in, a blur of maroon motion as her simple dress flared in her wake. She spun my chair with no notice or warning, rearranged my hair, and plopped a wig atop it. The rug was mostly brown—a couple shades lighter than my very dark locks—with some gray at the temples and the back. "I have a mole, colored contacts, and costume glasses for you, too," she said. "Your picture's online, so I figure you want to throw people off."

"Pretty much," I confirmed.

I put the contacts in place. They changed my eye color from emerald green to a dull brown. The glasses were a contemporary style with clear lenses slightly tinted. Cynthia showed me the best spot to add the fake mole, watched me apply it, and gave me three more if I needed to use this getup more than once. The mirror showed me I projected the image I wanted to. Minus the mole, and with my natural eye color, I could see aging gracefully like this. "You're worth twice what Joey pays you," I told her.

"Fuck off," my longtime friend said.

———

Once I had my new look, I needed to upgrade my wardrobe.

Nothing on Cynthia's racks qualified. The best thing anyone could have done with those clothes was stuff them into an incinerator. I would need to go shopping in my own closet. The drive from Greektown to Federal Hill was quick. Upstairs, I checked out my options. Thanks to Gloria needing part of my closet space, I rotated out-of-season items into another bedroom. My suits, separates, and tuxedoes remained, however. A man needs to have some standards.

I picked a pair of pressed chinos, a white shirt and navy blazer, and brown loafers. If no one believed I retired young, maybe they could hire me to work on a boat. I couldn't tie a nautical knot to save my life, so my employment would set the record for shortest tenure. Dressed for the marina, I drove back to the office.

When I opened the door, T.J. waited in a form-hugging powder blue dress. It stopped just short of her knees and accentuated all the right places. My assistant was a tall, pretty, young woman with athletic legs, and she picked a garment to show off all her attributes. The neckline stopped a little short of being called plunging, but it still took a fairly serious dip. T.J. wore a chain around her neck, and a brooch hung from it. It sat just above her breasts, so it gave my eyes something to focus on other than her cleavage. Her hair, normally pulled into a ponytail, hung free past her shoulders, and she'd teased the ends with a curler. I realized I'd been standing there in stunned silence when she asked, "How do I look?"

"Terrific," I said. "*Now* you look like a trophy wife."

She smiled. "Thanks." T.J. held up her left hand, revealing two gleaming rings on her fourth finger. They sparkled in the light, and one definitely looked like a wedding band. "The only good things I ever got from my mother besides height. The engagement ring is cubic zirconia, but I don't think anyone's going to pull out a jeweler's loupe on us today."

"I think you're right."

T.J. cast a scrutinizing look at my attire. "I need to make sure my fake husband is dressed well. Where's the suit? No tie?"

I scoffed. "Those are for the middle class. People who work for me have to wear suits and ties. I can't be bothered. The time it takes me to make a Windsor knot costs me ten grand."

My assistant chuckled. "Jesus, you certainly have the rich asshole part down."

"I listened to how some of my friends' fathers talked when I was in high school," I said.

We left the office and got into the S4. I wondered if I should have asked to borrow my father's Lexus LS sedan. Joey could have made himself useful and been the driver. Maybe next time—if we had to do this charade again. Early afternoon traffic on a random Monday cooperated, and we made good time heading toward Annapolis. En route, we planned our cover story and identities. T.J. insisted I be named Cyril Donaghue—"You should be used to a first name you don't like," she said, cutting right to the quick—and she was Margaret. "Definitely Margaret. No nicknames for a woman of my status. Maggie and Peggy are so *common*." She'd managed to inject the right amount of haughtiness into her voice. It reminded me of a few teammates' mothers and grandmothers I'd met back in the day.

"Why does Donaghue need a G?" I asked.

"The extra letter is more aristocratic."

Her reasoning was sound, and I couldn't find fault. With our false identities established, I used the GPS to guide us to the first marina on our list. At least twenty boats were docked at its pier or in slips. We got out and headed for the office. A restaurant sat beyond a pair of double doors, and the first sign I saw read *Members and guests should wait to be seated*. The place didn't seem large or quite fancy enough to have membership requirements, but I'd thought the same about homeowners associations in a lot of neighborhoods I'd visited over the years.

I asked the young lady at the counter if Gary was available. When she inquired, I offered a general answer as to why we were there. She said he could see us in a few minutes, and we were welcome to wait outside. It was the most polite dismissal I'd gotten in months. We used it as an opportunity to scout the pier and slips. I wondered if we would need a membership to venture far enough down the let's-host-a-harbor-party road. It might create a paper trail and lend an air of tacit approval the marina may not want. Gary as a solo entrepreneur made more sense. It also explained why he'd worked here for more than a decade. Toward the far end, I saw a large boat called *The Wayward Lady*. "There," I said, jutting my chin toward it.

T.J. nodded. "It must be the one Bree told us about."

I didn't know a lot about boats, but this one looked plenty big enough to have a dozen or more people on board with room to move around and party. On the deck, a musclebound man who looked like he had not been hired for his sailing acumen kept a watchful eye on things. "I'm going to guess he's not the harbormaster."

"Probably not," T.J. said.

"I think it means they're still using the boat for their parties."

"It's a good thing, right?"

Normally, I would have answered yes. However, the presence of a goon, as well as the specter of the mayor and his fixer, cast a pall over everything. "I guess we'll see," I said.

———

"What do you know about boats?" T.J. asked me as we waited.

"They're holes in the water you can only fill with money," I said. "Otherwise, not much."

"I'm a little surprised your parents don't have one."

"I think my mother prefers to be seen as the kind of person who gets invited to boat parties." My assistant rolled her eyes. "I know. I get it. They do cover for some of their peccadilloes with charitable work. Probably more than we can say for a lot of the people who own hardware here."

"True," T.J. said. Even though there was plenty of

sunshine, the lights of the marina made her dress pop. When I first met her, T.J. was eighteen, lanky, still in her old life, and desperate to make a change. Now, a little over four years later, she almost looked like a new person. Her eyes shed their dullness, she talked louder and with more self-confidence, and access to better food filled out her formerly malnourished frame. She was more convincing in her guise than I was in mine.

A middle-aged man with a head full of gray hair approached. He wore chinos in a color close to mine along with a striped polo. His beady eyes took in me and then T.J., lingering far longer on her. "Gary," he said when he walked up. He held out his hand, and I shook it. Gary was one of those guys who tried to dominate the greeting with a strong grip. I'd met men like him before, and digging my thumb into a pressure point made him wince.

I deigned a smirk. "Thanks for meeting us today."

He moved to my assistant. "I don't know you," he grumbled.

T.J. flashed her best high-wattage smile and wrapped his hand in both of hers. "We appreciate your time. I'm Margaret. This is my husband, Cyril Donaghue." She squeezed his hand again.

He colored slightly and gave T.J.'s chest a not-so-subtle look. "What can I do for you?"

"We're interested in some pleasure cruises," I said. Keeping my voice low, I added, "Emphasis on 'pleasure.'"

"I'm not sure I can help you." He didn't recoil or try to end the exchange, however. Gary was the right guy. We simply needed to overcome his reticence.

"Marcus told me you could." His face gave nothing away. "I've heard it's been a while since you put on a good harbor party. I want to bring them back." I pointed to the goon-manned vessel. "And I want to use *The Wayward Lady*. It's got the right name. Good vibes."

Gary stared at me. I stared back. After a few seconds, he bobbed his head a few times. "I can show you the boat. Not going to commit to anything else right now. You understand."

It wasn't a question. "I do."

He led the way to the ship in question. It sat near the end of the marina. I wondered if this enabled a faster getaway, though the position probably mattered less on the water. Gary held up a hand as he prepared to board *The Wayward Lady*. He exchanged a few words with the enforcer, who stared at T.J. and me before going ashore.

I played the dutiful husband and helped T.J. onto the deck. In her four-inch heels, she was nearly as tall as me. "She's a forty footer," Gary began his explanation. Based on my limited knowledge, I knew this meant the boat was a good size. "Egg Harbor's a great manufacturer. We use her for sunset cruises and those sorts of things." Gary leaned a little closer to me. "I've been hoping to get the harbor parties started up in force again."

"Why did they stop?" I asked. I knew the answer—the correct one at least—but I wanted to hear how our host spun it.

"Uh . . . general lack of interest at the time. We still do an occasional one but nothing more." This explained the ship being under guard. "Costs went up, the number of guests went down. You prepared for the expenses?"

"How much are we talking?"

"Significant."

I shrugged. "I retired at thirty-eight. Got myself a much younger wife." As if on cue, T.J. moved beside me and put her arm around my shoulders. I put mine around her waist. It felt too intimate, but we were trying to sell the image. To her credit, she didn't flinch. "I'm good for the money."

Gary looked out over the water. "It'll take some time. I need to make sure all the . . . amenities . . . are available. These have always been popular events."

"I understand." I jerked my head toward my fake wife. "Sometimes, I think I'm just trying to keep up with her."

Gary gave T.J. an appreciative and lascivious smile. Again, she didn't flinch or react. "I can see how it might be a challenge." He leaned in and whispered, "I like them young, too."

It took every ounce of my restraint not to throw him overboard. Instead, I smirked a second time. "Who doesn't?"

"You have other guests in mind?"

"Maybe. I'm open to . . . meeting new people with similar interests." My stomach lurched as if I were seasick and *The Wayward Lady* cut through the water at speed.

"All right," Gary said. "We're talking several hours at sea each time. There's always one stop, sometimes more. Want to see below deck?"

"Sure," I said. He led the way down the staircase. I again held T.J.'s hand both to feign helping my wife and because the steps were narrow. Three narrow doors were closed. Gary opened the first. It was a tiny empty room, maybe seven feet square, with a bare floor and no windows. Enough space for a twin bed but not much else. I didn't need to ask what went on in here. Beside me, I felt T.J. shudder.

"We used to have two rooms," Gary said. "Reconfigured the space to add a third after more people wanted to . . . celebrate below deck. You can even rent access to these."

"For a nice sum, I'm sure," T.J. said. Her voice didn't betray her disgust.

"Depends on the quality of the merchandise, but I'm sure

you could do all right." We headed back to the deck. Gary double checked the door to make sure it was locked before he joined us. "I can ask around if you're interested."

"I am," I said.

"Let me get your contact info, then."

I gave him our names—"With a G," I made sure to add when he typed them—and the number to a burner phone I owned.

"All right." Gary shook our hands again. This time, he didn't try to squeeze mine too hard. "You'll hear from me when I know something." We walked back down the dock. The guard took his post again, Gary returned to the office, and we kept going to the car.

"You think we'll hear anything?" T.J. said once we'd pulled out of the lot.

"I doubt it."

"They have to be careful and check us out."

"And they'll find nothing when they do. We might be able to have Joey whip something up, but if they start looking right away, it won't matter."

"I hope we rattled someone's cage, then."

"If not," I said, "I think we will when Gary runs this meeting up the chain."

She nodded and slipped her shoes off. "I can't wait to get back in regular clothes again."

"Hopefully, our fake marriage stops here."

"Cyril," she said, putting a hand over her chest and affecting the refined lilt to her voice again, "are you fake divorcing me?"

"I am," I said, "and I'm keeping the car."

CHAPTER 14

BACK AT THE OFFICE, I was glad to get out of my disguise. Off came the wig, glasses, and fake mole. I packed everything away and combed my hair while T.J. changed in our restroom. She emerged a few minutes later, her dress in a garment bag, wearing jeans and a thin sweater. Her hair was back in its familiar ponytail. Other than the extra makeup she didn't remove, there was no sign she'd just done an excellent job cosplaying as a trophy wife. I went in next and came back out in jeans and a black quarter zip. "You didn't need to change," T.J. said.

"I definitely did."

"You could at least work in your getup."

"I'd feel compelled to learn more about sailing and tying knots," I said. "We don't have the time to spare." She chuckled. "Besides . . . any more time dressed for the docks, and I'd be tempted to call Gloria a filthy landlubber tonight."

"What's the next move, Captain?" my assistant asked.

"I don't think we dress to the nines for Gary again. We got some confirmation out of him, and I doubt we'll see much else once he starts digging."

T.J. took the brooch on a chain off over her head, careful not to snag her hair in the links. I eyed it curiously. With it no longer sitting above an interesting neckline, something looked a little off about the piece of jewelry. "It has a small camera in it," T.J. said. "A while ago, I visited the spy shop you've mentioned a couple times."

I smiled. "Interesting place. More interesting proprietor."

"He certainly is." She twisted the faux gold backing, and it separated from the jewel. T.J. used a USB-C cable to connect it to her computer. "I started taking video once we walked into the office. It can record for about two hours total. I went everywhere you did on the boat, so I should have everything." She clicked her mouse a few times. "Uploading now."

"Good work," I said.

T.J. tried to lean back, but the legion of cardboard doom prevented it. "Damn boxes," she groused.

"Maybe we can get them out of here soon." I took out my phone and called Liz Fleming. "Darrell needs a new lawyer." A perky female voice answered. I explained who I was and—very briefly—why I was calling. The receptionist told me she would find out if Ms. Fleming had time to speak to me. A moment later, I had my answer.

"C.T. Ferguson," the attorney said. "It's been a few years." Her voice still sounded familiar because we'd worked together several times. "How are you?"

"Can't complain." I put the call on speaker.

"You get in trouble?"

"Probably, but I'm not calling for me. I have a client who needs your help."

"Lay it on me," she said.

I ran down how we came to take the case, what happened to Darrell Wilson, the mountains of paperwork we slogged through, and the dubious nature of the case considering our potential new suspects. I left out my annoyance at not getting a text returned. "Can you help him?" I asked at the end of my sales pitch.

"Maybe. Who was his lawyer before?"

"The public defender."

"Eight years ago." Liz paused, and I could almost hear her thinking. "I probably had just started there when his case would have gone to trial. Wilson . . . Wilson . . . oh! I remember. He got stuck with Go-to-Jury Drury."

"What?"

"Victor Drury. He was about a hundred and ten years old back then. Hated plea deals unless they were too good to pass up. Generally recommended his clients go to trial."

"Did it work out?" I wondered.

"Sometimes," Liz said. "These were people who couldn't afford an attorney, so they got stuck with the PD. What else were they going to do?"

"It's probably a good thing your last name doesn't rhyme with a legal term."

"Probably," Liz agreed with a laugh. "If this Darrell wants me as his lawyer, I'll take him."

"I doubt he can pay you anything."

"I do some *pro bono* work. Besides, if he's been wrongfully convicted and imprisoned, then the city or state will have to pay him. I'll receive a cut there."

"Can you get us in to see him tomorrow morning?"

"Sure," Liz said. "I'll text you the time. I know you like to be late. Maybe try showing up on time for this one." T.J. covered her mouth to avoid snorting or laughing.

"Thanks, Liz," I said. "See you then." I ended the call, and

T.J. stopped trying to suppress her amusement. "Have your fun."

"Did she give you shit for being late, too?" my assistant asked.

"Liz and I disagreed over the necessity for me to be on time."

"I'm sure you did. I like her already."

"Since you're so keen to track my hours, I'll probably go right to the jail in the morning . . . presuming Liz scores us a good time."

"Normally, I'd want to come along," she said, "but I don't mind skipping a field trip to prison."

"I'll bring you a souvenir," I offered.

T.J. grimaced. "Please don't."

———

"The prison?" Gloria wrinkled her nose over breakfast. We were both up early enough to eat at my kitchen table. "I offered to bring T.J. something from the gift shop," I said. "I'm happy to make the same offer to you."

Gloria chuckled as she picked up her coffee. "They don't have a gift shop."

"How would you know?" I asked, leaning closer and arching my eyebrows. "You have some extensive prison experience you didn't tell me about before we got married?"

"Yes," she said, struggling to keep a straight face. "I led a life of crime before I met you. You changed my life."

"Not the first time I've heard it from a woman." Gloria swatted my hand, but her cheeks flushed pink. "Though none of the others were scofflaws." I took the last bite of my multigrain bagel. For some reason, I awoke almost an hour earlier than normal. Picking up a dozen seemed like a great idea for breakfast—and also to negate the benefits of the three miles I ran.

"You really think you can get this guy out of jail?" Gloria wanted to know.

"Not today," I said. "I'm going to see if Liz Fleming will represent him. She's on board, but he gets to decide. If he agrees, she'll file a motion, and we go from there."

"Good luck. I'll be working at my house. A load of paperwork I'm starting to fall behind on."

I swigged the remainder of my coffee. "Seriously, ask T.J. to help. It sounds like you need it, and I'm sure she'd appreciate a little extra money."

"Maybe I will." Gloria stood and kissed me goodbye. "Maybe you can change my life some more later."

"Only if you've repented your evil ways," I said. We kissed again, and I left before my departure could become difficult and delayed. I pulled into the main lot at the correctional facility right on time. The prison was a hard, gray place made of stone, glass, razor wire, and despair. Guards walked the outdoor yard, and all the watchtowers were manned. It was a warm day, so I opted for a short-sleeved button-down over chinos. I had a feeling Liz would introduce me as her investigator to keep me in the room while she met with Darrell.

The attorney was already waiting inside, and she stood when I entered. Liz looked great in a white shirt, dark gray skirt, and heels. She was about five-six, though closer to five-ten with her current shoes, and styled brown hair spilled past her shoulders. Before Gloria and I made things official, Liz and I flirted a few times, though nothing ever came of it. She would make someone a lucky man if she weren't already wedded to the law and her career. "You're actually on time."

"I hate to be predictable," I said.

When the woman behind one of the counter stations called her name, Liz grabbed my arm to tug me along. "He's my investigator," she explained when the gray-haired woman eyed me askance.

"You have ID?"

I showed her through the thick Plexiglas, and she nodded. A few keystrokes followed, and two guest passes emerged from a printer. Liz and I each stuck one on our chests. "We'll call you again when the prisoner is in the attorney room."

"Thank you," Liz said. We waited once more. Liz flipped through emails on her phone, so I did, too. Nothing urgent. She dashed off a couple replies and muttered a few curses before a different guard called us back. This one was a tall, stocky fellow. He checked our IDs in the event they'd changed in the last several minutes before unlocking a room and letting us in.

Darrell Wilson sat on the far side of the metal desk. His wrists were cuffed together, and another chain held them to a bar drilled into the top. The space was about the size of a police interrogation room and featured similar poor lighting. Absent were the security cameras and one-way mirrors. The prison system monitored almost all inmate conversations, but they couldn't watch or listen in to any taking place in rooms earmarked for lawyer meetings. Darrell was a black man of light complexion. He looked tall even sitting in an uncomfortable chair. He was thin, and I wondered how much of a toll his time inside had taken on the man. "Who are you?" he asked when Liz and I sat down.

"Mister Wilson, I—"

"Call me Darrell. I ain't a mister in here."

"All right." Liz started over. "Darrell, I'd like to be your attorney. There's a new investigation into the murder of Alyssa Winters. My investigator here doesn't think you did it."

"I didn't."

"Great." She took a paper and pen from a zipped case which also held a legal pad. "This is an engagement letter. Sign it, and we can get started."

Darrell's dull brown eyes scanned the paper. He frowned after a moment of reading. "I gotta pay you?"

"No," Liz said. "My efforts to get you out will be free. Should we succeed . . . and should you decide to take the advice of your new attorney and sue the shit out of the state . . . I'll get a percentage if we win that action."

"All right." Darrell signed the paper as best he could with his wrists bound. Liz collected the agreement and put it away. "What do we do now?"

"First, I want you to know that anything you tell me is now covered by attorney-client privilege. This extends to my investigator C.T. when he's with me."

"All right. What about my case?"

"The challenge is you've already been convicted. A hallmark of our justice system is how everyone is presumed innocent. I'm afraid that doesn't apply to you. You've been judged guilty." Liz held up a hand to cut off her new client's protest. "It means we have to flip the script and actually prove you're innocent with a habeas petition. To do it, we need new evidence. The kind that will convince a judge."

"You have some?" Darrell wondered.

"Working on it," I said.

"You don't have anything yet?"

"Darrell, it's fine," Liz said. "We're not going to court tomorrow. These things will take time. When they put us on the docket, we'll be ready,"

Darrell's frown remained, but he bobbed his head. "All right. What do you need to know?"

"Any idea who killed Alyssa?" I asked.

"I wish I did."

"I wish you did, too. What about the mayor or his chief goon?"

"Dunning?" Darrell snorted. "Fucking snake. I don't know if they did it, but I wouldn't be surprised. They never liked me."

"Why?"

"I did some work for Hargrove's opponent in his first election."

"Sounds like motive to me," I said.

Liz nodded. "Me, too."

———

"I want to nose around the boat again," I said to T.J. later in the day.

"You think you'll find anything?"

"I don't know. At this point, it's been too long to uncover something like Alyssa's DNA. They've had eight years to clean up. There might be something there, though. Maybe it can tell us what's really going on."

"We know what's really going on," my assistant said.

"We need to be able to prove it. Especially if Darrell's going to get out of prison. New evidence, remember?" Sneaking around wasn't a legitimate means to get it, of course, but it could direct where the police looked later.

"Yeah." She frowned. "What if the guard is still there?"

"I can handle a guard."

"All right. Are we going once it's dark?"

"Yes," I said. "*I'm* going then."

"No way, boss. I'm coming along." She held up a hand to cut off my objection. I complied. "I'll be the driver and lookout. We've operated under the assumption they're going to realize someone might be onto them. If they do, there might be more than one guy. Maybe they're expecting you to come back and do what you're planning."

She had a point. "All right. Pick me up at my house. Eight o'clock."

"Will do," T.J. said.

We ended work a couple hours later. I went home and made dinner. Gloria was at her house, and when I talked to her, I suggested she remain there. "We're getting to the point where people might figure out who I am." I remembered confronting the mayor and Dunning. If they were involved to the degree we suspected, Gary and the goons could already know Cyril and Margaret Donaghue weren't who they claimed to be. "Some of them already know."

"I hope you can wrap this up quickly," my wife said. "I miss you."

"I miss you, too," I said. "I just don't want someone to look for me and find you."

Gloria understood. While most of my cases were pretty routine, I knew she didn't like it when they became dangerous. She also knew this was who I was. I ate dinner and caught up on a streaming show Gloria wouldn't want to watch. As the witching hour neared, I changed into black chinos and a matching lightweight sweatshirt. My hair was already a dark brown. Hopefully, it would be enough to avoid detection.

T.J.'s Mustang rolled down Riverside Avenue right at eight. This marked an occasion I was glad she'd chosen the four-cylinder turbo over the V8. We would be much quieter on approach. Maybe if some asshole blew up this one like her last pony car, I could talk her into a silent electric vehicle. Her apartment's parking lot featured dedicated spots with charging stations.

I hopped in the passenger's side. T.J. had her phone's GPS shared on the car's screen, and we were off. "You think it'll be dark enough?" she asked as we left the city.

"In the sky, sure," I said. "We don't know what the lighting situation at the marina is, but I can't imagine they bathe the area in floodlights at night."

"I guess we'll find out."

About forty minutes later, we neared the parking lot. T.J. killed the headlamps without me needing to suggest it. The lot itself—now holding only a single vehicle—was lit well enough to see where we went. T.J. guided the Mustang near the SUV, a late-model RAV4. If a chase ensued, I liked our odds against it. We could see *The Wayward Lady* and a good bit of the piers. I waited. A guard walked a regular patrol. I watched him go through the circuit twice to make sure I knew the pattern. The place probably had cameras, but electric eyes always carried a question: was someone watching them? Still, real-time or after-the-fact monitoring, I didn't need to become the state's most wanted and most handsome burglar.

I put a small earpiece in my ear. T.J. did the same. I called her, and we verified the comms worked. "Remember, you're pulling double duty," I told her. "Driver and lookout." I pulled a ski mask over my face. "Stay low," I added as I slipped out of the car.

A low fence now separated the main office and dock from the pier area. I hopped it easily, moved in a crouch, and kept close to the boats as I padded along. With the office and restaurant closed, the smell of the salty sea air was more prominent.

Most of the boats had pedestrian names painted on their hulls. The one docked just before *The Wayward Lady* was called *Better than Alimony.* If I wore a cap, I would have tipped it based on the name alone. *Better than Alimony* also stood out for being a rich blue as opposed to the white paint job many of the other crafts carried. Whoever owned it didn't mind the attention it drew. Respect.

The sentry was still on his appointed rounds. He had a few piers and many boats to cover. I remained low and hopped aboard *The Wayward Lady.* Illumination in the area allowed me to see my surroundings, but it proved poor for investigating. Once I got below deck, I could use my flashlight and look around better.

"We got a car, boss," T.J. whispered in my earbud. "They're parking close to the building."

"Let me guess," I said. "Two guys inside."

"Looks like it." She paused. "Yeah, two. They just got out and are heading your way."

"Shit." I looked for the guard. Rather than finish his normal route, he ran toward my position. I liked my chances against him, but two more guys—trained officers if they were really with the harbor patrol—changed the calculus.

He made it to *The Wayward Lady* faster than I thought he could, and he vaulted onto the deck. "You ain't going nowhere," he said. Either he added a growl to his voice for intimidation, or he regularly gargled with nails and broken glass.

"I must be going somewhere, then," I said. He frowned and cocked his head to the side. "Double negative."

Rather than debate me on the grounds of both math and English, he came at me. I leaned out of the way of a haymaker, blocked two more, and answered with a short jab to his gut. It had the desired effect of creating a little space. Footsteps ran closer as I kicked the guard in the gut, drew my leg back again, and gave him another right under the chin. His head snapped to the side, and he dropped like he'd been shot.

As I turned away, the other two walked aboard. They moved with the easy confidence of men who expected things to go their way. They didn't carry guns—this was a good thing, as I'd come unarmed. Both were at least as big as me. "You're tres-passing," one of them barked.

I held my wrists out. "Arrest me, then," I said, knowing they wouldn't. They couldn't. The men who pulled their strings had too much to lose.

"I think we've moved past arrest."

CHAPTER 15

"GOSH," I said, feigning ignorance. Like always, it took considerable effort. "What's past arrest?"

One of them pounded his fist into his palm. These two looked like they came from similar molds in the Goon Factory. Both were about six-three, built like they knew their way around the gym, and kept their hair short. Nothing to grab onto in a fight. Neither had any distinguishing features like a scar. They were large, menacing to many people, and anonymous. The perfect pseudo police organization who could do off-the-books work when the boss required it.

We didn't have a lot of space on the deck especially with the prostrate form of the first guy splayed out. "You want me to call the cops?" T.J. whispered.

"No," I said, trying to disguise it in a deep breath. Neither fake cop accused me of talking to a confederate.

"You can make this easier on yourself," one of them said. He was the same one who'd spoken before. His hair was a shade lighter than his friend's. "We'll even overlook the assault charge you should be facing." I said nothing. "Drop the investigation, stay out of Annapolis, and everybody wins." The ski mask obviously did little to conceal my identity. I tended to like standing out and being distinctive. There was a time and place for everything, however, and right now was neither.

"Especially your bosses," I said. "What's the next office after mayor? Is he going for governor?" No reply. "I don't think a history of hookers, shady building deals, and using pricks like you for his personal goon squad will play well with most voters."

Both showed thin smiles. The pair's apparent spokesman replied, "We gave you a chance." They fanned out as best they could in the confined space. I stepped on the downed man's fingers as I backed toward the rear of the deck to try and gain some room to maneuver. It was an accident, but I'll admit the crunch felt satisfying. The talker surged toward me. I blocked his strikes as his partner waded in.

Fighting two opponents is never easy. Even unskilled ones can capitalize on the advantage, and lucky blows hurt just as much as well-practiced ones. When your foes have done this sort of thing before, the difficulty goes up even more. They were smart. While Mouthy engaged me up high, his friend went for a body shot. I blunted it with a raised knee and kicked out, hitting the second man in the midsection. It wasn't hard enough to drop him, but I only needed him to back off for a second.

He did.

When the spokesman threw a hard right, I stepped to my left, caught his wrist in my right hand, and drove my left elbow up under his chin. He rocked back on his heels but didn't go down. The other one recovered and glowered at me. I grabbed the back of Mouthy's head, hit him in the stomach to start him bending in the proper direction, and bounced his skull off the deck railing. He rebounded and landed hard on his back.

The other one let out a guttural yell as he fired punches at me. When you piss people off, even skilled fighters can trade technique for anger and speed, trying to get their revenge quickly. I turned them all aside, answered with a short jab of my own to give me some space to operate, and then hit my foe with a left elbow strike. It was the second one I'd delivered, and his head was pretty hard. My arm hurt, but I tried to ignore it as he wobbled on his feet.

I tried to shake the pins and needles from my left forearm and hand. My opponent backed away from a right cross, and the numbness made me late blocking his kick. It took me in the left side. Pain blazed along my ribs, and my next breath didn't fill my lungs. I took a step back only to feel two arms wrap around me. "Got you now," the guard growled in my ear. While I struggled against his hold, the second harbor patrol guy gave me a good punch to the gut.

The spokesman got back to his feet, shaking his head to clear the cobwebs. His eyes scanned the area and eventually focused on us. A smile like that of a predator spread across his face. I kept trying to break free, but the burly guard was strong, and he'd wrapped my arms in a way to deny me much leverage. I wriggled my left hand free. It mostly felt normal again. "You want to know what's past arrest?" he said, his tone mocking me. "I'll show you."

He pulled the Taser off his belt. "Great weapon," he continued. "Locks the muscles up. Nonlethal . . . unless you 'accidentally' fall into the water a few seconds later. It takes a few minutes to move again after you get tased. Plenty of time to drown." T.J. asked what was going on in my ear. I didn't answer. I got my second hand free but still couldn't make much headway.

Then, I remembered stepping on this guy's hand as I

moved across the deck. Sure enough, the last two fingers on his left hand were twisted, and he wasn't using them to hold me at bay. Mouthy grinned and raised the Taser. I used my free left hand to grab those broken fingers and twist for all I was worth. The guard howled. I dug my feet in. His grip loosened.

I used all my weight and leverage to jerk my torso to the right.

The taser fired with a dull *thunk.*

I finished my turn.

The guard, having come along for the ride, soon howled in pain. I felt him stiffen, and a jolt of electricity coursed through me. I managed to squirm free. The second harbor goon moved to intercept me. The guard, his muscles locked up from the Taser, wobbled a little and fell forward. His shoulder clipped the back of my thigh as he collapsed, his chest hitting the railing and his stiff form going over the side with a loud splash.

I stumbled forward, unable to regain my balance. The railing loomed. I put my hand on it to steady myself, but I'd built too much momentum. Just like my foe a couple seconds before, I, too, toppled over the side of *The Wayward Lady* and splashed into the water.

———

Before I went over the railing, I had the presence of mind to draw in a big breath.

Whatever residual jolt I got from the guard touching me while getting tased didn't seem to affect me much. Maybe it was the rubber soles on my shoes. Either way, the list of things right with the world at the moment was extremely short, and these two items formed the entirety of it.

The last time I took an unexpected dip in a body of water,

it was the Baltimore Harbor, and I had two bullets in me. One in the side and one in the back. They cost me my spleen, a lung lobe, and a few percentage points on my ability maximums. Memories of going into the harbor assaulted me. The water had been cold then. Today, in September, it still held some warmth from the summer. Unable to take a breath in my current predicament, I focused on this difference to try and remain calm.

My earbud fell out at some point after I went under. I'd been at the stern. *Better Than Alimony* would be to my right. In the murky depths, its dark hull stood out. I stayed under and swam toward it. Only when I felt my way around to the far side did I stick my head up.

"Get him back!" Mouthy shouted. "He's gonna drown!"

"Where'd the PI go?"

"Who cares? We know who they are. We'll see what they have soon enough."

"Shit," I muttered under my breath.

"We need to find the detective," the second fake cop said.

"Maybe he'll do us a favor and drown," the spokesman said. "Let's get Andy out first."

I went under again as someone else splashed into the water. I popped up twice, hiding between boats to get more air each time. Eventually, I reached the end of the pier and pulled myself out of the drink. Water poured from my clothes. I stayed low and ran to T.J.'s Mustang. Her eyes widened as she saw me approach. She unlocked the door, and I climbed in. "Sorry in advance about the seat," I said.

She took off. "Forget it. What the hell happened?"

I looked over my shoulder, but *The Wayward Lady* was too far away to make out what happened. "The guard came back early. I guess I tripped a camera or motion detector somewhere.

Dealing with him wasn't hard, but then two assholes with the harbor patrol showed up."

"They must have been nearby already."

"Probably expecting us to do something like this."

"You all right?"

"I'm more annoyed than anything," I said. "I like these clothes."

"I'm guessing you want to go home from here?" T.J. asked.

"I think they're onto us." I looked in the passenger's mirror for a tail and didn't see anything. "One of the harbor patrol pricks said, 'We know who they are. We'll see what they have soon enough.' Plural. We cleaned up well, but I don't think the Donaghues fooled anyone."

"You think they know who I am, too?"

"Probably. You and Lexi were there when we talked to the mayor and Dunning. I'm sure they got screen caps of all of us from their cameras. Easy to compare Margaret Donaghue to you. From there, I'm sure Dunning knows people who could run your file." Including Leon Sharpe, but I hoped he would take selling us out as a bridge too far.

We were on the highway. My assistant drove well above the suggested speed. "We'll get to my apartment first," she said. "I don't want to check it out alone."

"All right." I texted Gloria to be careful, lock the doors, and turn the alarm on. She said she would. By now, she knew the time for questions would come later. I could practically feel T.J.'s tension in the cabin. "We'll be okay."

She offered a small nod but kept driving in silence.

CHAPTER 16

T.J. WAS full of nerves as they neared her building.

She'd chosen The 501 for several reasons. Its location was great, most renters were young like her, the rent wasn't eye-watering—though it was definitely aspirational for her at the time—and most of all, the place got high marks for security. Now, as she guided her Mustang into the lot, she hoped the last one held true.

A few months ago, her prior Mustang blew up in this very same parking area thanks to a murderous duo collectively branded as Vox Populi. The fallout had been mild, with The 501 admitting to gaps in their security that enabled the duo to access the lot and spend the time it took wiring a car to explode with no one seeing them. Inside the building, T.J. had always felt safe.

She wondered if this would remain true.

After parking the car, she hurried inside. C.T. moved at a more normal pace, probably owing to his sodden clothes and recent fight. When she got to her apartment, the door was open just a crack. T.J. stopped. C.T. approached a few seconds later, a pistol already in his hand. "I thought you went unarmed," T.J. said, keeping her voice to a whisper.

"To the boat. I left the gun in my door pocket."

"You could've told me."

"Can we review my sins and failings after we check this out?" T.J. shrugged and bobbed her head. C.T. went in first. He moved from the living room to the kitchen and then down the hallway. T.J. stopped and took in the scene.

The place was trashed. She'd seen movies and TV shows where criminals—or sometimes the police—completely ransack a house looking for something. Somehow, her apartment looked even worse. A lamp lay broken on the floor. Books were everywhere. Even the couch cushions were sliced open and stuffing left strewn all over. Tears welled in T.J.'s eyes as she looked around.

She needed to feel safe in her own space. For years, she didn't. It was the opposite. Even when she had a place to stay, it came with unpleasant strings attached. For about eleven years, her mother provided a safe home. Then, her marriage fell apart, her mental health went right behind it, and the string of lovers—some of whom went looking for younger entertainment when the lady of the house fell asleep or passed out—ruined everything.

T.J. couldn't lose her apartment, too.

"All clear," C.T. said. "Whoever was here is gone now."

"This is a disaster," T.J. said, her voice small in her own ears.

"It's just stuff."

"Don't tell me it's just stuff!" It sounded harsher than she'd intended, so she dialed it back a few notches. "This place means more to me than that. I didn't grow up like you did."

C.T. put his hands up. He tried his best to understand, but

he really couldn't. "You'll need to look around and see if anything is missing."

T.J. snorted. "How the hell would I even tell?"

"It's probably hard. You'll need to call the police."

"I know." She sighed. "It's never fun to deal with them."

"Gloria has a guest room if you don't feel safe staying here."

"I'll be all right." T.J. managed a small smile. "Thanks, though. While I call the cops, why don't you dry off?"

"I think I will," C.T. said. He headed for the bathroom while T.J. took out her phone and tapped out 9-1-1.

———

While she waited for the police, T.J. tried to take inventory of her apartment.

Everything being on the floor or otherwise in disarray made it challenging. She didn't have much when she moved in, and while she'd accrued some things since, the place wasn't cluttered or packed full of random stuff. A quick check of valuables —TV, the rings from her mother, a couple other pieces of jewelry, and her laptop kept in a hidden place—showed nothing was missing. This eliminated robbery as a likely motive.

C.T. walked out of the bathroom. His clothes were drier, though his hair remained mussed like he were a boy and his grandmother had ruffled it. "I didn't want to use your brush," he said.

"Do you have cooties?"

"Not the last time I checked."

"Go ahead, then." T.J. shrugged. "If we're always supposed to look better than the police, you need thirty seconds in front of the mirror."

He emerged again quickly, his hair back in place. "Thanks."

"What kind of trophy wife would deny her husband a hairbrush?" T.J. said.

A knock came from the front door. T.J. opened it, and two uniformed officers walked in. She didn't recognize either of them. C.T.'s frown told her he didn't, either. The man—white, tall, and wiry—was a sergeant whose name board read Windsor. His partner was a solid-looking Latina named Cabrera. They established who everyone was and took a tour of the apartment before diving in with the usual questions.

"I can't identify anything that was taken," T.J. said. "I guess it's possible someone walked out with a couple paperbacks, but my valuables are still here. I don't have many, so it was easy to keep track of them."

"Looks like there was some forced entry," Cabrera said. T.J. hadn't noticed. She'd been too focused on her space being invaded. "Any of your neighbors mention break-ins?"

"No. This is a safe building. It's one of the reasons I picked it."

"So you think you were targeted?" Windsor asked.

"Yes," T.J. said.

"Why?"

"I work for him." She jerked her thumb toward C.T. "He's a private investigator, and I'm his assistant."

"You have a case?" Cabrera wanted to know.

"We always have a case."

Windsor said, "One worth breaking and entering for? If you're right, someone came here looking for something and trashed your apartment in the process of conducting their search."

"Apparently so."

"Want to tell us what you're working on?" Cabrera prompted.

"My cousin is a homicide lieutenant," C.T. said. "Rich Ferguson. He can fill you in on what we've been working on and why someone might take an unhealthy interest in it."

"You can't just tell us?"

"Not without violating our client's confidence."

Both officers stood and stared as if doing so would make T.J.'s or C.T.'s resolve crumble. Both said nothing. After a moment, the cops put their notebooks away. "All right," Windsor said. "We'll file a report. If you discover something is missing later, let us know." He handed her a business card.

"Thanks," T.J. said. The uniforms left. T.J. sighed as she took another look around. "They must have known we were in Annapolis."

"I didn't see anyone following us," C.T. admitted, "but I'm not exactly a savant when it comes to picking up a tail."

"Anything at your house?"

"No. I checked the camera feeds on my phone. It survived my dip in the bay. A few people walking or driving by, but no one stops or tries to break in."

"I'll check the office." Both C.T. and T.J. could access the security systems at Manny's—the one covering the whole building and the separate system for the upstairs area. C.T. installed and configured both. She spent a couple minutes going through photos and footage. "Nothing looks amiss. Someone could have driven by and thought better of it."

C.T. looked up from his phone. "Quiet at Gloria's, too. Maybe someone followed you from here."

"Maybe," T.J. said.

"You want help cleaning the place up?"

"No." She smiled. "It's nice of you to offer, but I got it. Wait . . . don't you want me to drive you home?"

"I'll get an Uber or Lyft."

"All right. See you tomorrow."

C.T. left, and T.J. stared at all her possessions strewn about the floor. She needed to tidy it all, but more than anything, she burned to kick something.

———

Even though it was late, T.J. got out the heavy bag and set it up.

It took longer than she'd wanted because she had to straighten the mess in her bedroom first. Her closet looked like someone tossed a grenade in it, but her clothes and fitness gear remained intact. She changed into athletic attire, strapped on a pair of MMA gloves, and picked a playlist designed to get the blood flowing. If any of her neighbors got annoyed by the sounds of her workout, they could get over it. With earbuds in place, she pressed play, clapped her fists together, and got busy.

Her apartment getting tossed bothered T.J. more than she thought it would. The 501 had a great reputation for safety. Whoever broke in either walked past the man on duty at the desk or found another way in. The cops would look into it, but T.J. thought it best to talk to the guy, too. He knew her. If he saw anything, he would tell her.

This place also represented the most stable and secure housing she'd had in ten years. After her mother's string of short-term boyfriends, T.J. left home. Her life, already veering out of control by that point, went fully off the rails. She ended up in a profession it took her years to break free of.

A few faces of her mom's lovers shimmered into view in the

bag. T.J. had the distinct displeasure of seeing more than one up close in the middle of the night. Her shoes whacked into the canvas a few times, followed by some hard elbow strikes. T.J. took a deep breath, bounced on the balls of her feet, and waded back in.

Her last pimp was an asshole with the stupid but appropriate moniker of Weasel Boy. Even thinking of his stringy hair nearly made her gag. The girls worked out of several hotels, motels, efficiencies, and other buildings in various states of disrepair. A few months before she got out, Weasel Boy accused T.J. of keeping too much money for herself. She hadn't, and she showed him, but he was high or in a bad mood and didn't want to hear it. His muscle, a big idiot named Jocko, smashed up her room, beat a pleading T.J. to within an inch of unconsciousness, and then invited a couple friends to have fun with her.

Thankfully, she had no recollection of the last part. Black-outs could occasionally be good things.

T.J. pounded the bag with a flurry of hard punches. Right, left, right, left. Her triceps burned. Her hands ached. She kept going, slamming her gloved fists into the conjured faces of her former tormentors until she was spent. T.J took a couple steps back and sat—it was more of a collapse, but she didn't want to admit it—on the floor. She took off the gloves and spiked them off the carpet. If she weren't surrounded by neighbors late at night, she probably would have yelled.

She'd come to terms with her old life. Sometimes, memories bubbled to the surface. She'd gotten better at dealing with them. These—combined with the break-in—were the worst yet. She picked up the gloves, tossed them toward her closet, and focused on her breathing. *I'm not going to cry. I'm not going to cry.*

After a few minutes, T.J. got some water, took a long shower, and went to bed.

She didn't cry.

CHAPTER 17

I GOT HOME and checked out my house.

The security system didn't show any disturbances. I'd made some serious upgrades after I caught two idiots wiring a bomb in my basement a few months ago. Only one of them survived to go to trial, and the gun I used to put half of *Vox Populi* down now led my way inside. The kitchen was clear, and I moved through the rest of the first floor before heading upstairs and then to the cellar. No one.

I reactivated the alarm and drove to Gloria's house. Her system was armed, too, and I turned it off only long enough to walk through the door. "I was worried," she said, tying a robe around her as she came down the stairs.

"All good. Just being cautious."

"Why are you damp?" She looked at my hair and chuckled. "Trying a new look?"

"As a matter of fact, I am," I said. "I call it 'in the bay chic.'"

"You certainly have the first part down." She pointed toward the second story. "Tell me what happened once we're upstairs. You need to get out of those clothes."

"Are you offering to help?" I asked with a crooked grin.

"Dirty bay water isn't a turn-on."

I fetched a pair of pajamas from one of the dresser drawers Gloria's sprawling wardrobe allowed me to use. The shower felt good. It was hot, clear, and clean, the opposite of my recent immersion on every count. I dried off, made sure my hair looked normal again, and emerged in my dry PJs. Gloria sat on the king bed. She'd doffed her robe, and she now wore a pajama top and shorts, the latter earning their name by riding high up her terrific thighs. "What happened?" she wanted to know as I sat beside her.

"We found a boat used years ago was still in operation. Couldn't really see much during the day. They're not going to advertise what it's really for. I wanted to go back at night and check it out."

"And?"

"There was a guard in the area. He mostly focused on the boat I was interested in. I took him out, but then two assholes from the harbor patrol showed up. We all got into it . . . one of them had a Taser, the big guy went overboard and knocked me in with him. I swam away."

"Did they at least get their friend out of the water?" Gloria's brows knitted in concern even for a goon she'd never met. "If he got Tased, he couldn't swim, right?"

"Right," I said. "Someone dove in as I was headed back to the marina. I got in T.J.'s car, and we headed away. I overhead the two harbor patrol jackasses saying they knew who we were. T.J.'s apartment got tossed while we were gone."

"Is she all right?"

"She seemed a little shaken up, but I think she'll be fine."

"What if they come back?"

"I told her she could stay in the guest room here," I said.

"She didn't want to. I think whoever broke in was looking for something . . . like evidence we'd found."

"Do you have any?" Gloria asked.

"Not a ton," I admitted, "and even if we had a lot, it wouldn't be in her apartment. Call it part evidence search, part intimidation tactic."

"And you were worried they might come here?"

"It's a possibility. I'd expect them to check my house first, but it only takes a couple seconds for someone to learn we're married and get your address." I paused. "My place was fine. If anyone dropped by, they didn't try to get inside."

Gloria stretched out her legs and leaned into me. "There are times I wish you had a less dangerous job."

"There are times I wish I did, too. Just make sure you keep the alarm on . . . even if you're working from home."

"I will," my wife said. She reached an arm up, pulled my head down a little, and kissed me. "Now, let's talk about your definition of 'chic.'"

"I'm all ears," I said.

"I'm very glad you're not," Gloria said.

———

In the morning, I checked the security system at Gloria's house to allay her concerns. All the cameras transmitted. The break-glass sensors seemed to work properly—we obviously skipped a full test—and all the window sensors worked when we opened and closed the glass. The app received updates and displayed a feed in almost real time. We paid a decent price for it, and it looked to be worth the investment. "We're good," I said.

Gloria drank coffee at her kitchen table. Like everything in the house, it was larger than its analogue in mine. A family of six could have used this in their dining room. "Thanks. I don't know why, but I woke up a little nervous."

"It's a big case, and the people we're looking into know who we are. It's only right to be concerned." In addition to the alarm system, I previously insisted Gloria keep a shotgun in her home office. I had no idea if she'd be able to pull the trigger in the moment, but the weapon was ideal for home defense. Even its telltale *chick-chack* sound could deter many a home invader.

After breakfast, I kissed Gloria goodbye. She held our embrace a few seconds longer than usual. "Be careful," she whispered into my ear.

If recent events served as a guide, I probably wouldn't, but I still said, "You bet." I drove to the office to see two distinctive cars in the section of the lot where we normally parked—T.J.'s Mustang and a blue Honda Accord coupe. Sure enough, when I opened the door, both my assistant and our intern were already working. The aroma of coffee filled the office as the machine neared the end of the brewing cycle. "We just got here a couple minutes ago," T.J. said.

"I know it's not normally my day in the office," Lexi added. "But considering what happened recently . . ."

"We figured it was all hands on deck."

"What do you think?"

"I think I like it when you two tag-team the conversation, and I don't need to talk," I said.

Once we all cradled fresh mugs of java, T.J. said, "I told Lexi what happened yesterday. If the harbor patrol are involved, it has to be on the orders of Hargrove or Dunning."

"Most likely," I said.

"Those two have something to hide," Lexi said. "Probably a bunch of somethings if this is as serious as it appears. A scandal forces the mayor to resign, whatever next office he had planned isn't an option, and his longtime number two is missing a meal ticket."

"Maybe we can get them to kill each other," I mused. "Let the situation deteriorate a little more, make some popcorn, and watch the show."

"You really think that would happen?" T.J. asked.

"No. I think Hargrove would try to use the harbor patrol or the real Annapolis police to arrest Dunning. The problem is Dunning probably knows guys who work off the books, so the mayor would get popped outside his office or house one night."

Lexi shrugged. "Still not a bad outcome."

"It is if Dunning gets away with it," I said.

T.J. spread her arms. "We're all here . . . surrounded by a ton of papers. Let's make sure neither one can get away with it."

"I knew I hired you two for a reason," I said.

————

The office became a flurry of activity.

T.J. called Bree again. I didn't hear most of the conversation, but I knew she wanted anything else relevant about Alyssa. Lexi worked on digitizing all the notes we currently had about Alyssa—including those written in her own hand—plus Bree's current recollections. I focused on the duo of Hargrove and Dunning. They stood to lose if the harbor parties and Alyssa's murder came out, but how much? I needed to know what was at stake beyond the obvious.

I didn't have a lot to go on. Their public profiles offered plenty of information, but no avenues of attack besides the apparent ones. Lexi updated a shared document as she worked, so I opened a copy to see what kind of progress she was making.

I learned right away I'd missed some of Alyssa's notes. I could go back and read them in detail later. For now, I focused on names—both individual and businesses.

The people turned out to be unremarkable. A couple were women caught up in the same profession. The men were likely johns, and apart from the random assault charge or DUI, none made a compelling or convincing murder suspect. The businesses, however, proved to be a different story. The first three I looked into didn't exist. Not just closed. Nonexistent. Except for their initial registration with the state, I found nothing.

They were shell companies.

Now, the crucial information was what operations they concealed, and who owned them. T.J. thanked Bree for her time, put her phone down, and started typing. Her changes appeared live in the document. I added a few things to my search, but the results were the same. More shell companies. They were all registered by someone who must have been an agent for these sorts of things.

Simon Lawton was an attorney by trade, though his website looked barren, and I could find few mentions of him appearing in court for anything. Not all lawyers took things to trial, but all of them maintained online presences to attract new clients. Mister Lawton, Esquire, did not. It made me wonder why. Did he already have a full roster? Were the services he performed for them legit on the surface but shady underneath?

It only took a couple minutes to find connections between Marcus Dunning and Lawton. They shared memberships at several clubs important people liked to attend to remind others they were VIPs. They'd appeared in the same photos a few times. Apart from his club memberships, Lawton never sought the spotlight. Dunning soaked it up, and while the two men had never appeared together at anything, they'd both been snapped at the same events.

It wasn't a smoking gun. It really wasn't a gun of any kind. To continue the metaphor, I had a half-dull knife left out in the fog. But it was something. Three shell companies of interest pointed to Lawton, and by extension, to Dunning. All of them were related to construction or improvement in some way. I told the ladies what I'd found.

"It's pretty loose," Lexi said.

"We need to tighten it up, then," I countered.

"I'm sure Dunning didn't make it easy," T.J. said. "If we can do it, an enterprising reporter might be able to."

"With the help of a brilliant person well-trained in the cyber arts, sure."

"What does it all mean?" Lexi wondered.

"We're going to find out," I said. "Dunning is dirty, and so is the mayor. One might be muddier than the other, but they've both been rolling around in it long enough to be covered. We agree?" They both nodded. "To me, the question is . . . did Dunning do this at the behest of his boss, or did he go rogue?"

"Which do you think?" T.J. asked.

"I don't know yet. Him going rogue gets us closer to the scenario where they try to kill each other."

"I'm rooting for that one," Lexi said.

"Me, too," I admitted, "which means we're probably not going to get it."

CHAPTER 18

I'VE NEVER BEEN a fan of most unannounced visits.

The metal steps removed the surprise factor from anyone coming to the office. Over time, I've learned to pick out the sounds of Gloria, T.J., and Lexi on them. Goons always sounded heavy and plodding by comparison. The ones I heard just now fell more in line with the ladies. Either Hargrove and Dunning sent a female assassin to kill us, or someone like Naomi was popping in.

Sure enough, our client appeared on the camera a moment later. Today, she didn't keep her hair in a ponytail, so it spilled across her shoulders and down her back. "I know I could have called," she said, heading off my identical comment. "I was in the area and hoping you had something."

We all huddled around my desk after Naomi paused to admire our stacking of the case file boxes. "We're getting Darrell a lawyer," I began. "He had a public defender before, and the guy has since left the office. Someone I know is taking his case *pro bono*."

"Good. He should go free if he's innocent."

"He should, but because of what's already happened, we

need to prove it." Naomi frowned, and I waved a hand. "Legal stuff. Not important today."

"We found the boat used for some of the harbor parties," T.J. said. "It's still docked in Annapolis."

Naomi leaned forward in her chair. "Did you get to go on board?"

"Yes, but they do a good job cleaning up after themselves. There are three small rooms below deck probably used for . . . obvious purposes."

"How did you manage to see it?"

"Clever undercover work," I said.

"We posed as a rich married couple," T.J. added, "and dropped a couple names for legitimacy."

Naomi's eyes widened, and Lexi snorted. "C.T. was wealthy and retired early, and I was the trophy wife."

"I could believe the second part," Lexi said.

"I'm sure you look good all dolled up," Naomi pitched in.

"If I can stop dodging the slings and arrows for a second," I said, "the most distinctive feature about the boat was how closely some meathead guarded it. He was supposed to be there to keep an eye on the dock area, but he paid special attention to *The Wayward Lady*."

"So you didn't get to see much?" Naomi asked.

"We went back," I said. "I'd rather you not talk about this part on the podcast. I snuck on after dark to see if I could find anything."

"And?"

"I found the same guard I'd seen the day before. Plus two jackasses from the harbor patrol."

Our client's eyes went wide again. She had an expressive face, and limiting herself to an audio format removed a great way to connect with her listeners. "Did you get away?"

"I'm here, aren't I?"

"It must have been scary."

"It was definitely dangerous in the moment," I said. "They tried to tase me and throw me overboard."

"Wouldn't you drown?"

"Yes."

Naomi's brows knitted. "What happened?"

"The guard ended up taking the voltage. He and I both went into the water, but I managed to swim away. One of the harbor patrol clowns had to jump in and get the big idiot out."

"Now you're on their radar."

"We probably already were," T.J. said. "We've all been to see the mayor and Marcus Dunning. If they're behind all this, they could have seen through our ruse."

"Not because of my acting," I said.

"Or my dress."

"This will make for really interesting segments on the podcast," Naomi said, "even if I keep some of the juicy stuff back. I'm worried about you, though."

"Thanks," I said. "We're used to getting menaced and harassed. Me especially."

"Still. There have been enough casualties here. I don't want one of you to end up in the hospital . . . or worse."

"We'll be all right," T.J. said with a confident smile. It was good to see.

"Okay." Naomi stood. "Can you email me what you've done recently? It'll be easier to compile into my show notes that way." T.J. nodded. "Thanks. I'm going to start recording tonight. Should be another episode out soon."

"We'll definitely listen," Lexi said.

As much as I didn't want to when we took this case, I knew I'd be tuning in.

———

After Naomi left, I drove to police headquarters to see Rich.

In his days as a sergeant, my cousin spent most of his time in the field. Now, as the lieutenant, he was in the office more often than not. I knew he relished the added responsibility, but I also understood being chained to a desk would chafe at him. Despite the crap I gave him for riding my coattails in investigations, Rich was a very good cop. I didn't know if making him a supervisor constituted the best use of his skill set, but employees and enterprises struggled with this challenge when it came to promotions all the time.

Sure enough, Rich sat behind his desk. To his credit, the more sedentary nature of this job didn't show in his waistline. "Here to tell me what other cases we're getting wrong?" he offered as an opening jab.

"Not originally. If you want to give me some files to look over, though, I'm happy to point out your mistakes. Are red pens still a thing?"

Rich rolled his eyes and made a vague gesture toward one of his guest chairs as he looked at his monitor. His office was small. The desk, three total chairs, and a small bookcase consumed most of the square footage. I closed the door, but it and the primary wall were both made of glass. "What's up?"

"We've made some more strides in the Alyssa Winters case," I said. "He's getting a real lawyer, so there will be a push to get him out of jail at some point."

"Sounds like a problem for the state's attorney's office."

"And for the lead investigator who will get called as a witness."

Rich shrugged. "If the guy didn't do it, he should get out. What other strides are you talking about?"

I mentioned our foray to Annapolis to tour *The Wayward Lady*. Rich kept his expression neutral until toward the end, when he broke out in a laugh. "Wait . . . you and T.J. posed as a married couple?"

"Yes," I said. "I was the successful man wealthy enough to retire at forty, and she was my trophy wife."

"But you didn't take your actual wife."

"Gloria hasn't been working in an investigator's office for three-plus years."

"How'd T.J. look in the dress?"

"I'll admit she looked very good."

Rich spread his hands. The amused expression never left his face. "Did you tell Gloria?"

"No," I said.

"You don't think it'll be an issue?"

"I'm happily married. T.J. is like the weird younger sister I never had."

"You had an older one, though," he pointed out.

"And I remember her every day." Samantha, three years my senior, died when she was nineteen. Despite my parents trying to hide the details from me, I learned about five years ago she'd been murdered. Her killer rotted in jail where he belonged. "I did miss out on a younger one, though. T.J. is what I imagine she would have been."

"If you say so."

"Just like you're the very annoying and *much* older brother I never had," I said.

"I guess you didn't find anything on the boat?"

"No." I told Rich about our return trip and what happened on the deck of The Wayward Lady.

"Harbor Patrol is a legit agency," he said. "You might want to try avoiding them in the future. They can arrest you."

"The plan was to tase me and toss me overboard," I pointed out. "Like one of them told me, we were past the point of arrest."

"You think this means the mayor is in on it?"

"Or his chief of staff, yeah. Dunning gets a little shadier each time I look into him. Did you know Darrell Wilson did some work for Hargrove's opponent during his first run for mayor?"

"No."

"Want to bet Marcus Dunning knew?"

"I'm not taking those odds," Rich said.

"How come you latched onto him as a suspect?" I asked. "He wasn't even a particularly good one. More convenient than anything. It's not like you."

"What's not?"

"Sloppy police work."

Rich scoffed. "You have a funny way of paying me a compliment."

"I mean it. Yes, you've gotten a few commendations and attaboys because I did a lot of the legwork . . . and I'll always give you shit for it . . . but I know you're good at your job independent of me or anyone in this building. Two things can be true at the same time."

Rich leaned back in his chair and didn't say anything for a few seconds. "I was a pretty new sergeant at the time. Sometimes, I felt like I was on the fast track from my time in the army. Other times, not so much. Captain Sharpe . . . he was a lieutenant then . . . came up the same way, so I think he took an interest in me. I knew his reputation. Good and bad. The Alyssa Winters case landed in my inbox. Before we even got very far into it, Sharpe said he'd also been investigating and had a suspect. We shifted to Darrell Wilson, and I guess we never really got away from him."

"Tunnel vision."

"Yeah," he said. "It happens to all of us sometimes, I guess. If you can find a better suspect and get Wilson out of jail, good."

"It might not be good for *you*," I pointed out, "or Sharpe."

"Can't control it now." Rich lapsed into silence again. He tended to do this when I'd shaken his faith in the BPD as an institution. It didn't happen often, but when it did, my cousin went into something of a funk. One of these years, it might cause him to do something.

I stood. "I just wanted to give you a heads-up. It might get ugly once Liz takes Darrell's case to court."

"Liz Fleming?"

"Yeah."

"She's good," Rich said.

"She is."

"Good-looking, too."

"She is," I agreed, "though I cared a lot more about it before I was married." I started for the door.

"I'll help you," Rich said, and his words made me stop. "It'll have to be something unofficial for now, but I think you're right. This was a rotten case, and I don't know why Sharpe tainted it, but he did. We have to make it right. Let me know if you need an assist there."

"Thanks," I said. "I will."

———

"Did you have a nice lunch?" T.J. asked when I got back to the office.

"I haven't eaten yet."

"We got an extra sandwich coming just in case."

"Thanks." I sat at my desk.

"Lexi and I have been busy while you were talking to Rich," she said.

"I think I finally got him to crack," I said. "He's a little rattled. It happens from time to time when the BPD fucks something up. Just takes him a while to get there. He's willing to help us get to the truth."

"About time," Lexi said, and she wasn't wrong.

A few minutes later, an impossibly skinny fellow dropped off our lunch order. I thought about telling him to take my sandwich. He clearly needed the calories more than I did. The ladies ordered from some place I'd never tried. They got me chicken salad, and while it wasn't the choice I would've made the first time I ate somewhere, it ended up being a good sandwich. Their homemade chips were a touch greasy and needed more salt.

"Tell me how you were busy," I said when we'd all thrown our trash away and washed our hands.

"I talked to Bree again," T.J. said.

"Wow. We're going to need to put her on the payroll at this rate."

"She knows we're making real progress, so I think she's more willing to lend a hand. There's some risk for her in all this."

"I think we need to offer her benefits, too," Lexi added.

"You her agent now?" I asked.

"What if I am?"

"I don't negotiate with underlings."

While our intern rolled her eyes, my assistant continued. "I got names. Some former clients of Alyssa's. I wonder where Bree keeps this information."

"You and me both," I said in my best David Rose voice from *Schitt's Creek*.

T.J. either didn't get the reference, or I made a poor Dan Levy impersonator. Probably a little of both. "Anyway, we ran down the names. One is still active in Maryland politics. I . . . might have reached out on our behalf."

"I hope we were persuasive."

"He's willing to talk off the record."

"I'll take it. Let's get him on the line." A moment later, we listened to the ring tone for Maryland state senator Buddy Friedman. When he answered, I told him who I was and how my assistant made contact earlier.

"Off the record," he said in a nasal tone. He spoke quickly and carried a hint of a Baltimore accent despite being elected in Anne Arundel County.

"Sure."

"I don't consent to being recorded."

"No problem," I said. Lexi tapped a pen to her notepad and offered a thumbs-up.

"Whaddya wanna know?"

"Who would want Alyssa Winters dead?" I said.

Friedman snorted. "Christ. How much time you got? Could be a long list."

"Explain, please."

"Alyssa was smart. Maybe not in the book sense, but the girl had a brain. She knew why men came to see her, and she kept notes. Detailed notes. She documented connections between people she . . . uh . .. saw professionally. I even heard she took pictures of herself in bed next to guys who fell asleep. Could have been scandalous if they got out."

"Sounds like motive," I said, and both T.J. and Lexi bobbed their heads in agreement, their ponytails bouncing in sync.

"Could be," Friedman acknowledged.

"Would we recognize some of the names?"

"Definitely."

"You want to share any?"

"Definitely not."

"All right. Have you ever heard of harbor parties?"

"I don't think so," Friedman said.

"Alyssa mentions them a few times. As far as we know so far, they were cruises where women would join at various points maybe in different states."

"I'm going to guess referring to them as parties means those girls were getting onboard for an obvious reason."

"Yes," I said. "Covering up a possible federal crime is also motive."

"It is. Look, I know some of these guys. Let's just say they were the type to appreciate some variety, but they weren't the type to ask too many questions."

I knew some men like these, and T.J.'s glower told me she did, too. "All right. I think you've given us some more to work with."

"Feel free not to call me again." Friedman hung up before I could answer.

Lexi stopped writing and put her pen away. "I'll input these to our shared docs."

"Where's Alyssa's hidden trove of blackmail material?" T.J. asked.

"I'm wondering the same thing," I said. "I'm also curious if it's still out there or if someone found it eight years ago."

Lexi raised an eyebrow. "What's your gut tell you?"

"Considering the attempts made to stop us, my hunch is no one's found it yet."

"Let's make sure we're the ones who do, then," T.J. said.

CHAPTER 19

FOLLOWING OUR CHAT WITH FRIEDMAN, Lexi added notes to our growing online document collection while T.J. and I dug into Marcus Dunning.

After eight years in the Army, Dunning moved into the private sector. He enjoyed an entrepreneur's spirit and a prospector's luck at first glance. His official biography of course used empty platitudes like "visionary leadership," "resilient strength," "piercing foresight," unparalleled business acumen," and "market-shaping vision." They sounded like the powers of Superman if he were conceived by crypto bros. I figured Dunning wrote them himself or badgered some poor marketing intern to revise her already purple prose a hundred more times.

"What an asshole," I muttered.

"Let's make sure he ends up a guilty asshole," T.J. said.

Part of Dunning's collection of rejected motivational poster catchphrases was his alleged business sense. Using the list I'd discovered before, I did an even deeper dive for entities founded by Dunning, any he invested into, or those his lawyer buddy—and likely registered agent—was involved with behind the scenes. I also searched data breach records. Attorney-client privilege meant a lot less if someone got hacked.

Correlating all the information, a pattern emerged. Companies Dunning was involved with to some degree tended to get special treatment. This made sense. He was Mayor Hargrove's chief of staff, and the two worked together dating back to their days in real estate. Both knew how the game got played. I noted favorable issuances of permits, approved plans for construction, and similar perks a business with no important friends in Annapolis couldn't get.

"This doesn't mean much by itself," Lexi pointed out when she looked over what I'd added. "Dunning has friends and knows how to work the system. He should. He's a part of it."

"It's a start," I said. "He and Hargrove are doing worse stuff than this. I think the things I've found are probably what enable the sleazy shit we need to find."

"The stuff Alyssa knew about," T.J. said.

"It'd be nice to find a hidden cache of information," I said. "Everyone tells us she was smart, took pictures, kept notes. If those still exist, I'd love to uncover them." I figured they did, at least in part because Hargrove and his goon squad kept trying to deter us. It was logical to presume something remained hidden, and they wanted to leave the status quo in place.

"It's not like Alyssa had a steady house."

"And if she did," Lexi said, "the mayor would have bulldozed it and built something else in its place."

Her comment got me thinking about Annapolis's revitalization. Hargrove got a lot of credit for the renewal, or gentrification, or whatever buzzword people wanted to apply to it. The city had been in operation for centuries. Many people—me included—loved the old-world charm retained in certain areas. Others favored smashing anything older than fifty years and building cookie-cutter monstrosities of concrete, glass, and steel instead. Many of these "others" were people with money or reputations on the line.

It took a few minutes, but I compiled some more information. Public building records are surprisingly easy to access if you know where to start. Several historic buildings got renovated or replaced because of failed inspections. State law protected the old structures, and no company could knock one down without jumping through a lot of hoops and playing jump rope with lengths of red tape.

One of the ways to shortcut the process was failed inspections, especially with anything relating to public safety.

I had no way of knowing if these black marks were legit or part of some campaign by Hargrove and Dunning to remake Annapolis, take credit for it, and also profit from the whole thing. It made me wonder how much of the city's revitalization was built on favors, deceit, and sand. I added notes about my discoveries to our archive.

"Now, we might have something," Lexi said a few minutes later.

"Going to be hard to prove," T.J. said.

I nodded. "It will, and we can expect roadblocks from the administration at every step. There's something here, though. If I can use a construction metaphor, we need to keep digging."

Both ladies groaned. "You sure Gloria's not pregnant?" T.J. asked. "That was a classically bad dad joke."

"I hope not." I put those uncomfortable thoughts out of my head and kept working.

———

The rest of the afternoon didn't lead to any epiphanies. T.J. and Lexi left, and I locked up and headed to my car a few minutes later. Thanks to the situation we currently found ourselves in, Gloria had been staying at her house rather than our usual time-sharing arrangement. I wanted to get a couple things from my place, so I drove toward Federal Hill.

As the crow flies, getting from Fells Point to Federal Hill is fast and easy. Crows never drove in Baltimore traffic, however. The distance wasn't great, but Eastern to President to Lombard to Light to Key Highway involved a lot of red lights and a plethora of impatient fellow motorists. As I headed down Lombard, I noticed a police car change lanes to pull up behind me. I didn't recognize the colors, but the light bar on top was a dead giveaway.

Sure enough, the reds and blues flared to life. Still in second gear at pretty low RPMs, I knew I wasn't speeding. As I eased to a stop in the bus lane, I spotted the sedan's front plate in my rearview mirror. It bore the logo of the city of Annapolis. "Shit," I muttered to the empty car. One of these days, I needed to get a dash cam I could turn around for situations like these. Instead, while the two guys behind me sat in their car probably plotting how to abduct me, I set my phone to record video and dropped it in my shirt pocket. The lens peeked out above the top of the fabric.

I put the parking brake on, leaving the S4 running in neutral. Neither man behind me made a move. I couldn't see what they were doing. Most police cars in Maryland came equipped with computers taking up space from the front-seat passenger. Neither fellow looked busy. If they were indeed the harbor patrol, they knew damned well who I was. No need to run the plate.

Finally, they got out, so I did, also. "Stay in the vehicle, sir," the driver ordered. He was tall, blond, and dumpy. His partner was short but solidly built with a black mullet. Neither really looked like a cop.

"What's this about?" I demanded.

"Sir, get back in your—"

"What's this about?"

"Do you know why we pulled you over?"

"Do you?" I asked. Both frowned and looked at each other as if my simple question short-circuited their feeble brains. "It's not a hard question, guys. I wasn't speeding. My tags haven't expired. Taillights are intact." I shrugged. "What's going on?"

"Are you Coningsby Trent Ferguson?" the long-haired one asked.

"Really? I'm supposed to believe you don't know who I am?"

"We need to search your car," Blondie said. I noticed he dropped the pretense of calling me sir. Neither man was armed. Their uniform belts held flashlights, handcuffs, and Tasers. Not even the holster for a pistol.

"Sure," I said. "Let me see your warrant and have my attorney verify it."

"We don't need a warrant."

"What's your probable cause, then?"

"You were in Annapolis the other night," he said.

"Let's presume you're right. If I was there, so were a few thousand other people . . . none of whom I see pulled over with me. Kind of feels like you're singling me out." They didn't say anything. "You need some fashion advice? Those uniforms and haircuts really aren't helping either of you?"

"You a faggot?" Mullet Man said.

"No. Even if I were, I wouldn't take you up on your get-out-of-jail-free offer."

"Now wait just a—"

"The trunk," the blond one insisted. "We need to look in it."

"And your probable cause is?"

"You're a prick."

"If it were illegal," I said, "I'd get pulled over most nights."

The shorter one looked at the tailpipes. I could almost see the gears turning. Smoke is coming out. This means the engine is on. This means locks might not be engaged. Sure enough. he felt for the trunk release, found it, and opened the lid as I moved toward the rear of my car. Blondie tried to intercept me, but he was standing too far away.

"This is an illegal search," I said, making sure to raise my voice for the benefit of people walking past us. None of them seemed perturbed by these two clowns flouting the Constitution.

As the mulleted one reached inside the trunk, I spotted a small bag in his hand. After making sure my body was square to him for the cell phone camera, I called out, "You're trying to plant drugs in my car! I see the bag."

He straightened up, concealing the contraband in his palm as a few people looked at the scene while they walked past. "The hell I was."

"Bullshit. Your bosses want me out of the way, so you're trying to drum up some fake charges."

"We could charge you with trespassing."

"Go ahead, then. Seems like a lot of trouble for a misdemeanor."

"The two of us can arrest you," the blond cop said, a smile starting to form on his thin lips.

"Your two friends thought they could get rid of me," I said. "They even had some help. How did it go for them?"

"Turn around and put your hands behind your back."

"You're a little out of your jurisdiction here."

Blondie's face reddened, and he reached for his Taser. "Turn around and—"

"No."

When he drew the weapon, I moved forward. His hand came up. I chopped at it, striking his thumb. He barked in pain and dropped the stun gun. His partner had one, too. I couldn't rely on one idiot to tase the other two times in a row. As the blond one rubbed his hand, I kneed him in the groin. He doubled over, and I crouched, using him as a shield against the other cop who also had his Taser out. When the light-haired one almost slumped over, I planted my feet and pushed forward, using him as a ram to slam into his partner.

Both bounced off the hood of their car and fell into the left lane. Now, of course, people stopped to watch and film what went on. I couldn't wait around for these two to get back up and summon reinforcements. I hurried back into the S4, slammed it into first gear, and pulled away with screeching tires.

CHAPTER 20

AS I ZOOMED through a yellow light headed up Calvert Street, I called Rich. "Are you home?" I asked when he picked up.

"Yes. Why?"

"I'm coming over."

"Why are you—"

"I'll explain when I get there," I said and disconnected. Being in traffic complicated my escape, but I couldn't control the time of day and the volume of cars on the road. I could only control my route. Cameras on the highway and in toll plazas would track my movements via license plates. There were probably some in the city limits, as well, but they'd be fewer in number. I could stick to city roads and still get to Hamilton. With the traffic volume on I-95 this time of day, it might even be faster.

I headed right on Saratoga and then made a left onto Gay Street. Once it went through a couple of name changes, it would become Harford Road and continue northeast into the county it was named for. I checked my mirrors constantly for any sign of the two Harbor Patrol clowns. They were an actual police force, so they could have called the BPD to help. Doing so would make whatever they had in mind for me official, however, and harder to hide after the fact. Hargrove and Dunning probably wanted me to end up weighted down by bricks on the bottom of the Chesapeake Bay, and their badged goons could only try to make it happen if they operated alone.

As I got farther away from downtown, traffic eased, and I was able to gain a few miles per hour. At a red light, I turned my phone off and pulled the SIM card out. I kept a spare dumb phone in the glove box in case I ever needed it. As I idled at the next red signal, I swapped the card into the flip model and plugged it into the charger. The battery was at zero percent. I'd slacked off on keeping it plugged in once a week. Couldn't do anything about it now. By the time I got to Rich's house, it should at least be operational.

I drove past Lake Clifton High School and into the Waverly area of northeast Baltimore. From here, I could get to Hamilton in a number of ways. I took a right onto Walther Avenue as it offered the most direct route to Rich's house. Three turns later, I wheeled into the driveway of his pale yellow Victorian. He'd bought it a decade or so ago and fixed it up periodically. The neighborhood dated back eighty to a hundred years depending on which street you were on.

Rich's Camaro sat near the top of the driveway. I pulled onto the grass, steered the Audi past it, and stopped when the concrete ended and his backyard began. I was about as far to the left as I could get and still open my door. Considering the incline from the street—and the fact Rich's Camaro screened the S4 from view—my car would be hard to spot if someone drove by.

I got out and headed around to the rear entrance. Rich

opened the back door. He stared at me through the storm door and didn't look happy to see me.

———

"I hope my lawn comes back in the spring," Rich said as he frowned at the tire tracks where I'd steered around his car.

"I'll pay to resod if it doesn't."

We went back inside. Rich opened the fridge and pulled out two longnecks. He twisted the caps off both and offered me one. Miller High Life. I tended to favor imports, but I wasn't going to turn a beer down under the circumstances. We sat in his living room. The dark wood floors looked great. They were original to the house. The previous owner hid them with carpet which Rich ripped out a couple years ago. He'd paid a professional to restore the cherry hardwood—money well spent.

Once we'd each enjoyed a few swigs, Rich asked, "What the hell is going on? Why does it look like you're hiding?"

"I kind of am."

He sighed and leaned back in his recliner. I sat on a matching sofa. A coffee table which was almost the identical color as the floor stood between us. "What happened?"

"Two goons from the harbor patrol pulled me over," I said.

"They're a little outside their jurisdiction."

"I tried to make the same argument. They weren't amenable. I had a run-in with a couple of their brethren earlier. I don't think this pair wanted to arrest me, either."

"Explain," Rich said as if I were a beat cop who needed to answer for some violation of protocol.

"I started filming with my phone. They wanted me to open the trunk so they could search the car. I refused. One of them popped it anyway. I caught him trying to plant drugs."

Rich's eyes widened. "Really?"

"Yes."

"Jesus."

"Yeah. My guess is they'd then haul me away on drug charges and use it as an excuse to take me to some black site instead."

"Sounds a bit too CIA for these guys," Rich said, "but I think you have the right idea. They obviously want you out of the way."

"Can I use your laptop?"

"You're not going to do anything . . . weird with it, are you?"

"No," I said. "I want to transfer the file." Rich fetched his laptop and a cable. After my real phone was back on, I switched it into airplane mode and connected it to my cousin's computer. Windows recognized it as an external drive. I found the video file and emailed it to him, then sent it to Gloria, T.J., Lexi, and Liz Fleming. When I finished, I turned my phone back off and handed Rich his laptop so he could see what went down.

"What are you going to do with this?" he wondered when he'd finished.

"It's pretty damning."

"It is." He watched it again, his brows furrowed. "I don't know what they're going to try and do, but you could use this for leverage."

"If I need to," I said. "You definitely saw the bag, right?"

Rich bobbed his head. "I'm sure you could get a still from the video and see it clearly. Looked pretty big, too, as far as those things go. They were trying to pin something serious on you."

"It means we're getting close."

"To what, I wonder?"

The truth, I figured, but I didn't yet know what form it would take. "I want to call Gloria. She's going to get worried about me soon." I walked into the kitchen and called my wife on the flip phone.

"It can't be good if you're using this number," she said, concern darkening her tone.

I explained what happened after I left the office. "I'm all right. I'm at Rich's for now. Not sure where I'm headed from here, but it'll need to be some place they don't know to look for me."

"What are you going to do with the video?"

"So far, I've emailed to you and a few others," I said. "I might set up some kind of fail-safe where it goes to a few people if I'm not around to delay it."

"That sounds like your speed."

"Even Rich suggested I could use it for leverage."

"What if they come here?" Gloria asked.

"They'd be way out of their jurisdiction," I said. "If anyone comes, it'll probably be the county cops. Don't open the door if you can help it. Talk to them through the doorbell camera. Tell them I'm not there. You don't know where I am. Don't let them in without a warrant. If they have one, call a lawyer."

Gloria sighed. I sympathized. "All right. I hope you wrap this up soon."

"Me, too. I love you."

"I love you, too." I flipped the phone shut and rejoined Rich in the living room. He worked on his laptop.

"I've been looking over the case," he said. "Some parts don't sit right with me. Probably never did if I'm being honest."

"Good thing to be," I said. "Unless the harbor patrol guys come here looking for me."

"Fuck 'em. I'm with you on this one . . . wherever it goes."

"It might not be pretty."

"I think it's already ugly."

"Yeah."

"We might need a little more help."

"You have anyone in mind?"

"As a matter of fact," Rich said, "I do."

———

"I want to call Casey Norton," Rich said.

Having worked with Norton a few times, I agreed. He worked for the Maryland State Police and would have way more jurisdiction than Rich in case the Harbor Patrol continued to be a problem. "He still a captain?"

"I think he's going to make major soon."

"Good for him," I said.

"Maybe not for the rest of us. I like being able to get him involved. If he gets kicked up the ladder, he'll probably do more delegating."

"Sounds familiar."

"What?"

"Heavy is the head that wears the crown, right?"

"I wish someone would give me a crown," Rich said.

"You'd need several," I said. "They have to go with your daily suit rotation."

Rich grinned, shook his head, and took out his mobile. A moment later, we had Captain Casey Norton on the line. Rich brought him up to speed on the generalities quickly.

"You have the video?" Norton wanted to know.

"Give me your email, and I'll send it to you," I told him.

He provided his address, and I shipped it off. The playback sounded tinny through Rich's phone's speaker. At the end,

Norton sighed. "I always knew the Harbor Patrol was a bad idea."

"What do you mean?"

"Mayor Hargrove wanted them. Some initiative to clean up crime on the water and at the docks, I think. He and his chief of staff are good at making friends and collecting favors, so they managed to talk the colonel into accrediting the agency." The head of the Maryland State Police—a man whose name I didn't know—carried the official rank of colonel.

"Sounds like you could also render them null and void," Rich said.

"If we need to. I'll keep this video and present it."

"What if they come after me?"

"I'll make sure they don't hold you," Norton said.

I appreciated the offer, but I doubted detaining me would be high on their list of priorities. Still, getting cooperation from high up in the MSP was important at this juncture. "Good. I need to keep investigating. I think we're close."

"Keep me in the loop. I don't like the mayor, and I especially dislike Dunning. I'll be happy to see them carted off to jail."

"Thanks, Casey," Rich said, and he ended the call. "I want to look over the old case notes some more. What are you going to do?"

"I brought a tablet," I said. "Always have it in my bag. T.J. and Lexi were working on digitizing everything we've compiled so far. I'll see if there's anything interesting."

Rich carried his computer to the dining room. I stayed where I was. The ladies finished getting everything online, so I started going through what we had of Alyssa's notes and journal. On my second read, I noticed something.

I've always had a thing for fireplaces, but this one is the best.

I'm not sure I even need to put a log on the grate. The idea of it is enough to warm me.

One of these days, when I have a man and a house, I'm going to make sure it has a great open hearth like this one.

Despite these frequent mentions, Alyssa never named the building. I wondered if it still stood, what happened to it, and what she might have used the fireplace for.

CHAPTER 21

I WOKE up and briefly wondered where I was.

The bed and room were unfamiliar. I slept on a double surrounded by walls painted a very light blue. Then, I remembered driving to Rich's house. This marked the first time I'd slept in his guest room, and as much as I appreciated it, I hoped not to need it again tonight. A quick glance at my phone showed me it was just after seven. Way too early to be awake, which meant Rich had already been stirring for at least an hour.

The smell of coffee coming from the first floor wafted up the stairs. I couldn't go back to sleep with the sirens singing so clearly. I made sure I was presentable before trudging downstairs. Rich was already in a suit as he sat at his dining room table drinking a mug and looking over an actual physical newspaper.

"You always take your antiques out so early?" I asked as I headed into the kitchen.

"What?" Rich frowned and looked around his area. The paper rustled when he moved, and the lightbulb went on. "Force of habit at this point."

I mentally did the math on my parents' ages. Everything was harder before coffee. "If it's any consolation, you're probably *The Sun*'s youngest subscriber by about twenty-five years."

"It's really not."

"You eat yet?"

"I was gonna get something on the way in," Rich said.

"I'll whip up some breakfast."

"You don't need to."

"Least I can do," I said. I checked out my cousin's fridge and pantry. A few minutes later, I fried four eggs in a pan, bacon sizzled in another, and four slices of bread went into the toaster. A couple slices of mozzarella later, we each had hearty breakfast sandwiches.

"Wow, thanks," Rich said when I set his before him. "This looks way better than what I normally buy."

"Damning with faint praise."

"You're not as pretty as the girl working the counter, though."

"We all have our faults," I said. "Even me." Rich finished his sandwich, told me I could stay as long as I needed to, promised to keep my visit a secret, and then left for the office. Casey Norton said the state police would get me back if Dunning's uniformed goons nabbed me. What if the Harbor Patrol took me to a secret location, however? A bag over my head, an injection of something to make me pass out, and a toss into the water, and their problem was solved. Norton would only find out when the report of a handsome body washing up somewhere landed on his desk.

I appreciated his offer, but I couldn't count on it.

I also couldn't count on getting a lot of work done on my tablet. T.J. would be awake by now, so I called her. "You all right?" she asked.

"For now."

"Where are you?"

"At an undisclosed location. I need my laptop."

"You realize you'll have to tell me where to bring it, right?"

"I do," I said. "I'll send you a message." I ended the call and sent her a text via Signal. *I'm at Rich's house. Not sure if the HP are still looking for me, so make sure you're not followed.*

She replied a minute later. *See you in about an hour. You're making the coffee.*

It was a fair tradeoff.

———

T.J. kept her word and arrived fifty-seven minutes later.

I opened the door just wide enough to let her in and then closed and locked it again right away. "No one followed you?"

"Aren't you being a little paranoid?" she asked.

"Two sort-of cops tried to plant drugs in my car so they could arrest me and do who knows what from there," I said. "You're not paranoid if they're actively trying to remove you."

"All right." T.J. put up her hands. "I doubled back on myself a couple times and took an inefficient route off the highway. I also brought your laptop." She unslung a backpack from her shoulders. I extracted the computer I used at the office. It was already connected to all our shared resources. I could have mapped them on my tablet, but the laptop featured a much larger screen and an actual keyboard. "You going to survive without your multiple monitors?"

"Barely."

"You want me to stay and work here?"

"Wherever you're more comfortable."

My assistant made a show of sniffing the air. "Is that coffee I smell?"

"I made it a little while ago," I said.

She poured herself a mug and came back. We set up shop at the dining room table. Like most surfaces in Rich's house, it was free of decoration and dust. He must have used a cleaning service. The promotion to lieutenant increased both his responsibilities and hours spent in the office. I doubted the ratio was equal, but my cousin rarely complained. "Did you find anything in what we've compiled of Alyssa's notes?" T.J. wondered.

"I did. She makes several references to a fireplace she loved."

"You know where?"

I shook my head. "She never mentions the building. We know she didn't keep a steady address. It could be just about anywhere."

"Why do you think it's significant?"

"When she was murdered, I'm sure her killer searched for whatever dirt she had on people."

"Your theory is she stashed it in a fireplace?"

"Considering everything we've seen," I said, "I think we can presume her cache is still unaccounted for. Hargrove, Dunning, and their goon squad are desperate to find it. Granted, they want me off the case, which will probably tamp down Naomi's podcast. I think there's more there. They might be convinced I know where Alyssa hid everything. Hell, they might be working on the assumption we've already found it."

T.J. frowned. "Wouldn't people look in a fireplace?"

"Sure. They might not look up the chimney, though. Carefully remove a sooty brick or two, and you create a place to stash things."

My assistant arched an eyebrow and chuckled. "Did you learn this because you needed to stow your weed in college?"

I scoffed. "No. A few of my more . . . security-conscious hacker friends in Hong Kong did it. Even when the police raided our place and hauled everyone away, they missed a few things."

"You're not denying you had weed in college."

"I didn't," I said.

"Really?"

"Really. I was too busy playing lacrosse, sleeping around, and rushing through my assignments at the last minute." T.J. wrinkled her nose and got back to work. An idea came to me. "Think about how Hargrove has done a lot of the revitalization."

"By bulldozing perfectly good buildings," my assistant said.

"Which were designated as historic in some cases. He followed the process. Got permits, the works. If they have an idea where Alyssa's stash might be—"

"They'll want to knock it down," T.J. broke in.

"Yes. Keep an eye on the construction permitting out of Annapolis and Anne Arundel County. If something comes through with a short deadline until work begins, it's bound to be the place."

"And we would need to get in before they knock it down."

"Seems a lot better than sifting through the rubble," I said.

———

The sounds of water lapping against hulls and shorelines heralded another podcast episode.

"Welcome back to *Harbor Homicides*. I'm Naomi Chambers.

"Normally, I put these out in the evenings. If you're waiting until after sundown and drinking some wine, I'll be doing the same. This is an unusual year. Normally, I do my own investigations and break up the case into logical episodes. I know what happened and what's going to happen.

"This time, though, I'm almost as much in the dark as the rest of you. I'm not doing ninety-plus percent of the legwork this time. I decided to put this podcast out because the story of Alyssa, Darrell, and the people who tried to destroy them shouldn't wait for the end of the workday."

She chuckled. "Wow, that was a long preamble. I think I've rambled enough. Let's get down to why we're all here.

"In our previous episodes, we've examined the inconsistencies in Alyssa Winters' murder investigation, the suspicious staging of her death, and the evidence she had been gathering about human trafficking operations in Annapolis harbor. Today, we're going to focus on two critical developments: the legal fight to free an innocent man, and the floating den of exploitation that may have cost Alyssa her life.

"First, let's talk about justice delayed. Darrell Wilson has spent eight years in prison for a crime he didn't commit. But finally, there's hope. A prominent criminal defense attorney—whose name I'm withholding for now—has agreed to take Wilson's case pro bono. She's preparing what's known as a habeas corpus petition, essentially asking the court to review Wilson's conviction based on new evidence that wasn't available at his original trial."

A sound effect of papers rustling yielded to somber music. Naomi continued to excel in the audio arena.

"The petition includes the forensic timeline discrepancies I detailed in earlier episodes, witness statements that were never properly investigated, and most crucially, evidence that Alyssa

Winters was murdered because of her investigation into a trafficking operation—not because of any connection to Wilson.

"But here's what makes this case particularly compelling from a legal standpoint: the new evidence doesn't just suggest Wilson is innocent. It actively points to a different perpetrator with both motive and opportunity to kill Alyssa Winters."

Now, the music became a little more upbeat. I could almost see a conductor pointing an accusing wand at someone.

"Which brings us to the centerpiece of today's episode: a forty-foot boat called *The Wayward Lady*.

"*The Wayward Lady* has been docked in Annapolis for years. The boat is available for private charter, hosting what the marina's booking system lists as 'exclusive corporate events' and 'private dinner cruises.'

"But according to multiple sources, *The Wayward Lady* serves a much darker purpose. Three former employees of various Annapolis-area escort services have now come forward to me—speaking on condition of anonymity—to describe being transported to *The Wayward Lady* for what they were told would be 'party hosting' jobs. What they found instead was systematic exploitation."

A different voice spoke next, this one distorted electronically to preserve the victim's privacy. "They told us it was just cocktail service, maybe some dancing. But once you were on that boat, they made it clear what was really expected. And once you were out on the water, there was nowhere to go."

"The same source describes seeing girls who appeared to be minors at these events," Naomi continued, "exactly matching what Alyssa Winters had documented in her journal entries.

"But what makes *The Wayward Lady* particularly significant is who was protecting it." The score took on a more ominous tone. If this were a TV show, the villain would be onscreen. "According to sources who have conducted extensive investigation into this case, *The Wayward Lady* is surrounded by an unusual level of security involving both private guards and members of the Annapolis Harbor Patrol. This level of protection is extraordinary for a simple charter boat. It's the kind of security you'd expect around a crime scene or something someone desperately wants to keep hidden

"But even more intriguing is who might be behind *The Wayward Lady*. A web of financial entities ultimately connect to Marcus Dunning, chief of staff to Annapolis Mayor Robert Hargrove." I'd never established Dunning as a partner in the ship, but maybe Naomi took our work and ran with it. She'd done her own investigations for years, after all.

"Dunning has built a reputation as the mayor's 'fixer'—the man who makes problems disappear and deals get done. But according to sources familiar with his business dealings, Dunning operates through a sophisticated network of shell companies that obscure his true financial interests.

"The pattern is consistent across multiple enterprises: a Delaware-registered company owns the asset in question, but when you trace the ownership chain, it leads back to entities controlled by or connected to Dunning. The same structure appears in several Annapolis development deals that received favorable treatment from city government.

"What makes this particularly concerning is that Dunning's public role gives him access to inside information about city planning, zoning decisions, and law enforcement priorities. If he's also secretly profiting from enterprises like *The Wayward Lady*, that represents a massive conflict of interest at best and active corruption at worst."

After a brief pause to build suspense, Naomi continued. "Sources close to the investigation describe Dunning as operating like a shadow mayor, wielding power behind the scenes while maintaining plausible deniability through his network of shell companies and intermediaries.

"And if Marcus Dunning was indeed connected to the trafficking operation that Alyssa Winters was investigating, that would give him a powerful motive to silence her permanently.

"The Harbor Patrol's involvement is particularly troubling. According to investigators, certain Harbor Patrol officers appear to be providing unofficial protection for *The Wayward Lady's* operations, ensuring clear waterways during its nighttime excursions and deterring anyone who gets too curious about the vessel's activities.

"This represents a serious breach of public trust. The Harbor Patrol is a law enforcement agency, funded by taxpayers, tasked with ensuring boating safety and marine law enforcement. Their job isn't to provide private security for boats involved in potentially criminal activities."

Another pause. I was riveted. It worked.

"Remember, Alyssa had told friends she was 'sitting on a bombshell' that could 'bring down powerful people.' She had photographs and documentation of trafficking operations connected to what she called 'harbor parties.'

"The Wayward Lady represents exactly the kind of operation Alyssa was investigating. And the level of official protection it receives suggests connections reaching into law enforcement itself."

The music shifted in tone again, now becoming contemplative.

"Which raises uncomfortable questions about the original investigation into Alyssa's murder. If Alyssa was killed because she was exposing a trafficking operation protected by both private security and Harbor Patrol officers, how thorough could an investigation be when some of the same people might have been involved in the cover-up?

"We know that witness statements pointing away from Darrell Wilson were minimized or ignored. We know that the investigation was closed with unusual speed. We know it was also closed with a lack of care.

"*The Wayward Lady* continues to operate. The same private security continues to guard it. The same Harbor Patrol officers continue to provide protection during its nighttime excursions, and they harass legitimate investigators."

The score became more forceful, punctuating the hostess's words. Naomi did a good job matching her cadence to the rhythm.

"But things are changing. The habeas petition for Darrell Wilson is moving forward with new evidence that could finally free an innocent man. Law enforcement agencies with no connections to the original investigation are now taking interest in both *The Wayward Lady* and the circumstances surrounding Alyssa's death.

"Most importantly, Alyssa's story is finally being told. The trafficking operation she died trying to expose is finally facing scrutiny. The powerful people she threatened are finally being held accountable.

"Eight years ago, someone thought they could silence Alyssa Winters by killing her and framing an innocent man. They were wrong.

"The truth has a way of surfacing, like debris washing up on the shore after a storm. And sometimes, it takes a while for the tide to carry it home."

The music built to a crescendo before mellowing out and fading.

"Next time on Harbor Homicides, we'll examine the political connections that may have protected *The Wayward Lady*'s operation . . . and why certain city officials seemed so eager to see Alyssa Winters' investigation buried along with her."

I sat in silence for a few minutes. Naomi used what we gave her, added some of her own work, and wrapped the whole package in a compelling bow. It made her a great podcaster.

It might also make her a target.

I called and got her voicemail. When prompted, I left a message. "Naomi, it's C.T. Great episode. I want you to be careful. The Harbor Patrol has taken a keen interest in me. I'll send you a video I took. Don't let it happen to you. We're dealing with the kind of people who will definitely kill the messenger." I ended the call, set my phone down, and hoped Naomi was safe.

ABOUT AN HOUR after I left Naomi the message, Rich returned home. He said he sometimes ate lunch at his own table, but I knew he came by to check on me—and maybe to make sure I hadn't turned his computer into a hacking machine. "I thought you only had a tablet."

"T.J. dropped off the laptop."

"She still here?" Rich asked.

"No," I said. "She stayed for a little bit and then went back to the office. I listened to the new podcast episode. T.J.'s listening to it now."

My flip phone vibrated in my pocket. I hoped it was Naomi calling to tell me she was safe, but I realized I'd never told her how to get a hold of me. By default, my burner didn't register on caller ID. A little contribution I made to its operating system. Not many people had this number. The simple screen showed a phony business name called Lin's Foods which meant Liz Fleming called. I answered.

"What the fuck are you involved with?" she demanded.

"You have no idea how often I ask myself the same question."

"Ever come up with a good answer?"

"Not really," I admitted.

"The video you sent. I . . . don't even know where to start."

"Sure you do. You love taking on the system."

"These clowns are the system?" she asked.

"A small and mostly incompetent part of it, but they're a police force. Ostensibly."

"I need some context, but first, I want to be sure I'm your lawyer. You on a smartphone?"

"No."

"Have a computer handy?"

I logged back into my laptop. "I do."

"Good. Venmo me twenty bucks."

"On TV, PIs and lawyers do this for a dollar."

"Inflation," Liz said. I signed into the site and sent her the amount she asked for. "Done. You know, you really could get a higher retainer if you asked for one."

"This is about to be the shortest attorney-client relationship in history," she said. I heard the amusement in her tone, and it made me chuckle. "Now, tell me what the hell is going on."

I ran down the situation for her, providing a little background on the case, minimizing the illegality of my second trip to the docks, and focusing on the general goonery she could see in the video. "I didn't even know there was such a thing as a harbor patrol," Liz said.

"Me, neither . . . until I started this investigation."

"You have help on this one?"

"I have a contact with the state police who promised to make sure these assholes don't disappear me," I said. "Now, I have you."

"I'll handle whatever comes up."

"I like the confidence, but I don't think you'll get a situation to handle. I've tangled with these guys twice now. The first time, they tried to tase me and throw me in the Bay. Last night, two different ones tried to plant drugs in my car. My guess is the contents of the bag were enough to add a distribution charge. Then, it's a major felony, and they take me to a black site somewhere you won't even know to ask about."

"Sounds serious," Liz said.

"Very much so," I confirmed.

She paused and blew out a long breath. "What do you want me to do with this clip?"

"I was thinking of setting up some kind of fail-safe. If I'm not around to keep a timer alive, the press gets the footage."

"You definitely watch too much TV."

"As my very well-compensated lawyer," I said, "what do you and your usurious rates recommend?"

"Don't do a damn thing for now. Leave it with me. I'll act in your best interests."

"Liz, are you saying I don't always act in my own best interests?"

She snorted. "Do I really need to?" she asked before clicking off.

"Sometimes, a big retainer goes to people's heads." I put the flip phone away.

"Liz . . . Fleming?" Rich wanted to know. I nodded. "She's your lawyer?"

"Yes."

My cousin offered an appreciative bob of the head. "Good-looking woman." It was the second time he'd made the observation.

"Not as good-looking as my wife," I said. "Maybe Liz is single and desperate to meet a police lieutenant facing an existential crisis about his own agency while helping his younger and much more handsome cousin."

"The cousin's not more handsome," Rich said, "just full of himself."

I shrugged. "If the shoe fits."

"You've cobbled a very specific shoe there."

"I've never seen Liz's feet," I said. I'd definitely admired her legs in the skirts she wore every chance I could. "Maybe they match."

"I'll be all right." Rich munched a sandwich. Maybe he really did come home for lunch. The bread was pale. Not toasted. The scent of peanut butter reached my nostrils. As a lieutenant, Rich made enough money to get something delivered every day. If he wanted to drive a half hour each way enjoy his midday meal, his fridge held ingredients to make something better.

"I will, too, you know."

"Never hurts to check."

"Liz accused me of not always acting in my own best interests, too."

"I think I might be in love with her now," Rich said.

———

While subjecting myself to the local news, I heard one of the anchors say something horrifying.

"We'll be going live to Annapolis in a few minutes where Mayor Hargrove will be making a major announcement."

"Fucking hell," I muttered. "I'm glad I haven't eaten lunch yet." I called T.J. to apprise her of this new miserable development.

"What a prick," she said.

"It was true before he called this press conference. Doubly so now."

"You think he's announcing a run for governor?"

"Has to be it," I said. "I think there's a negative nine hundred quintillion percent chance he's going to fall on the sword for the Alyssa investigation."

My assistant chuckled. "I don't think you'll find anyone to take those odds."

"If you can stomach it, you might as well tune in. The stakes just got a lot higher. Hargrove has even more to protect."

"Lucky us," she said and ended the call.

On Rich's fifty-five-inch TV, the steps of Annapolis City Hall had been transformed into a campaign stage, complete with harsh television lights that made the municipal building look almost gubernatorial. Mayor Robert Hargrove stood behind a podium bristling with microphones, flanked by his carefully assembled power tableau.

Marcus Dunning positioned himself directly behind the mayor's right shoulder, his expression radiating the kind of confidence that came from decades of political maneuvering and commanding a goon squad. To Hargrove's left stood his wife Helen, a pleasant-looking woman in her forties who smiled with what appeared to be genuine warmth. Completing the group was Maryland State Police Commander Patrick Wells, his dress uniform immaculate and his bearing military-straight.

"Good afternoon," Hargrove began, his voice carrying the practiced cadence of a man who'd been rehearsing this moment for months. "Thank you all for being here on this beautiful Maryland day."

Beautiful Maryland day, my ass, I thought, glancing out my window at the gray sky. It wasn't the only thing contributing to the general pall. Politicians could make a tornado sound like a gentle breeze.

"I stand before you today not just as your mayor, but as a lifelong Marylander who believes our great state deserves better," he continued. "For too long, we've watched as career politicians in Annapolis have failed to address the real issues facing working families."

The irony wasn't lost on me. Here was a guy who'd been in politics for over a decade, backed by a man who'd been pulling strings at least as long, complaining about career politicians. Considering they both did well in real estate before moving into the political arena, I doubt either man knew much about the "real issues facing working families," and I was certain they didn't much care.

People like Hargrove were why I never voted.

"Rising crime, failing schools, an economy that works for the wealthy but leaves everyone else behind," Hargrove continued. "These are the things we need to change. They're not all unique to us here in the great state of Maryland, but we still have to put in the work if we want conditions to improve."

Behind him, Dunning nodded at all the right moments, his face a mask of concerned gravitas. The commander maintained his thousand-yard stare, while Helen Hargrove beamed at her husband like he was announcing the cure for cancer instead of another gubernatorial campaign.

"That's why today, I'm proud to announce my candidacy for Governor of Maryland."

"There's a shocker," I muttered to the empty house. "Next, he'll tell us water is wet, and politicians lie."

The speech rolled on for another ten minutes, a dreadful greatest hits collection of campaign rhetoric about jobs, education, and public safety. Hargrove was smooth, I'd give him that—he managed to sound passionate about the most generic policy proposals, and he knew how to work a crowd even through a television screen.

What fascinated me was what he didn't say. No mention of recent events in his city, no acknowledgment of ongoing investigations, nothing whatsoever to remind voters about dead sex workers, innocent men in prison, or questions about police conduct. It was political amnesia in action.

When he opened the floor to questions, the assembled reporters served up softballs a beer-league all-star could have smashed over the fence again and again. Campaign organization, fundraising goals, potential running mates—nothing that might actually challenge the candidate or force him off message. The Alyssa investigation and Naomi's podcast were big news and not just in Maryland. I wondered if Hargrove chose these reporters because he wanted a collection of lickspittles. I certainly wouldn't put it past him.

Then Jim Breslin from the *Capital Gazette* tried to earn his paycheck: "Mayor Hargrove, can you comment on the recent murder investigation involving—?"

"I'm here today to talk about Maryland's future," Hargrove cut him off. His smile never wavered, his tone never changed. "My focus is on the issues that matter to families across our state . . . good jobs, safe neighborhoods, excellent schools. Next question."

It came off as a good dodge, but a dodge nonetheless. Hargrove probably practiced it in front of a mirror this morning on the off chance some journalist would actually do his or her job.

The softball questions continued for another ten minutes. Tax policy, climate change, economic development—all safe territory that allowed Hargrove to recite his prepared talking points without breaking a sweat. It was political theater at its most polished and least informative.

"Maryland deserves leadership that puts working families first," Hargrove concluded, delivering his closing lines with the same practiced confidence he'd shown throughout. "Together, we can build a state that works for everyone, not just the wealthy and well-connected. Thank you all for being here today."

As the cameras continued rolling, Hargrove worked the rope line like a seasoned pro, shaking hands and posing for photos and selfies. Dunning remained in the background, but I could see him watching everything, cataloguing every interaction, every angle, every potential problem. I could imagine the calculator in his head keeping tabs on the transactional nature of the interactions he witnessed.

The whole thing had been a masterclass in saying nothing while appearing to say a great deal. Not a single substantive policy detail, not one concrete proposal, nothing to pin him down or create controversy. Just pure, distilled political ambition wrapped in patriotic bunting and served with a side of false modesty.

Watching from my cousin's couch, I felt like I'd been witness to something genuinely dangerous. Hargrove and Dunning needed to be stopped, and they'd just put a few sizable roadblocks in our way.

———

Later in the afternoon, T.J. called.

"I got something on the building angle, boss."

I didn't expect it to pay off so fast. Maybe the gubernatorial announcement moved the timeline forward. "Go ahead."

"It's a place called the Waterside Hotel," she said. "Looks like it was a mix of nightly rooms and short-term rentals. Alyssa could have stayed there from time to time. As far as I can tell, the same company has owned it for almost twenty years."

"Let me guess. Now, some arcane finding or policy violation means it needs to be demolished."

"You've played this game before. It was being renovated anyway. Closed for repairs about three weeks ago. Here's the best part . . . one of the rooms marked as a short-term rental has a fireplace."

"Pretty good odds this is the right building," I said. "Great work."

"Thanks. The permits all came through very quickly."

"Kind of like the mayor or his chief fixer put a rush on things."

"Kind of like that, yeah," she said. "What are you going to do?"

"When is demo supposed to begin?"

"The paperwork got finalized yesterday. A quick turnaround. They want to start in two days."

"On a Sunday?"

"That's what it says."

A Sunday night demolition would make sense. By then, weekend visitors to the city would have left. Police could cordon off a perimeter and allow the dynamite crew to do their thing. It wouldn't disrupt Monday morning traffic because the only thing left would be the cleanup.

I must have gotten lost in thought because T.J. asked, "What do you want to do?"

"I need to go there," I said.

"By yourself?"

"Probably not, but it has to be soon."

"I don't have any plans."

"Good," I said. "I think we need to drive down there tonight. I'll have to take a circuitous route to avoid the Harbor Patrol and whoever else is looking for me now. We'll have to drive separately. I'll call you later." She agreed, and we disconnected. I called Gloria, and after a couple minutes of catching up and confirming she'd seen no goons or creeps at her house, I hit her with what I hoped would be good news. "I think I'll make a lot of progress in the case tonight."

"Does that mean you'll come home?"

"Yes."

"Thank goodness." I could almost feel her sigh of relief in my ear through the connection. "What do you need to do?" I explained the importance of Alyssa's missing notes, the people who very much would not want them found, and our working theory about where they might be. "Hang on. You're going to go to this building and look in the fireplace?"

"And chimney, yes," I said.

"When it's scheduled to be blown up?"

"Not for a couple days."

"Do you think they're going to wire it the morning of?"

"I'm sure they've already started."

"Don't you see the danger?" Gloria asked.

"They have plenty of ways to try and stop me without blowing up an old hotel," I said.

"That doesn't exactly fill me with good thoughts."

"I'll be fine. If what we want is there, I'll get in and out."

"You don't think they've already looked?"

"If they found it, why detonate the hotel?"

"I guess." Gloria released a breath. "Be careful. I really don't like these dangerous cases."

"I will. Love you."

"Love you, too," she said. "Remember . . . if you die, I'm going to kill you."

"I'd expect nothing less," I said.

CHAPTER 23

I WAITED for darkness to fall before I left Rich's house.

He must have been working late. I didn't see or hear from him after he popped back in for lunch—and probably to check on me, though he'd be loath to admit it. If I had known a drive to Annapolis and the jurisdiction of the Harbor Patrol were in my future, I would have suggested we swap cars. They wouldn't know to look for a blue Camaro. Alas.

On my escape from Baltimore, I'd been careful to avoid major roads, toll plaza cameras, and other highway-mounted electric eyes as much as I could. Getting to Annapolis without driving past at least some of them would be impossible. I knew how these things could be set up. Cameras scanned license plates and converted what they saw into searchable text. An operator could create an alert to go off when a device detected a certain text string—like my license plate.

The trouble with alerts is someone needed to monitor them.

One of my college professors loved to say, "Detection without response is useless." I hoped for a profound lack of utility tonight. As I got onto the highway, I called T.J.

"I'm headed to Annapolis," I told her.

"You still want me to come, right?"

"Yes. Lexi, too. We might need all the help we can get."

"What are you going to do if those goons try to stop you again?" she asked.

"I guess we'll see what happens." A thought popped into my head. "I'm going to call Joey and tell him to bring a gun. You pick him up before heading down."

"You got it, boss."

"I'm not sure where I'll exit the hotel. Guess it depends on the resistance I run into. Make sure you're covering the front and rear."

"We will."

I ended the call and pressed the phony contact for my long-time friend. "Need your help," I said when he answered.

"What's going on?"

The answer would be a long story, so I gave him the Cliffs Notes version, covering Alyssa, Darrell, Naomi, the investigation, and the actions taken to dissuade me from pursuing it. "I want you with T.J. in case the shit hits the fan."

"I had plans for tonight," he said, "but I'll cancel them. You owe me a dinner."

"Good thing we're being paid well for this case," I said.

"Am I driving to Annapolis?"

"T.J. will pick you up. She's probably texted you by now."

Joey paused. "I just felt the buzz. See you soon." He rang off, and I made the rest of the drive in silence. When I exited the highway, I took a long and random route to get to my destination. I didn't encounter any police cars. Not willing to chance it, I left the S4 in a restaurant parking lot about a block away and hoofed it to the site. As I got closer, I lingered in the shadow of a building across the street.

The Waterside Hotel didn't look like it needed to be demolished. I'd seen many edifices worse for wear remain in service for years. After a light refresh, this would be a great place. It was a long building and two stories tall, likely a motel at some point which went upscale after an ownership change. The location proved convenient for anyone wanting a place to stay within walking distance of downtown Annapolis. Some of the upper rooms probably offered a view of the water. At the far end, a chimney stuck up from the roof.

Maybe Alyssa had an arrangement with the manager to use the room with the fireplace on a semi-regular basis. She could have stashed something in the fireplace or—with a little craftiness—up the chimney somewhere. The brutes who worked for the Harbor Patrol wouldn't come up with a creative solution to a problem, and their bulky frames prevented them from searching narrow spaces.

There were no lights on inside. The lot remained empty. Yellow tape formed an X across the entryway. The darkness prevented me from reading a sign posted there, but it no doubt mentioned the facility's status of being under construction. Or demolition, as the case may be. There would be liability concerns galore if a kid or homeless person wandered in and stayed long enough to get crushed by the rubble.

Hargrove, Dunning, and company probably wanted nothing better than to find my broken body amid a pile of concrete, plaster, and glass. I checked the street. A man and woman walked hand-in-hand across the road to a restaurant. The occasional car drove past. No one took an interest in me. I texted T.J. and Lexi from the burner phone and told them I'd be heading in. I made sure the coast was clear with a final look in each direction before hoofing it across the street toward the doomed hotel.

———

The front door was locked.

It was a sliding model designed to open when pressure plates on either side of the entrance detected a person. Considering glass formed most of its surface, I figured it would have been smashed and covered with plywood by now. I slipped thin gloves on, pretended to look at my phone as someone walked by, and then pulled my snap gun from my jacket pocket when the passerby left.

The lock yielded quickly. The door didn't automatically retract, so I pushed it far enough to slip inside and shut it again. Enough ambient light came in for me to look around and conclude I stood in what had been the lobby. A long counter stood on the left half of the area. On the opposite side were a couple of tables. One featured a rack selling actual paper maps. I wondered if people my age bought them for the curiosity value.

Two elevators were situated past the lobby. Beyond them was a door leading to the stairs and another to the corridor of guest rooms. I couldn't discount the possibility Dunning stashed a couple of his Harbor Patrol goons here to make sure I didn't nose around. The .45 now in hand, I retraced my steps back to the former lobby and cleared it before moving on again.

Checking every door would take time. Jiggling the handles told me the ones I tried were locked, and they opened with card readers. No keyhole for the snap gun. I would cross this bridge when I came to it for Alyssa's room. I focused on common areas on the ground floor—a small business center whose computers had been removed, a space with tables setup for eating but no kitchen, and a gym I could barely turn around in even with the equipment gone. No one stayed here for the amenities, but with some rehab, this could have been a nice place. A musty smell hung in the air. Water was close, and I wondered how much had seeped into the basement.

So far, I'd been using my cell phone flashlight to help me see. On a lark, I flipped a wall switch before I left the microscopic fitness center. The overhead bulbs flickered to life. I turned them off again, but it was good to know the power still worked. The staircase at the far end of the building was damaged to the point of being unusable—something else fixable in rehab—so I walked back down the hall and took the steps up. Again, I encountered no resistance.

Before I opened the door to step into the hallway, my phone buzzed. T.J. texted to say everyone had arrived. I put an earpiece in, and we set up a call. "I'm inside," I said, keeping my voice to a whisper. "So far, it's quiet. I'm going to look around. For now, hold your positions."

"Copy," Lexi said. T.J. also offered confirmation. I pushed the bar to open the door, hoping it would be quiet. It wasn't. The process itself made a thunk anyone could hear in an empty building. I waited. No one approached. No other doors opened. I closed the blasted thing as quietly as possible, which is to say not very quietly at all. Other than a small area with an ice machine, there were no common spaces on the second floor. I proceeded down the corridor. The room with the fireplace would be at the end.

When I got there, the sign identified it as *Suite #1*. No other placards trumpeted suites two or three. Maybe the promise of others sold guests on the place. As with the rooms downstairs, this one opened via a keycard. Before busting out a credit card and going old school, I tried the handle.

It was unlocked.

A shudder crawled down my back. This had to be a trap.

Three armed goons must have been camped out on the other side waiting to blow me away. I moved to the side, reached as far as I could, and nudged the door open. It swung into the suite with a quiet squeak. No bullets flew out at me. I didn't hear anyone in the space beyond. "Found the room," I whispered. "I'm going in."

The interior was empty. The wall to the adjoining room on the left had been knocked down, and it yawned open. There was no furniture left. A TV mount sat naked on the wall. The suite comprised two rooms, and the fireplace was not in the first.

Before I could advance, I heard footsteps.

I swung the .45 toward the open wall, but someone's boot kicked it from my hand. The gun slid across the carpet and thudded to a stop under the window AC unit. One man stood to face me, and another moved to join him. Other walls had been knocked down, as well, and the area beyond the suit was basically a large open space. Neither of the two men before me looked familiar. "Trying to beat me down hasn't gone well for your friends," I said. Neither replied. "I came here to get one thing. If you let me get it and go, we don't have to see each other again."

"Can't," one of them said.

"You ain't making it out of here alive," the other added.

Neither held a gun, and both lacked any telltale bulges under their shirts. They weren't armed. Unless they were deadly cage fighters, I couldn't see how they'd take me down let alone kill me.

Then, I heard a muffled boom.

The building shook, and I wobbled on my feet.

Both my foes smiled like wolves.

CHAPTER 24

T.J. HOPED the Alyssa Winters case would wrap up soon.

She'd wanted to work it at the beginning because she saw something of herself in the dead woman. It was impossible not to. Now, she wanted it to conclude for the same reason. Every new piece of evidence kept inviting the inevitable comparison. Even though there were many differences between her and the late Alyssa, T.J. couldn't help but run down a checklist in her head.

Prostitute? Check.

Bad circumstances? Check.

Faced violence on the job? Check.

Murdered? Thankfully, T.J. found Melinda and got out before the same thing could happen to her.

"Jesus! Get it together," she chided herself in her apartment. Maybe another night of pounding the punching bag was the therapy she needed. Her phone buzzed, snapping her from her rare moment of self-pity. C.T. called. It was after dark and later than normal hours. She wondered what he was up to and figured it wasn't good.

"I'm headed to Annapolis," he said.

"You want me to come?"

"Yes. Lexi, too. We might need all the help we can get."

"What are you going to do if those goons try to stop you again?" she asked.

"I guess we'll see what happens." T.J. frowned. This seemed a little reckless. C.T. sometimes took chances she wished he wouldn't. "I'm going to call Joey and tell him to bring a gun," he added. "You pick him up before heading down."

"You got it, boss."

"I'm not sure where I'll exit the hotel. Guess it depends on the resistance I run into. Make sure you're covering the front and the rear."

"We will," T.J. assured him. C.T. ended the call and got Lexi on the line.

"I guess I should bring a gun, too," the intern said.

"I figured you carried no matter what," T.J. said.

Lexi chuckled. "I do. You want me to pack an extra for you?"

"No. I'm bringing Joey. We'll meet you at the hotel. I'll text you the address."

"See you soon."

Six fast-driving minutes later, Joey dropped onto the passenger's seat of the Mustang, and they were off to the Maryland capital city. "I'm giving up a date to be here," Joey said, buckling his seatbelt as T.J. sped through a yellow light.

"I'm sure you worked something out with C.T."

"This seems like a shitshow."

"Pretty much," T.J. said. "I think we're near the end now. If anything, our success will keep it from becoming an even bigger shitshow."

When she was about fifteen minutes out, T.J. initiated a

quick call to Lexi, who said her ETA would be similar. T.J. tried calling C.T. next.

No answer. She and Joey exchanged a worried glance before she tried again.

No answer.

———

T.J. curbed the Mustang about 500 feet from the hotel on the opposite side.

She snagged a spot in front of a small restaurant. Another car hovered in the area, and the driver honked a few times after T.J. sniped the space. She and Joey sat in silence. Both looked at the old building. It might have been a motel in a past life, upgraded and prettied up over the years into its current form. Now, for reasons unclear on paper, it faced demolition. T.J. knew the reason. Hargrove and Dunning couldn't run the risk of Alyssa's undiscovered cache falling into the wrong hands.

Would someone comb through the rubble and uncover it? What if it was a small flash drive? A crumbling building could destroy the device, but it might be tiny enough to slip through the rocks and land unmarred on the ground. Anyone could potentially find it then. It would be like looking for a very short needle in a chaotic pile of hay.

T.J. wondered what went on inside. The interior remained dark. Not many people milled about. This location was far enough from the main attractions to see lighter foot and car traffic. Still, had it been Friday night instead of Thursday, the scene could be quite different. A blue Accord coupe approached in the rearview mirror and parked somewhere behind the Mustang. She sent her boss a text. *Joey and I are here. Lexi just pulled up. All good?*

A moment later, she got a thumbs-up emoji in response. After a quick sigh of relief, T.J. gave Joey an earpiece, and they both popped them in. She worked on getting everyone onto the same call. Once the line was established, C.T. whispered, "I'm inside. So far, it's quiet. I'm going to look around. For now, hold your positions."

"Copy," Lexi replied.

"We got you," T.J. said.

Everyone climbed out of the cars. T.J. muted her mic. "How about Lexi and I take the front? Joey, are you good with the back? We'd be on both sides and have a gun at each position." Joey nodded and jogged down the cross street.

"I don't like this," T.J. said.

"Me, neither."

"I hate to use a cliché, but it's too quiet."

"We could go in," Lexi suggested.

"No. You heard the boss. We hold for now."

"Why are we here tonight, by the way?"

"We think it's where Alyssa kept her stash," T.J. said. "No idea if it's still here or not. All of a sudden, though, this place gets a demolition permit approved at record speed."

"Someone wants to make sure anything remaining is never found."

"Yep."

"I want to look around," Lexi said. "Back in a few." She padded off in a crouch. T.J. pretended to be looking at her phone to avoid the appearance of standing alone in front of an abandoned building. A few minutes later, Lexi returned. "Just the one way in or out."

"There's no rear exit?" T.J. asked.

"Chained and padlocked shut," Lexi said. "They're serious about keeping people out."

Or trapping them inside, T.J. thought, but she didn't want to spread her anxious musings to her friend. They stood far enough away from the entrance to not draw suspicion and to keep an eye on the second floor. Lights came on toward the area with the chimney. A lone figure moved behind a window at the end. Two others advanced toward it. All disappeared behind a wall.

Then, a muffled explosion went off, and the building shook. A few loose stones fell near the front door.

T.J. unmuted her mic. "Boss! Get out. The building is coming down."

"No," he said. She heard sounds of a struggle on his end of the connection.

"We're coming in."

"No," he repeated. "Under no circumstances are any of you to come inside."

"But—"

"I mean it, T.J. None of you."

Before T.J. could answer, the building shook again.

———

"What the hell is going on?" T.J. shouted. Another muffled boom near the front of the building preceded another tremor. More stonework came loose, and a large window cracked down the middle.

"They wired it to blow already," Lexi said. "Someone must really want whatever's in there to stay hidden."

"Boss, get out of there," T.J. said. C.T. didn't reply. She tried a different tactic. "Joey, do you see anything?"

"Not really," he said. "I can only see in some of the

windows. There's a lot of movement. Probably a fight. No one's running down the hall, though."

This was ridiculous. C.T. and T.J. figured out the truth about buildings getting knocked down in Annapolis and knew to look for one coming soon. They found it, thought it might be the big break in the case, and it turned out to be a trap. Maybe a literal death trap. Another bang shook the structure again, and T.J. felt the rumble through the sidewalk and into her core. She heard another, this one coming from higher up. A gunshot? C.T. must have gone in armed. Did he have to shoot one of Dunning's men?

Did one of them shoot him?

"You have to get out of there," she yelled into the mic.

"No," came C.T.'s reply. "Not yet. Stay outside."

Farther down the street, a few people had stopped, and they looked in the direction of the old hotel. The reverberations from the blasts must have reached farther than T.J. thought. None of them moved, but one man was on his phone. "I think someone's calling the police," T.J. said. "Which might mean the Harbor Patrol. Let's cut our losses."

Over the sound of a scuffle, C.T. again said, "No."

"Boss, I—"

"Call Rich. Tell him to call Norton." The sound of a fist striking flesh and bone rang in T.J.'s ear, and C.T.'s line went quiet. A moment later, a loud static pop made her wince, and the silence resumed.

"I think we've lost communication with him," T.J. said.

"This is bullshit," Lexi said. "I'm going in."

"No." When the intern started to walk toward the entrance, T.J. grabbed her arm. "You heard what he said."

"The building's coming down, and he's alone. He needs our help."

T.J.'s heart beat faster, and she heard the blood rushing in her ears. "You might not make it out."

"I need to try." Lexi jerked her arm free, nearly lost her balance when the place shook again, and then headed through the front door ahead of more stones breaking on contact with the sidewalk.

"Dammit!" T.J. hollered. She took a few steps to follow her friend but stopped. Even apart from the fact it might collapse at any moment, this hotel reminded her of too many she'd been forced to toil away in over the years. While there had been no explosions, T.J. had seen and experienced more than her share of violence in places bearing superficial resemblances to this one. The moment's pause saw another window fracture, and falling glass chased her back a few steps. T.J. ran around to the back. The exit may have been chained up, but there were still windows.

Worrying about one person surviving the chaos had been stressful enough. Now, she fretted over two and couldn't bear to lose either of them. Another rumble reinforced the possibility that neither C.T. nor Lexi might make it out alive.

CHAPTER 25

DEMOLITION OBVIOUSLY STARTED EARLY.

All the "It's a trap" memes I'd seen over the years flashed into my mind. If only I had heeded the wisdom of Admiral Ackbar. The two men standing before me didn't seem bothered by what went on around us. My pulse quickened to the point I could feel it in my chest and hear it in my ears. I also heard T.J. telling me, "Boss! Get out. The building is coming down." My mind flashed to Gloria. Alone in her house. I needed to get out of here to see my wife again.

Both guys rushed me. My pistol, across the room and under the air conditioner, might as well have been in the next city. I didn't see any other weapons on their belts. Maybe Dunning's goons had learned from their two aborted attempts to tase me. I blocked a couple punches, shoved the first guy into the second, and backed away to position myself better in the space. "No," I told my assistant as my foes glared at me anew.

One was a tall, burly ginger with a Conan O'Brien haircut and a mustache. The other stood a couple inches shorter than me at six feet even, was bulky to the point of being top-heavy, and shaved bald. They didn't wear uniforms identifying themselves as the Harbor Patrol, security guards, or anything on the spectrum of officiality.

They shared a quick glance before rushing me again.

The shorter one went low and arrived first. He sort of lunged at me in a way suggesting he was new to this tactic. He also left himself open to a knee in the face, so I gave him one. He fell off to the side. The other guy reached me the instant before my foot hit the floor again. Off balance, I toppled over when he did his best middle linebacker impression and tackled me. "We're coming in," T.J. said in my ear. It would be a complication I didn't need. If someone really did wire the place to blow up, no one else needed to be inside.

"No," I insisted as I struggled to keep my opponent at arm's length. "Under no circumstances are you to come inside." His meaty hand shoved my face away, and he took the opening to slip behind me and go for a chokehold.

"But—"

"I mean it, T.J."

I pulled on his arm. It didn't budge. A muffled boom came from the far end, and the building shook and wobbled again. It rocked us enough to allow me a little purchase in my quest to get free. I moved my foe's forearm suffciently to sink my teeth into it. He howled in pain. His grip loosened the amount I needed to squirm free, elbow him in the head, and slip out of the hold. I got to one knee as he rubbed his jaw. We both stood. The other guy remained on all fours trying to shake his head and clear the cobwebs. "You must be getting paid well," I said.

The ginger shrugged. "Well enough."

"How about your families after you're dead?" He said nothing. "You know your odds of making it out of here are as bad as mine, right?"

"We outnumber you," he pointed out. "I think our chances are better."

Bantering back with absurd logic could only mean slow recovery from my knock on his noggin, so I followed with two quick strides and a hard boot under Baldy's chin. His head snapped back and then slammed into the floor as he slumped flat. "How's this strategy working out for you so far?" Faux Conan shrugged again. "You might want to double-check your math."

Another set of footsteps approached. Silence prevailed on the connection. If it was T.J., Lexi, or Joey, I would be upset. Instead, it was another brawny guy. "I like my numbers," the red-haired one said. The newcomer stood about six-four, wore his dark hair short, and looked like he knew his way around the gym. He said nothing and charged toward me. I deflected a couple punches before landing a knee in his gut, kicking him in the back of the leg, and laying him flat with an elbow strike.

It all gave Ginger time to get back in the fray. He'd staked out a good spot, and I couldn't quite turn around before his punch caught me in the side. I retreated and played defense while breathing proved difficult for a few seconds. When I thought I might have an opening, another rumble rocked us. I staggered back, and my foe shifted to the right. I tried to go for the fireplace, but he grabbed my arm.

Rather than try to dislodge my enemy's grip, I stomped hard on his toes. He yelped, I jerked my arm free, and drove the air out of his lungs with a shot to the solar plexus. Ginger tried to back away, but I kicked him in the face, and he sprawled on the floor. The first man remained unconscious.

The third reached under his pants leg for a revolver.

I ran toward him. He got it clear of the holster, but I got my hands on the gun before he could bring it to bear. We struggled over it. He was bigger and stronger, but he also remained on his backside. I enjoyed the advantage of leverage and twisted. When his finger inside the trigger guard threatened to break, he let go. I wrenched the gun free, reversed it in my hand, and put a round through his knee.

His scream pierced the quiet. Ginger recovered enough to thwack this gun away from me, too. His eyes looked glassy, however. Right then, T.J. implored me to leave again. "You have to get out of there," she yelled in my ear.

"No," I growled. "Not yet. Stay outside."

Ginger tried to get me in another hold. I wriggled free as the dark-haired man moaned and sobbed, holding his knee as blood collected around his leg. The redheaded goon went back to the chokehold well. I evaded him and punched him in the jaw. It turned his head but didn't drop him.

"I think someone's calling the police," T.J. said in the earpiece. "Which might mean the Harbor Patrol. Let's cut our losses."

"No," I told her again as he sidestepped my follow-up strike.

"Boss, I—"

"Call Rich. Tell him to call Norton." Dividing my attention distracted me long enough for his right hook to take me just under my left eye. The earpiece flew out and landed with a soft thud.

Ginger stepped to the side, ground his heel on it, and took the time to taunt, "Hope you said goodbye to your girlfriend."

I kicked him in the right side. It wasn't hard, but he'd shifted his weight, and the blow caused him to teeter. He couldn't focus on defense. I hit him with a left jab before dropping the man with a right cross of my own. "She's my assistant, you prick."

I shook my hand out as I walked to the fireplace and looked for anything which might have fallen out. Nothing. The mantle was empty. Despite the detonations, the stonework appeared structurally sound.

I was about to reach inside when another shock knocked me down.

"I don't want to die," Ginger said in a small voice, his words a little slurred.

"Should've thought about it before you took Dunning's blood money."

"Please." I ignored him. He persisted. "You have to help me."

"I have my own problems right now," I said. Even if I found what I came for, I still needed to get out of a building which might come down around me at any moment. Ginger displayed the classic symptoms of a concussion. I had no idea how I would make it out by myself let alone dragging him along with me.

———

Something had to be here.

We'd done the work to get to this point. If Hargrove and Dunning wanted to kill me, there were myriad options easier than luring me to an abandoned hotel and blowing it up. The Harbor Patrol tried twice already, but those were amateur attempts. Someone with Dunning's reputation and connections could have hired a sniper to follow me from a distance and plug me on my way into the office one day. Clean, simple, untraceable, done.

No, they were worried we would find something. Probably because they tried and failed. This meant Alyssa must have hidden it very well. I got down on all fours and felt around the hearth for anything like a loose stone. Nothing. I moved into the firebox and did the same along the floor and walls. Again, I came up empty. Touching all the stones was taking time I might not have.

The building shook again to remind me of the ticking clock.

My pulse increased as time wound down. I'd never met Alyssa, but descriptions of her said she was five-five or five-six and pretty slim. I was taller and broader. She could stand up in the flue, and my shoulders barely squeezed inside it. All she would need was a phone flashlight to hide things and find them later. I felt around as high up into the flue as I could. My finger scraped something I would swear felt dodgy, but I didn't know if I'd be able to reach it. I'd never been claustrophobic, but I'd also never tried to cram myself into a stone-enclosed space while a building crumbled around me. It struck me as a suboptimal test for a common fear.

A boom sounded from somewhere below me, and I felt everything thrash and shake. I scrambled out of the fireplace as a bunch of rocks came down. The stonework no longer looked structurally sound. Along with the falling bricks and rocks, I heard a different kind of thud. A small black metal box lay amid the rubble. Ginger wobbled on his feet—for reasons beyond the demolition, I suspected—and made no move to get it. I grabbed it and put it in my jacket pocket.

The problem now was getting out. I stood at the far end of the second floor. The exit closest to me had been boarded and chained up. The nearest staircase was a deathtrap. Walking through the entire hotel while bombs went off in the basement struck me as a decidedly poor idea. I moved to the window. After a narrow strip of concrete below, I could aim to land on a grassy hill. A fifteen-foot drop but to a softer landing. Somewhere to the right, I spotted Joey down there. He waved. I waved, too.

"You gotta help me," Ginger said. He moved to stand beside me. "I don't wanna die."

"What about your friends?"

"Not my friends. Fuck 'em."

I nodded. "I like the cut of your jib. You seem like you have a concussion, though."

"Probably do. Had one in high school, too. Never played football again."

I got him turned around and positioned in front of the window. It extended almost to the ceiling, befitting a room billing itself as the penthouse. This would be our way out. I couldn't tell Ginger in case he suddenly became a chicken about the whole thing. "All right," I said. "I'll help you. We're getting out of here."

His stiff posture relaxed. "Good. How are we doing it?"

"You're gonna help me, too." I stood a few steps away. Ginger's eyes were still glassy, and he couldn't focus on me or anything else in the room. I rushed forward, slamming my hands into his chest and propelling him backwards. "Tuck and roll, Red," I said as a surprised expression replaced his blank one before his back broke the glass, and he fell out of sight.

I looked through the now mostly empty space. Ginger lay with his face planted in the grass. Joey looked at him and then up at me. "I'm coming now," I said, and my longtime friend nodded. Shards still clung to the frame in a few places. I took a deep breath, backed up a few steps, ran forward, and leaped through the opening.

———

After passing through the remains of the window, I turned my body even as gravity did its work.

Air rushed past me. It felt like I fell for minutes even though it was less than a second. My back hit the grass. Thanks to a lack of rain recently, it felt hard and unforgiving. I tucked my chin to my chest, preventing my head from taking the blow. Landing like I did still knocked the wind out of me. Thirty-two feet per second per second didn't seem like a lot of speed until you stopped at the end. I lay on the hill and groaned. To my right, Ginger was sprawled out face down and not moving. His left arm lay under his body.

Joey rushed to me. "You all right?"

I coughed a couple times. "I will be."

T.J. dashed toward me from the opposite direction. "You made it!" She threw her arms around me and wrapped me in a tight hug. "Your comms went out. I was so worried."

"Discount Conan O'Brien here stomped on the earpiece," I said. "Check his wallet. He owes us for it." To my surprise, T.J. actually did fish the unconscious man's billfold from his rear pants pocket. She grabbed a few bills and stuffed them in her jeans. Another low rumble boomed. I watched the building shimmy as more stonework came free. "We should probably move farther away."

"Did you find anything?" T.J. wanted to know.

I patted my jacket. Another reason to land on my back was minimizing the odds of anything happening to Alyssa's secret cache. "I think it found me more than the other way around," I said, "but I got it."

"Good."

I scanned the grass and concrete. Someone was missing. "Where's Lexi?"

T.J. frowned and wrung her hands together. "I tried to stop her, but she went in after you."

"What!?"

"She got free. I tried to keep her back."

"Goddammit." I got to my feet. My back still hurt, but I would be all right. Another boom—this one louder—caused violent tremors in the structure. "Joey, can you get this guy out of the danger zone? I apparently need to risk death to save our bull-headed soon-to-be-former intern."

Despite the damage the old hotel had already suffered, most of the interior remained intact. A few windows were broken. I could go through one, but then I would be in a random room somewhere. What if the door to the hallway wouldn't open? No, I needed to waste precious time and go through the front. As I moved toward the main entrance, another explosion knocked me from my feet. Joey dragged Ginger to safety. T.J. also lay prone. She got up and started toward the door, also, but I held her back. Many buildings wired for demolition imploded. Not all, however. If the old hotel scattered its debris outward when the death knell sounded, we'd all be in serious danger.

"We need to get away." As if on cue, a persistent low rumble heralded the collapse of the building as we ran to a safe distance. It started at the middle, and each of the ends turned to rubble next. A cloud of gray dust rose higher than the hotel ever stood. All in all, a pretty clean implosion, though some rocks fell where we stood a scant few seconds prior.

"Lexi!" T.J. shouted as she fought against my attempt to keep her from rushing to her death.

All we could do was hope Lexi made it out.

CHAPTER 26

"I CAN'T BELIEVE IT," T.J. said, tears spilling from her eyes and running down her cheeks.

"Maybe she got out," I said.

T.J. muttered something I couldn't understand as she put her head to my chest and cried. I put an arm around her and let her grieve. We were far enough away now for the continuing crumbling of the building not to be a threat even though fragments of stone and bits of glass kept falling. Stone dust filled the area, and we coughed.

"What are you crying about?" a voice asked from behind us.

It was Lexi. Her clothes and face were dirty, but she was alive and looked unhurt.

"Goddammit," T.J. said, grabbing the intern's arm and pulling her in. With me already there, it ended up being a group hug. I was happy to see Lexi was all right, but I extricated myself and let the two friends cling to each other another moment.

"What happened?" I demanded. With Lexi safe, my pulse finally slowed. It had been elevated since I first walked into the

Waterside Hotel. I felt like I'd run a marathon and then jumped out a window past the finish line.

"I . . . well . . . I went in after you," Lexi admitted. "T.J. tried to keep me back, but I got my arm free and walked in. It was dark and smelled musty. Little explosions kept going off below me. I made it to the far end and tried to use the stairs, but they came down." I'd seen the same steps and didn't even attempt to go up. Ah, youth. "That's when I figured I should get out. I didn't want to leave you there, but I also didn't want to die. Was there a gunshot on the second floor?"

"Yes. One of the goons brought an ankle rig."

"What happened to him?"

"I shot him in the knee before the gun got kicked away," I said. "Either he's the luckiest man in Maryland, or he's somewhere in the rubble with his friend. I managed to get one of them out alive."

"I was headed up the main hallway," Lexi said. "Part of the ceiling collapsed as I got closer to the exit. I ended up going into one of the rooms and using the chair to break the window and clear the glass. I got out and moved away as the whole thing came down."

Sirens approached now. I didn't know who would respond and how loyal they might be to Hargrove and Dunning. "You do something like this again," I told her, "and you're fired."

"Understood." Her bemused expression told me she did, in fact, comprehend my words but had little intention of following them.

I handed T.J. the package. "I think this is what we all came for."

"Where was it?"

"In the chimney. My guess is Alyssa could fit in there because she was slim. She'd rigged a hole and used the façade of a brick to cover it. I only found it because the tremors shook everything loose."

She held it in her hand and stared at it. "I hope it's what we need."

"We should go," Joey said.

"Right. The three of you, split now," I said. "Take the package and get out of here."

"What about you?" T.J. asked.

"Did you call Rich?"

"Yes."

"I'll be fine. There are enough people nearby to prevent Harbor Patrol from going rogue." I jerked my head toward the street. "Make yourselves scarce. Start working on whatever's in the case. If Rich did what we asked, I'll wait for the real cops to show up."

They left, taking a circuitous route around most of the onlookers. The sirens grew closer. My back still hurt from slamming into the hill, so I sat at the curb and waited. I texted Gloria to let her know I was all right, and I'd see her later. Her relief came accompanied with a gaggle of heart emojis in many colors. Blue and red lights colored the area as a police car stopped a short distance away.

———

Of course, it was the Harbor Patrol.

Annapolis city cops arrived, too, but they were second on the scene and stood down after a chat. Hargrove and Dunning must have ordered their uniformed goons to listen for any calls coming in about the Waterside Hotel. As far as I knew, the men inside never signaled anyone. Neither man looked familiar to me. Both were brawny, though the shorter of the two looked like a fire hydrant stuffed into a police Halloween costume.

They cuffed me, sat me back on the curb, and rattled off my Miranda rights. More onlookers gathered, no doubt drawn by the collapsing building and emergency response. I alternately heard, "You ain't goin' nowhere" and, "You'll be leaving with us soon" from my captors, so I asked a clarifying question.

"Which one is it?"

"Huh?" the taller one said, displaying his eloquence.

"Am I not going anywhere, or are you taking me somewhere?" He continued to wear a blank expression. "Am I Schrödinger's Prisoner?"

"Who?"

"Schrödinger," I said. "Had a cat. Quantum decay." I shrugged. "Never mind."

"You think you're smart?" he barked.

"Yes."

He leaned down to growl in my ear. "If you were smart, you'd shut up." He straightened, sneering at me and clearly enjoying the power trip.

"Are you threatening me, officer?" I asked in a voice loud enough to draw attention. "I'm already handcuffed despite being innocent." I shrank away from him as if afraid of catching a beating. "What more are you going to do?"

"Shut up," he muttered, but the damage was done. A lot of eyes were on us now, and a few members of the throng pointed their cell phones in my direction.

"It's hard to follow your boss's orders when you're being filmed, isn't it?"

"I told you to shut up." His leg tensed as if he wanted to kick me, but he restrained himself.

Members of the fire department took cautious steps into the

rubble as more sirens approached. Captain Casey Norton stepped out of an unmarked SUV. He was in plain clothes, his badge hanging from a chain around his neck. He was about my height and build but at least Rich's age. Gray intruded on the dark hair at his temples. "Who's in charge of the scene?" he asked.

"I am," the burly guy near me said. "Harbor Patrol."

"Not anymore." Norton ducked under the yellow tape and handed my captor a piece of paper. "As of now, MSP is taking over, and I'll be in charge onsite. Your agency isn't recognized anymore. No police or investigative powers."

"Says who?"

"Read to the bottom."

"You're asking a lot," I said.

"It's signed by two people," Norton explained. "One of whom is the governor. Now piss off and get out of my crime scene." Neither Harbor Patrol man made a move. Norton showed a tight smile. "You can either leave on your own or be escorted out. I kinda hope you pick the second option, but I'm still offering the first." Three uniformed troopers walked close to stand behind the captain, steely eyes never left the two dressed-up goons.

"Fine," Fire Hydrant said. He started to walk away, but one of the troopers stopped him.

"Not so fast," Norton said. "I'll need your badges and weapons."

"And handcuff keys," I added.

A couple minutes later, the two clowns left without incident. Norton gestured for me to stand. I did, and he undid the cuffs. I flexed my fingers. "You all right?" he wanted to know.

"More or less."

"Find anything?"

"Discovered I'm pretty good at jumping out of windows and landing on grass."

"How nice for you. I meant for the investigation."

"When I know, you'll know."

"Not good enough. Step into my office." Norton pointed to the Explorer. I climbed into the passenger's seat.

"I love what you've done with the place," I said. "Have you thought about hanging some curtains?"

"I'm serious. I want to know what you found."

"We suspected Alyssa Winters kept a cache of information somewhere. A few people made reference to what she knew and how it might bring some powerful folks down. If Hargrove and crew found it, they wouldn't need to go so aggressively after me and my people. We saw this place got on the demolition list quickly, so I came to check it out."

"Did you find this cache?" Norton pressed.

"I think so. I found *something* in the fireplace."

He held out his hand. "Which you'll now turn over to a sworn officer of the state police."

I patted my jacket theatrically. "Gosh, I must have left it in my other coat."

"Where is it?"

"Somewhere safe," I said. "I'll be happy to turn it over to you, but I'm making copies to review everything first. This was my investigation before it was yours, and I did a lot more than roll up in my SUV at the eleventh hour."

"I suppose you did." Norton sighed. "Fine. I'm coming to collect it in the morning." He jabbed a finger at me. "I mean it. I'm coming to collect. You and your cousin are reliable, but I set a good many things in motion based on promises from the two of you. Hell, I got an entire agency decertified in short order."

I snorted. "Come on. They were Mayor Hargrove and

Marcus Dunning's personal enforcers cosplaying as cops. I figured you'd be offended by their mere existence."

"Maybe I was," Norton admitted. I shifted in my seat. It was hard to get comfortable as the thick bolstering landed somewhere on my back no matter how I sat.

"You sure you're all right?"

"I've survived worse." I opened the door and stepped out.

"See you tomorrow," the captain said. "Don't play games with me on this."

"Should we keep the Scrabble board in the closet, then?" Norton rolled his eyes. "It's for the best. I'd beat you."

"Yeah, yeah." I shut the door, and he drove away. I unlocked the S4, lowered myself gingerly into the seat, and headed out of the city.

———

As I drove away from Annapolis, my phone buzzed. T.J. texted. *Lexi and I opened the package. Come to the office.* I wasn't surprised. I knew she was invested in this case from the start. Lexi ran into a crumbling building on the chance she might be able to find me and help me get out before we both got buried in a coffin of rubble. Her continued involvement came as no surprise.

I didn't need any additional prompting, but another text came in. *I made coffee.*

How could I say no at this point?

I flouted the road rules of Maryland, jotting off a quick reply to say I was on the way as I drove. With the Harbor Patrol no more, I could go back to using my real phone and sleeping in my own—or Gloria's—bed. The promised coffee would keep me going for a little while, but I needed a good night's rest—and probably some Advil for my back. With little traffic on the highways at night, I made good time getting back into Baltimore. I parked next to T.J.'s Mustang and Lexi's Accord. When I walked into the office, the two ladies were still there, and Joey remained with them.

My friend gestured to a box of donuts on the table. Based on the size, it should have held a dozen but currently contained only five. "I only had three," he said, no doubt figuring I suspected him of consumption in a five-to-one-to-one ratio as compared to T.J. and Lexi.

"I have some catching up to do, then," I said, adding a glazed and chocolate to a plate.

"We paid," T.J. added.

"Yeah," Joey said. "You still owe me a nice meal. Don't think you're getting out of this for a box of donuts."

I sank into my chair. "Wouldn't dream of it." After a few bites, I asked, "You find anything yet?"

"We got the good stuff," T.J. said, smiling. "A notebook, some CDs, and a flash drive."

"Wow." I chuckled. "CDs. How quaint."

"They might make sense depending on when she recorded the data," T.J. pointed out.

"Yes. Let's pretend I know a few things about technology as we go along. What's on them?"

"Looks like much of the content is duplicated," Lexi said. This made sense. Recordable discs were popular before flash drives took over. "We're copying everything and digitizing the notebook."

"A lot of photos?" I asked.

Lexi nodded. "And some documents . . . but more pictures."

"Good. Let's make sure we get it all. Captain Norton is

coming tomorrow morning, and he's going to expect us to hand over what we found in Alyssa's stash."

T.J. frowned. "We're just going to give it all to him?"

"Once we have copies, yes. Norton's one of the good ones. He got the Harbor Patrol axed from the list of actual police agencies in the state. I'm almost surprised he didn't follow me here and demand everything tonight."

"All right." T.J. put up her hands. "We'll double and triple check we got everything."

I yawned and stood. "I'm going home. Don't stay too long."

"We'll be all right," Lexi said, patting her side. I couldn't see from my angle, but I figured it meant she was armed.

"I mean it. Get the cache online and then go home. We can comb through it in the morning when we're more awake and alert. I think each of us had a pretty rough night." I glanced at Joey. "Well . . . most of us."

"I had to get Ginger away from the hotel before it came down," he protested. "He was a dead weight."

"Fair enough."

He grinned. "Needed some donuts to replenish the calories." The ladies chuckled. I grinned. Joey could get self-deprecating in his humor, but I knew he was more athletic—and sensitive—than he let on.

"Want a ride home?" I asked my friend.

"Sure."

"Does hitting a drive-through on the way to your house count as a nice meal?"

"No."

"I had to try," I said.

CHAPTER 27

AFTER DROPPING Joey off with another fresh bag of food, I drove to Gloria's house. She stood ready to greet me as I walked through the door from the garage. Her arms wrapped tightly around me. I missed her, and there were a few moments in the Waterside Hotel when I didn't know if I'd see her again. We stood in the kitchen, holding the wordless embrace for a good minute. The hug didn't help my aching back, and my breathing must have cued her in because she released me and frowned. "You all right?"

"Mostly."

"Any more rogue cops after you?"

"Their agency got decertified," I said. "I suppose Hargrove or Dunning could still give them orders, but they have to be a lot more careful acting without official cover."

"Was the Annapolis trip worth it?" my wife asked.

Before answering, I grabbed a beer from the fridge. I held a second bottle up for Gloria, but she shook her head. I carried mine into the living room, taking a long pull as I sank into the couch. Gloria sat right next to me. "I think we found what we were looking for."

"Now what?"

"We copy everything and turn it over to the police."

"Really?" She arched an eyebrow. "You? Turning things over to the police?"

"I'm getting soft in my mid-thirties, aren't I?"

"Is it Rich?" Gloria wanted to know.

"No." I shook my head. "The state. If we can give them enough, they can go around the Annapolis PD and haul the mayor and his chief goon away. Captain Norton is coming by in the morning."

"You need a good night's sleep, then." To my surprise, she let me get one. When cases have kept me away and in potential danger, Gloria has been very demonstrative about how happy she's been to see me arrive in one piece. Normally, I appreciate and reciprocate. Tonight, however, I was exhausted and drifted off a few seconds after my head hit the pillow.

My phone alarm jolted me out of a deep slumber. I staggered through a shower and making coffee. Gloria padded downstairs as I was about to leave. I apologized for not making breakfast, she kissed me goodbye, and I picked up bagels for everyone at the office on my way in. T.J. and Lexi were already hard at work when I got there. Both happily chose bagels from the bag and toasted them. I finished my sausage, egg, and cheese sandwich and polished off a coffee before we got down to business.

Alyssa's notes told a compelling tale. We filtered out data she'd amassed on anyone not relevant to the investigation. She knew Hargrove and Dunning were dirty, and even though some details were missing, the rest of the evidence we'd gathered filled in any gaps. The flash drive held scads of incriminating photos. Her journal confirmed she took certain clients simply to have access to their phones and what might be on them later. It was a dangerous pursuit, and she paid the ultimate price for it.

We worked on compiling information for Norton and for Liz Fleming. Combined with what she already had, there was enough to get Darrell Wilson out of prison. We also shared links to everything with Naomi. As important as it was to take down the Annapolis duo and get Darrell released, Naomi paid the check. The material we sent her would provide several episodes' worth of material and maybe even win her podcast some awards.

Rich needed the data, too. As the officer of record, he might still be able to go back in and update the case. I knew it could complicate things for Leon Sharpe, but the captain made his bed when he threw in with Dunning. I still wanted to know what they were meeting and shaking hands about. Maybe once we got everything disseminated, I could spare some time for a visit to police headquarters.

This represented another high-profile case. We'd hit a pretty good run of them recently. One of these months, I would need to take my assistant's persistent advice and bring in another investigator, at least part-time. Today, however, we needed to hand everything to Casey Norton. I needed more coffee before dealing with the cops.

———

Footsteps on the metal steps heralded Norton's arrival. I let him in. He wore his tan uniform shirt, olive pants with a brown stripe up the outer seam, and a ten-gallon hat. He tipped it to Lexi and T.J. before stepping inside and removing it. "Stop any cattle rustlers recently?" I asked.

"There's plenty of farmland in Maryland," he said. "You might be surprised."

"I just might." Norton shook a paper cup out of the plastic sleeve and poured himself some coffee. Like a lot of men in law enforcement, he took it black. I wondered if they spent days gulping down increasingly bitter coffee in police academies. He carried it to my desk and looked around at our collection of file boxes.

"What the hell is all this?"

"The BPD's notes on their Alyssa Winters investigation," I said.

Norton snorted, took in the scene again, and laughed. "Seriously?"

"Yes."

"I got everything on a flash drive."

"Dammit." I wondered at the reason. If the case records were digital—and they clearly were—Rich could have handed me a memory stick. Maybe Leon Sharpe told him to bury us in paperwork. It would be another question to ask the man.

"You might help the city hit its recycling goal all by yourself," Norton said.

"In the meantime, we can make some killer forts." Both my assistant and our intern rolled their eyes. "Or we could . . . if I weren't surrounded by two boring old grumps."

"I hope you don't expect me to take all this cardboard."

"Do the state police have a recycling goal?" I said.

"No."

"We have a flash drive, too," Lexi said. She set a small USB-C model on the desk. "It has all the photos and documents we found on her portable media plus the scanned pages from her journal."

"There should be enough there to go after Hargrove and Dunning," Lexi added, "and get an innocent man out of jail."

"The last one is a little above my pay grade," Norton said. "I can tell you I'm working on a task force. We want to bring in the mayor and his chief of staff without any political influence. I know there's the possibility of Leon Sharpe being tight with Dunning, so we're not including anyone from the BPD. This has to be above board and get fast results."

"Are you concerned they're going to flee the state?" T.J. wanted to know.

"No. I have people watching both of them. They're not going anywhere." He collected the small flash drive. "Good thing I got a new laptop last year. Thanks."

"You bet," I said. "I hope you end up throwing the book at them."

"We'll do our best." Norton stood and headed for the door. He put his hat on and tipped it toward T.J. and Lexi again. "Ladies." The captain left.

"He's not bad for an old guy," T.J. said.

While the girls objectified the captain, I checked to see if Rich had replied to our email with links to all the information. Nothing. I couldn't be surprised. While Sharpe wasn't his direct supervisor—and their methods often diverged wildly—I knew Rich thought of the man as a mentor of sorts. I liked Sharpe, so I didn't want him to get tossed out on the street. However, the task force would need to run down his potential involvement with Dunning.

It might not end well, but murder investigations rarely did.

———

We were about to call it a day when my phone rang.

Lexi had left earlier. As an intern, she was only supposed to give us a certain number of hours per week while taking classes, and—as usual—she'd exceeded her allotment. T.J. looked at me. Naomi's name appeared on the caller ID. "Not much time to look over everything we sent," my assistant said.

I nodded. Something bothered me about this call, but I didn't know what. We'd found the evidence and given it to the people who turned it into arrests and convictions. I answered on speaker. "Hello?"

"I think I'm being followed," Naomi said quickly. Her breathing suggested she'd done a fair bit of running.

"Do you know by whom?"

"No. I'm scared, C.T."

"Call the police."

"I can't trust them thanks to the Harbor Patrol."

"They're done," T.J. said.

"I can't trust them," Naomi repeated. I wondered if the way she took on law enforcement made her concerned for the kind of response she'd get when she needed them. It was a conversation for another time. "I'm sure someone is following me."

"Your phone," I mouthed to T.J., holding my hand out. She gave it to me, and I turned away to make a call while T.J. picked up my mobile and took it off speaker.

"Can you get somewhere safe?" she asked before I put in a call to Casey Norton.

"Norton."

"It's C.T. You said you had troopers on Hargrove and Dunning, right?"

"Yes, why?"

"Our client thinks she's being followed."

"Your client . . . the dramatic podcaster?" he asked.

"Can you check with your people?"

"Sure. I'll call you back." He rang off. T.J. stood near the opposite corner, my cell pressed to her ear. She shook her head.

"Naomi, can you tell us where you are?" I couldn't hear the response. "Good. Is there a safe place you can get to? A crowded building. Somewhere out in the open."

Norton called back. "Bad news. Dunning slipped his tail."

"Shit. I think he's after Naomi."

"Where?"

"I'll let you know when I know," I said and ended the call.

T.J. frowned. "Naomi? Naomi?" As I moved closer, she put the call on speaker in time for me to hear the connection drop. "Shit."

"Norton told me Dunning got away from whoever was watching him."

"And now he's after Naomi," T.J. said. She held my phone in a white-knuckle grip and paced as much as the towers of file boxes would allow. "Shit. We have to get her back."

"Let's get going, then."

Her eyes widened. "You know where they are?"

"No," I said, "but I have a good idea where they'll go."

CHAPTER 28

T.J. DROVE us to Annapolis as I continued trying to reach Naomi.

We hit a little traffic, but my assistant proved deft at getting around slow drivers, merging in and out quickly as needed, and generally setting an aggressive pace. Repeated attempts to contact Naomi failed. It had been about fifteen minutes since we lost contact with her. This would be plenty of time for Dunning or some of his paid goons to do something horrible.

While I thought I knew where they would end up, I didn't know when. Police and law enforcement have to jump through a lot of hoops to get near-real-time location data on someone's phone. Those of us who don't have to file our forms in triplicate can take shortcuts. An app on my mobile allowed me to track other people's. I only used it when I needed to, and now was one of those times.

I entered Naomi's number and a general area to start searching. The app populated her carrier and other relevant information. The screen filled with a display which looked like the radar screen in an old naval battle movie for a few seconds. Then, a map replaced it, and a blinking red dot showed

Naomi's location. "She's headed to Annapolis," I said, "but whoever took her has a head start."

T.J. pressed the accelerator. Her Mustang downshifted and revved higher as she moved to the left lane and kept going. "Where is she now?"

"About five minutes out of the city."

"And you still think they're going to the marina?" T.J. asked.

"I do."

"They'll get there at least five minutes ahead of us."

"I'm going to call in support." I left the tracker app open and dialed Casey Norton. "Dunning has Naomi Chambers," I said when he answered.

"You're sure?"

"As sure as I can be without looking in his trunk, yes."

"Where are they now?" Norton wanted to know.

"Headed to Annapolis."

"How are you tracking them?"

"Let's leave a little mystery in my methods," I said. "I'm pretty sure I know where they're going."

"Tell me, and I'll make sure we have a presence."

"The Bayshore Marina. You know it?"

"No, but we'll find it. We need a water team?"

"If only there were some reliable agency to patrol the harbor," I said. "You could even call them the Harbor Patrol."

"If only," Norton said. "I'll make sure we have a couple boats in the area in case they try to get away by water. What makes you think they're going to this marina?"

"One of the ships docked there was a big component of the investigation. It was used for trafficking and sex parties years ago . . . and I doubt everyone on board was in a state of mind to consent."

"Jesus Christ."

"It's a mess. We're headed there now. The boat in question is called *The Wayward Lady*."

"Little on the nose."

"When you don't expect to get caught," I said, "I guess you can give out careless names."

"We'll be there," Norton confirmed.

"Don't go charging down the dock. I think Dunning will be volatile. He's going to blame Naomi for a lot of what's happened, but I hope he'll see me and shift his anger away from her."

"You're a damn fool if you get on the ship with him."

"I guess I'll be a damn fool, then. Just make sure I don't end up a dead one." I ended the call and went back to the tracking app. Naomi's phone had stopped moving. Cell tower data is rarely so precise as to provide an exact location. Depending on the coverage, there can be a margin of error up to a hundred yards. In a city like Annapolis, we would have more precision. "She's in the area of the marina," I told T.J.

We got off the highway and onto the city streets. "Is her location steady?"

"The app says she hasn't moved for three minutes." As I watched, the little red dot stopped blinking and soon went out entirely. "Shit."

"What?"

"It's gone."

"Maybe Dunning turned her phone off."

The app reported the last location. "Maybe," I said. "Or maybe it was in her pocket when he tossed her in the water. Let's hurry." T.J. blew through a light changing from yellow to red. We'd be there in five minutes, maybe less.

———

Sirens began a quiet approach as we skidded to a stop in the marina parking lot.

I bolted out of the car and sprinted for the dock. T.J. was a few steps behind me. I made it over the fence and turned. My assistant told me to run ahead, so I kept going. Pole lights along the dock were already on. A couple boats were missing. All were dark except for *The Wayward Lady*. I heard T.J. land behind me as I dashed along. One of the Harbor Patrol's paid bullies I recognized from a prior encounter emerged from the shadows of another vessel and approached. "You shouldn't have come," he called.

I didn't break stride. His eyes widened as I closed the distance at a run. I drew my fist back, and he raised his hands to block a punch I never intended to throw. My left foot hit the wood. My right kept going forward, and I directed my shoe right into his groin. The force lifted him off the planks as I came to a sudden stop. The man's face contorted in pain. He would have fallen if I didn't grab him by the collar. I marched him to the boat he was hiding near, rammed his face into the hull, and tossed him in the water.

T.J. had pulled even with me now. I'd lost my trusty .45 when the Waterside Hotel came down, so I drew my 9MM and kept going. *The Wayward Lady*'s deck lights were on. Dunning stood in the open, a gun held in his hand, and Naomi standing near him. The tracks of her tears reflected light off her face. Her clothes were intact, and she displayed no visible injuries. "I didn't even need to call you," Dunning snarled as we neared.

"You could have picked up the phone instead of kidnapping someone."

"You're both messing around in things you don't understand."

"Enlighten us, then," I said. "Are you something more than the mayor's well-paid fixer and chief goon?"

Dunning snorted. "You have no idea. Hargrove is going places."

"To jail, yes. Maybe you can even be on the same cell block and share a prison boyfriend."

"Fuck you," he spat. "This doesn't end in jail."

"You hear the sirens?" They were louder now. Probably still a couple blocks away, but Norton and company would have boots on the dock in about three minutes. I didn't see or hear any boats in the water yet. "The only way this doesn't end with jail for you is if you make me or the state police shoot you."

"You think you're so goddamn smart?"

"Yes."

"Get up here, then," Dunning said. "We'll settle it."

"Sure. You can shoot me as I'm coming aboard. Pass."

Dunning stopped pointing the gun at me to grip it in a way suggesting he might surrender the firearm before tossing it into the water. "You're not going to kill me in cold blood."

He was right, of course. I wasn't Lexi's father, who would have fired the second Dunning's weapon splashed into the bay. I handed the 9MM to T.J. "If he tries to pull a fast one," I said loud enough for the disgraced chief of staff to hear, "shoot him."

"I will," she said. T.J. handled the pistol like she'd put in a little time at the range. She didn't point it at anyone but could easily bring it to bear if need be.

"I'm coming to you," I said.

"You sure this is a good idea?" my assistant asked in a whisper.

"No, but it's our only play. If the state cops swarm the area, we lose control, and it's a shitshow."

"I'm waiting," Dunning bellowed. He clenched his hands into fists and shadowboxed the air between himself and Naomi.

I walked down the pier to climb aboard *The Wayward Lady*.

––––––––

I knew I'd be vulnerable going aboard the boat.

Dunning's military history suggested he would be an honorable man and not exploit such an opening. His recent behavior, however, indicated the opposite. I would need to get onto the deck and have solid footing quickly. I noticed no ropes held the boat in dock and wondered when Dunning had undone them. The water was calm, but this made the initial step onto the bottom rung longer than normal. Dunning stared me down as I put my hands on the short ladder and started to climb.

While I knew I could scale it quickly, an opportunist would still have a chance to gain the upper hand. Dunning surged forward. Naomi, apparently realizing what he planned to do, hip checked him like she'd been playing hockey her whole life. It didn't knock the man down, but he rocked to the side and needed to break stride to keep his balance. It gave me a chance to vault onto the deck of *The Wayward Lady*.

"You bitch," Dunning growled, turning around. Naomi cowered as if she expected a blow to come.

"Hey, asshole," I called. Dunning stopped, turned around, and glowered at me. "You didn't invite me on board so you could beat up a woman."

His gaze swept over T.J. before returning to me. "When you're down, looks like I'll get a two for one."

He came forward. Many opponents I've gone up against have been bigger and stronger than me. Power represented the lone tool in their arsenal, however. Block the big strikes, and they grew tired, leaving themselves open for counterattack. Dunning wasn't in this class. He used his full body to put power behind his punches, but I knew he wouldn't wear himself out after a dozen swings. We moved away from the pier. Out of the corner of my eye, I saw Naomi bolt for the ladder. Smart woman.

"You could have let it go," Dunning said. He fired off two quick strikes. I blunted both and tried to hit him with a jab, but he turned it aside.

"You could have not killed an innocent woman," I pointed out.

"The whore was a threat to everyone and everything."

"Because you and your boss are assholes ruled by your ambition."

Dunning snarled and threw a series of rapid-fire punches. I raised my arms a little more each time, forcing his a little higher. The risk was he would notice what I did and attack while I was vulnerable. He didn't. I blocked a strike, stepped to the side, and hammered him in the midsection. My foe grunted. Before he backed away, I tagged him in the head with an elbow strike. It didn't put him down, though.

Footsteps hurried along the dock. "Give up now," I said.

"Go to hell." Dunning threw another set of jabs. A stance and weight shift heralded a roundhouse kick. Sure enough, he spun, but I ducked under his foot. It was a major blow which could have sent me for a loop. It also opened the attacker up to a counterstrike, but Dunning was a good combatant and blunted my jab with his trailing arm.

"Hold your fire," a man on the dock said. "Captain Norton is en route."

I hoped the state cops didn't hassle T.J. She didn't have the best history with law enforcement and tended to distrust most wearers of the badge. Dunning kept me at bay with a set of snap and side kicks. I caught one against my body and used my right foot to push his free leg out. Before I could get a hold locked in, though, he scrambled away and got back to vertical quickly.

"You're not going to win," I said. "Surrender now and make it easy on yourself. It's over."

"Maybe it is," Dunning said, "but I don't have to play nicely. What are they going to do? Give me two life sentences?"

Before I could answer, he came at me again. My arms ached from blocking so many strikes. I would have some impressive bruises over the next few days. I turned a few more blows aside and caught Dunning with a kick to the chest. It sent him staggering backwards toward the boat's controls.

I didn't have a chance to set my feet before he got on the throttle and took *The Wayward Lady* away from the dock. Dunning left the throttle open, and he got me in a chokehold before I could recover. There would be no tapping out here. He meant to lock it in until I passed out or died—and the former would just see my unconscious body thrown into the water. I'd be dead either way.

Dunning was strong and knew how to apply the hold. I couldn't wrench his arm free. I reached behind to poke an eye, but he turned his head. I was running out of air. Lying on my side with an enemy behind me didn't give me a great amount of leverage. I shifted to try and stand. Dunning moved with me. I grabbed his right leg, pulled it toward me, and wrenched his ankle. He groaned but didn't release the hold.

I twisted harder.

Dunning howled in pain. His grip loosened enough for me to dislodge his arm. I elbowed him in the head and rolled away, drawing in a deep breath as I did. My lungs burned, but I got back to my feet. Dunning, clutching his leg, remained on his side. I gave him a hard punt to the midsection. When he folded in half, I booted him in the head until he lay still.

The challenge now was getting the boat under control.

The Wayward Lady still moved with speed through the water. I eased off the throttle and let the boat slow down before turning the wheel and pointing us back toward the marina. A couple minutes later, I pulled close to the dock. Norton had arrived while we were away, and he directed some of his men to help me get the ship stopped and tied down.

Once a couple ropes were in place, I cut the engine. Dunning stirred but remained prone. I walked toward the ladder. Norton and a couple troopers waited to board. "Avast, me hearties," I said in my best pirate voice.

"Dunning up there?" Norton asked.

"Aye, the filthy landlubber is napping on the poop deck. Arrrr."

"Do you even know what a poop deck is?"

"No," I admitted, "but it sounds like a very unpleasant place."

CHAPTER 29

THE STATE POLICE put Dunning in handcuffs, read him his rights, and escorted the surly jackass to a nearby Explorer.

"How'd you know they were coming here?" Norton asked me.

"Seemed like the best option," I said. "The boat was a big part of the operation. We discovered it in the investigation. They've had it under guard. In the end, if the shit hit the fan, Dunning could make a run for it in open water."

"Strikes me as a bit of a lucky guess."

"A well-educated one." He didn't need to know about my illicit app.

He smirked. "You were big in this. We're going to take him to headquarters for questioning. You want to observe?"

"Hell yes," I said.

Norton pointed sharply at me. "Observe only. You'll be outside the room. I don't need any distractions or bullshit Dunning and his lawyers might try to bring up at this stage."

I put a hand to my chest and gasped in mock indignation. "Moi?"

"Yeah, yeah. Give us an hour or so."

T.J. sidled up once Norton walked away. "What's going on?"

"He's inviting me to observe Dunning getting questioned."

"You gonna take him up on it?" she asked.

"I think so."

"You remember I drove you here, right?"

"Shit," I grumbled. In the brouhaha on the boat, getting a ride back slipped my mind. "It's fine. We can expense an Uber to our client."

"Should I go, then?"

I could tell T.J. didn't want to stand here with a phalanx of strange cops around her. "Hang on a second." I texted Norton to tell him I would need a ride to HQ. He replied and said someone would collect me when they were leaving. "I'm good. See you Monday."

She hugged me all of a sudden. "This one has been a bastard. I'm glad you're all right."

"Never a doubt," I said.

T.J. snorted. "Keep telling yourself that." She headed away from the scene. I stayed out of the way while the cops worked. After about forty minutes, a slender male trooper with *LAWRENCE* on his name plate offered me a lift. As we pulled away, he asked if I was hungry. I told him yes, and we drove through a McDonald's en route. By the time we pulled into the lot at MSP headquarters, I'd finished my double cheeseburger, fries, and apple pie.

Lawrence led me inside. I waited on a padded bench past the lobby. The bullpen here was larger than in other stations but laid out much the same way. A gaggle of desks took up the central area, offices and a breakroom ringed it, and interrogation spaces were down the hall. I texted Gloria, let her know I was fine, and told her I'd be home after being a good boy and staying quiet while Norton questioned Dunning. She sent back a heart followed by a couple full rows of laughing emojis.

My reputation preceded me.

While I remained on the bench, a man wearing a five-thousand-dollar suit, very expensive shoes, and enough cologne to be fragrant from orbit walked in. He knocked on an office door. When he opened it and walked in, I spotted Norton manning the desk. My vast sleuthing powers told me the newcomer would be Marcus Dunning's high-priced lawyer. I doubted he would get much satisfaction from the captain. The pace of his exit and the sound of him stomping across the floor a short while later confirmed my theory.

After another few minutes, Norton stepped out of an office and jerked his thumb for me to follow him. He led me to a door and opened it. "You're in here." I would be on the observational side of the one-way mirror. "Audio will come in through two speakers. There's a microphone, but I might break your arm if you use it."

"They teach you much about the eighth amendment in the academy?" I wondered.

"Sure," the captain said. "It was on the list of suggestions."

Norton left me in the long, narrow space. Two stools which looked like shopworn rejects from a nearby bar comprised the entirety of the seating. I parked myself on one, wishing I'd noticed them before so I could have made a crack about beer and peanuts. Dunning and the expensive attorney already sat on one side of the table. They remained silent. Dunning's right arm was cuffed to a steel ring in the table. A moment later, Norton and another male trooper walked in and shut the door.

He was a little younger, shorter, and skinnier than the captain. It looked like Norton cloned himself but left the copy in the dryer too long. The other guy was probably around my age. Norton took a recorder out of his pocket, set it on the metal tabletop, and pressed a button. He started with the current date and time and kept going. "This is Captain Casey Norton and Corporal Peter Sutherland. Also in the room is Marcus Dunning, represented by Jerome Moses. We are here for several crimes, chief among them being the murder of Alyssa Winters eight years ago. Mister Dunning has been advised of his rights already. Can you—"

"I didn't kill the damn whore," Dunning barked. Moses put a hand up to silence his client. For now at least, it worked.

"Can you confirm a trooper read you your Miranda rights?" Norton asked as if he hadn't been interrupted.

"Yeah."

"Great. Let's talk about the boat we arrested you on."

"Never seen it before," Dunning muttered.

"Really?" Norton pressed. Sutherland opened a manila folder and put a paper on the desk. From my distance through the glass, I thought it was a map. "This is Naomi Chambers' cell phone."

"Who?"

Norton threw up his hands. "Come on. Counselor, if your guy's just gonna sit there and be an asshole, we're done. I hope he enjoys the rest of his life behind bars."

"Hold on," the attorney said as Norton stood. Client and lawyer huddled together. Moses remained so quiet I couldn't hear him, but he accentuated the points he made with sharp hand gestures. "My client will answer the question."

"Great." Norton crossed his arms and remained standing. "For someone who'd never heard of the goddamn boat before, you sure seemed to know how to get to where it's docked."

"All right," Dunning said. He put his head back and sighed like everyone in the room was imposing on him simply by being present. No one reacted to the obvious performance. "I know the boat. So what?"

"So we have a large number of firsthand accounts of some activities it was used for over the years." Dunning said nothing. "Ever hear of harbor parties, Marcus?"

He shrugged. "They sound like a good time."

"Not for the women brought on board and used for sex."

"I don't know anything about them, then."

Norton showed a thin smile. "You know we arrested Mayor Hargrove, too, right? He's already announced his future plans for office. I'm sure even the accusations of a bunch of terrible crimes would spell the end of his gubernatorial bid. He might think he can salvage something with a deal, though. Another term as mayor. Congress."

"What's your point?" Moses wanted to know.

"My point is, Counselor, the mayor is an ambitious man. He won't let something like a longtime friend and associate get in the way of what he really wants." Norton walked around the table, put his palms on it, and leaned down until he spoke a few inches from Dunning's face. "He will throw you under the bus. Then, he'll run over and back over your body until your blood is ground into the asphalt." The grisly image didn't seem to faze Dunning, who offered no reaction even as his attorney grimaced. "If he talks before you do, you're screwed."

"I need a moment with my client." Moses leaned closer to Dunning again. Norton moved back to where he stood before. After a minute of more whispers and gesticulation, Moses straightened. "Mister Dunning will tell you what you want to know, but we want a deal."

"What he gets is up to the state's attorney," Norton said. "I'll recommend something in his best interests." He nodded toward the prisoner. "Start talking."

For about twenty minutes, Dunning laid it out with minimal interruptions. Alyssa was one of Hargrove's favorite call girls. She knew plenty of women in the industry, so they both tapped her to set up the harbor parties. She didn't understand the scope at first, and once she did, her fee went up significantly. They paid to keep buying her silence and because rich guys were lining up to shell out money for easy sex on a boat. At some point, Alyssa threatened to go public with what she knew, and it obviously would have toppled many people. Dunning didn't kill her, but as the fixer, he paid someone to take care of it. The man had since died of natural causes. Darrell Wilson—working for the opposing candidate at the time—made a good scapegoat.

"I think my client has cooperated," Moses said after Dunning lapsed into silence.

"He has," Sutherland said.

"He'll need to do it again," Norton added.

"What do you mean?"

"The state's attorney is in possession of evidence detailing how some of these women came from other states." Dunning began a study of the tabletop. To his credit, Moses offered no visible reaction, but I imagined his blood pressure rising by the second. "She'll be turning it over to the FBI for an interstate trafficking investigation. Nothing to say now, Marcus? How long did it take to get to Delaware . . . or Virginia . . . or North Carolina?"

"I don't think we need to give anything to the FBI," Moses said.

"Out of my hands. I'd advise you to tell your client to take whatever deal a US Attorney offers. You know their win rate when they go to court, right?" I did. It was over ninety-nine percent. One of my history teachers in high school loved to say a line popularly attributed to Otto van Bismarck: "God loves fools, drunkards, and the United States." Only a fool or drunkard took on Uncle Sam in court. "Your client might get something from Maryland, but he'll be up on federal charges soon enough. If he's lucky, maybe he can serve all his time concurrently. I'd buy a funeral plot now, though." Norton jerked his head, and Sutherland got up to head toward the door. "Thanks for your cooperation. Interview concluded." Norton stopped the recording, and the troopers left the room.

For a change, I was glad I didn't say anything.

———

The weekend passed without incident.

Gloria and I normally did a lot of things, saw many people, and graced a host of establishments with our presences. I didn't want to do any of it. The case had been trying in many ways. I was exhausted, my back still hurt, and my biggest goal was to be a homebody who went out for morning runs. Having skipped Saturday, I did an extra mile on Sunday. We bunked down at Gloria's place over the weekend. She was happy to stay in with me, and not just for the time we spent not getting out of bed. My difficult cases affected her, too. "You're the Lois Lane to my Superman," I said.

"I always figured you to be more like Batman."

"Okay, but then you're either Catwoman, Vicki Vale, or Talia al-Ghul."

"I don't like those options," Gloria said, wrinkling her nose.

"How many have you heard of?"

She grinned. "Just one. I'll settle for being the queen to the King of the Nerds."

"I'll allow it," I said.

Monday morning, T.J. was already at her desk when I walked in. The aroma of coffee filled the space—as did the file boxes we still needed to get rid of. I would have to ask Rich what we should do with them. Norton got all the details digitally, so electronic copies existed. Still, I couldn't take boxes of official BPD documents to the nearest dumpster as much as I might want to.

After an exchange of pleasantries, T.J. said, "Liz Fleming wants to come by this afternoon."

"Tell her to bring lunch."

"Why?"

"My guess is she's going to say Darrell Wilson is getting released," I said. "It's step one. Step two is suing the shit out of the state for putting him in jail when they shouldn't have. She's going to do pretty nicely in the settlement. Lunch is on her."

T.J. chuckled. "I'll let her know."

We spent the morning going over invoices a couple people still needed to pay as well as some inquiries which came in over the weekend. We would need to tally up the bill for this venture before I seriously considered taking another case. At 1:30, Liz texted to say she was on her way. A second message indicated she was bringing lunch, and the string of middle-finger emojis conveyed how she felt about it. I answered with an equally long block of dollar emojis.

A few minutes later, Liz arrived with two paper bags full of food and displaying a proper amount of grease spots. "Hope you like The Abbey," she said as she set everything on our table.

"We love it," I said. T.J. and I spread the food out. Liz brought three burgers along with enough fries and onion rings to feed twice our number.

After a few minutes of chowing down, she said, "Darrell's habeas petition was granted this morning."

"That's great news," T.J. said.

"I officially filed it Friday evening once Hargrove and Dunning's charges appeared on the books."

"Quick turnaround," I said, "especially with Saturday and Sunday in between. Don't judges take those days off?"

"Sure," Liz said, "but they read the news. They know what's going on. Judge Taylor didn't see any reason to delay considering two people got charged for Alyssa's murder with much better evidence."

"When does he get out?"

"He should be a free man again by the end of the day."

"And when do you file your next set of papers?"

Liz grinned with an onion ring most of the way to her mouth. "By the end of the week."

"How much do you think he'll get?" T.J. asked.

"I don't know." Liz shrugged. "There's a recommendation, but these things never go to court. We're going to ask for the moon and stars, of course. My guess is we'll shake hands somewhere north of five hundred grand but less than three million."

"Not a bad paycheck," I said. "You can afford to get us lunch every day for a year."

With her mouth full, Liz allowed her middle finger to speak for her.

T.J. and I were packing up when Rich called. "You still at the office?"

"For now."

"Mind if I come by?"

"I can just Venmo you for the night in your guest room," I said. "Don't charge too much. You don't offer many amenities."

"Not really why I'm stopping by."

"I'll be here."

Rich ended the call, and T.J. asked, "What does he want?"

"I don't know. If he's come for the file boxes, he'll need something with a much bigger trunk than his Camaro."

T.J. slung her bag over her shoulders. "Mind if I take off?"

"See you tomorrow." She left, and I wondered what my cousin wanted to talk about. With the state filing charges against Hargrove and Dunning—with the feds to follow—the original case would come under scrutiny. This meant Rich, as the official investigating officer, would come under the same scrutiny. No cop got things right a hundred percent of the time, and I figured Rich's percentage was higher than most. He shouldn't get sanctioned for it, but then again, department politics were an animal unto themselves.

About ten minutes later, Rich's footsteps rang on the metal stairs. He carried a brown paper bag. Before sitting, he fetched a disposable coffee cup and carried it to my desk. To my complete non-surprise, the bag held a smallish bottle of bourbon. Rich poured some into his cup and an equal measure into my mug. He leaned back in the guest chair, sighed, and downed the whiskey in a single gulp. I didn't try to initiate or steer the conversation. Rich would talk when he was ready.

He poured a couple fingers into the foam cup and swirled the contents around. "This case sucked."

"It did," I agreed, "and you weren't even in a building wired to implode."

"I'm kind of hoping my *career* doesn't implode," he said.

I waved a hand. "You'll be fine. The investigation was eight years ago. No one gets everything right."

Rich didn't answer for several seconds. "I let myself get railroaded."

"You were still fairly new to the department then."

He frowned. "I'd put in a couple years. Enough to make sergeant. I wasn't a newbie."

"I imagine Leon Sharpe has exerted his influence on people regardless of their tenure," I said.

"He probably has," Rich allowed, "but I think I shouldn't have let it happen."

"You talk to him about what went down?"

"Like his handshake with Dunning in Annapolis?"

"Yes."

"I did." Rich swirled his whiskey some more and took a small sip. When he was surly, extracting information from him was harder than extracting teeth.

"And?" I prompted.

"Told me he and Dunning go back years," Rich said. "Sharpe knew there was an investigation brewing. He insists he didn't share any intel or do anything inappropriate. It just looks bad."

"*Very* bad. You believe him?"

"I think I do, actually. In the end, you and Norton hauled Dunning away, and Hargrove's arrest soon followed. The good guys won, and the bad guys are going to rot in prison cells."

"The result is good," I said, "but getting there was a little messy."

"Yeah." Rich downed the rest of the bourbon and set the cup down. "Sharpe's been on the hot seat before . . . especially in the last ten years. He's an old-school door-kicker and face-puncher. Those don't tend to play well with things like de-escalation training, consent decrees, and all."

"You think the BPD will broom him out?"

"Wouldn't surprise me."

"What about you?"

"Me?" Rich frowned. "I thought we agreed not much would happen to me. Can't get them all right."

"Not what I mean," I said. "I know you've flirted with going state before. Maybe this is a good time to jump ship."

"Maybe," he allowed with a slight incline of his head.

"Can you do one thing first?"

"What?"

"Take all these goddamn boxes with you."

Rich chuckled. "Go to hell."

CHAPTER 30

ON THURSDAY, Rich texted and offered to bring lunch. Not being a buffoon, I obviously agreed.

"What do you think he wants?" T.J. asked when I told her.

"I honestly don't know."

"You think he's leaving the BPD for the state police?"

"I doubt it," I said. "He might still be kicking it around, but he didn't decide this quickly."

"It's been a few days."

"This is Rich we're talking about. He has six pairs of suits so he can wear a particular color on a certain day all the time. Having two of each leaves one free while the other is at the dry cleaner's."

"Really?"

"Really," I said. "Rich loves routines. He's not going to throw his professional life into chaos after a few days of consideration."

"I guess we'll have to wait to hear what it's all about," my assistant said.

"Today is Thursday. He's going to be wearing a dark blue pinstriped suit."

"Maybe he'll surprise you."

"He won't," I said.

He didn't. Rich came up the steps about twenty-five minutes later. When I let him in, he carried a paper bag stuffed into a plastic one. As I'd predicted, he wore a dark blue pinstriped suit, pairing it with a white shirt and a red tie with navy polka dots. T.J. caught my eye and nodded. Rich set the bag down. "I stopped at a sub shop near HQ."

"We're not picky," I said.

T.J. got three paper plates, and between them, they set out a trio of cheesesteaks and bags of crinkly fries. I pulled six paper towels off the roll and sat down to join them. I ripped the white paper covering my sub and peeled back the foil. Steam rose, carrying the aromas of grilled steak and onions to my nose. I inhaled the pleasing scents. "When did you get rid of the file boxes?" Rich wanted to know.

"I told Paul King I would toss them in a dumpster behind the *Sun* building," I said. When Rich got his promotion to lieutenant, King earned a bump to sergeant, working under my cousin in the homicide unit.

"He believed you?"

I shrugged. "A couple uniforms picked them up the next day."

"I hope you wouldn't really give it to the paper," Rich said. I munched a couple fries in silence.

"What brings you by today?" T.J. asked after a few seconds.

Rich took another bite of his cheesesteak. "It's about Sharpe?"

"He get the sack?" I said.

Rich snorted. "No, guvnah, he didn't," he answered in a bad British accent. "'Get the sack.' Wow. He's suspended for two weeks, and when he comes back, he's going to be heading up a cold case squad."

"For how long?"

"No idea. It might be permanent. The department is doing damage control after your client made sure to drop Sharpe's name as steering what ended up being a lousy investigation."

"Where an innocent man went to jail for eight years," I added.

"You don't need to rub it in," Rich said.

"What about you?"

"I'm cleared. Sharpe is the one spending time in purgatory."

"It's probably a fair punishment," T.J. said.

I bobbed my head. "The right people are going to pay for it, and Darrell Wilson can get back to his life."

"I know it ended up well," Rich said, "and I realize Sharpe exerted undue influence eight years ago to help his friend. I don't think he knew what really went on. He took the word of someone he shouldn't have believed." My cousin sighed. "Sharpe can be complicated, but I've always seen him as something of a mentor . . . even when I haven't followed his example."

"Sounds like he'll be all right," I said. "He didn't get a demotion or anything?"

Rich shook his head. "Just an exile of indeterminate length."

"I don't like the sound of working cold cases." I wrinkled my nose.

"Sharpe probably doesn't, either." Rich picked up a fry and used it to point at me. "Maybe he'll call you in for a consult."

"I doubt his little squad could afford me."

"He'd still have a budget from the BPD."

I waved a hand. "I'm sure he'll have a motley crew of cops the commissioner doesn't like ready to help."

"You never know," Rich said.

———

Two uneventful weeks and a few days later, a bunch of us gathered at Gloria's house to listen to the final *Harbor Homicides* podcast of the season.

It was Sunday evening. Rich declined our invitation, but T.J., Lexi, Melinda, and Liz all attended. Every lady wore jeans in varying shades of blue and sweaters of different colors. It was like they all agreed on the loose parameters of a uniform. Clad in dark jeans and a maroon quarter-zip, I almost fit in. Gloria set a few bottles of wine out before everyone arrived, and because she can't help but serve food at things like this, a delivery of appetizers would provide our guests with something to munch on. I finished arranging the plates, bowls, and glasses a few minutes before the first guest—T.J.—knocked on the door.

We all lounged in the living room as we waited for the episode to go live. All the ladies wanted some wine, so Gloria and I retreated to the kitchen. She smiled at me. "You certainly surround yourself with pretty women."

"None as lovely as you," I said.

Color came to her cheeks. "Thank you. I'm sure I'm not the only one who's noticed, though."

I traced the area around my face with my hand. "Have you seen me recently? I have standards to uphold."

She chuckled, and we filled five wine glasses. Along with a bottle of beer for yours truly, we carried the beverages into the living room on two trays. Everyone settled in with their drink of choice and some finger foods as the opening music played through Gloria's speakers.

"Hello, *Harbor Homicides* listeners. I'm Naomi Chambers, and this is our final episode of what has been the most challenging, heartbreaking, and ultimately rewarding season of the podcast yet.

"When I started this four years ago, I never imagined I'd be sitting here today having witnessed justice finally served for Alyssa Winters. More importantly, I never imagined that our investigation would help free an innocent man who spent eight years behind bars for a crime he didn't commit."

As she did so well, Naomi paused a beat to let her words resonate.

"If you just found us or you've been here the whole time, you know this season has been different. Instead of presenting a completed investigation, you've been with us every step of the way as we uncovered a conspiracy that reached into the highest levels of Maryland politics. You've heard the frustration in my voice, the dead ends, the moments when I wasn't sure we'd ever find the truth.

"But we did find it. And today, I can tell you that Richard Hargrove, the mayor of Annapolis, and his chief of staff Marcus Dunning are both in custody, facing charges that include first-degree murder, conspiracy to commit murder, racketeering, evidence tampering, perjury, civil rights violations under federal statute, and obstruction of justice. The federal charges alone could put them away for life. Uncle Sam's lawyers don't lose in court."

A few bars of music preceded a sound effect of shuffling papers.

"Let me take you back to where this all began. Alyssa Winters was a call girl found murdered in a motel room. The police quickly arrested Darrell Wilson. The case seemed straightforward . . . they had a suspect with opportunity, some circumstantial evidence, and an overworked public defender who never really fought back against the state.

"But some people never believed it. The more I looked at things, neither did I. I took my concerns to a local private investigator, C.T. Ferguson, who accepted the case. What his agency found . . . what we all found together as this season unfolded . . . was a web of corruption, murder, and cover-up that goes back almost a decade."

"It would have been nice to get mentioned by name," T.J. said.

"Maybe you'll get a shout-out in the show notes," I said.

"The breakthrough came when C.T. recovered Alyssa's personal notebooks from the Waterside Hotel just moments before the building's demolition. A demolition hastily arranged by Dunning and Mayor Hargrove to try and destroy the evidence, I'll point out. Those notes and photos, which Alyssa had hidden behind a brick in the chimney of a suite, contained detailed records of what she'd discovered working as a call girl whose client list included some important men.

"Alyssa had stumbled onto something that would get her killed: evidence that Hargrove and Dunning were doing more than just running the state capital. They had . . . varied interests, you might say. The mayor's revitalization efforts largely happened to properties owned by Marcus Dunning's shell companies. Then, there were the so-called harbor parties where rich, well-connected men paid to have sex with women on a boat. If you were to guess the women were paid, you would be correct. If you were to guess not all of them consented to being there under the circumstances, you would also be correct. And if you were to guess some of the women came from neighboring states, you're three for three. Needless to say, this is where the federal prosecutors come in, and they almost. Never. Lose."

Naomi added another pause for emphasis before she continued.

"Alyssa's notes documented many such cruises over the three years prior to her death. In her later entries, she wondered if anyone is on to her. I don't know how Dunning and Hargrove figured it out. Alyssa was careful, but those men had a lot of friends. And in Darrell Wilson's case, they had an enemy . . . a man working for the mayor's opponent. Why not murder the woman who's on to your scheme and damage a political rival in the process?

"The notes showed that Alyssa had been planning to take her evidence to the cops. She never got the chance because Hargrove and Dunning ordered her to be murdered, and then whoever carried out the dirty deed planted evidence to frame Darrell Wilson. To be clear, we don't know who actually killed Alyssa. We know who ordered it and who bears the ultimate responsibility. Right now, her actual murderer hasn't been identified. My guess is the identity of the killer will come out in court. Someone will take a deal and hand over the information.

"During the course of the investigation, C.T. Ferguson and I discovered that Wilson's so-called confession was obtained through coercion and psychological manipulation, and probably not helped by his lousy public defender. The evidence was circumstantial. The timeline never made sense. But it doesn't need to in a railroad job."

Light music filled the silence, and then the sound effect of a gavel banging led to Naomi's next segment.

"Part of this was discovering who killed Alyssa, of course. It's what we do at *Harbor Homicides*. In this case, however, the wrong man was in prison. C.T. arranged for defense attorney Liz Fleming to represent him. Based on what the investigation turned up, she filed a motion to get him released, and it recently happened.

"I want to read you something. This is from an email that Darrell Wilson sent me earlier this week, after his release.

"*Ms. Chambers, I spent eight years in prison for something I didn't do. I lost my mother, my sister, my chance at a family, my career—everything. But I never lost hope that someday, someone would care enough to look for the truth. Thank you for caring. Thank you for not giving up. Thanks to you and the investigator, I got a good lawyer, and I can finally try to get my life back. Alyssa doesn't have this chance, though. She deserved justice, and now she has it. So do I.*"

Hopeful music played for several seconds before the hostess continued.

"That letter . . . it reminds me why we do this work. Why we ask the hard questions. Why we don't accept easy answers when they don't fit the facts.

"This season has been different in so many ways. Usually, I complete my investigation before recording begins. I present you with a finished story, a complete picture, in stages. But this time, you were with us as we followed leads, hit dead ends, made connections, and slowly built our case. You heard my frustration when officials stonewalled us. You heard my excitement when we found new evidence. You heard my anger when we realized how many lives had been destroyed by two corrupt men who used their power to harm and kill innocent people.

"Some of you have asked if I'll continue with this real-time format. The honest answer is . . . I don't know. This season nearly broke me emotionally. There were nights I couldn't sleep thinking about Darrell Wilson in his cell, thinking about Alyssa's family never getting answers. There were days I wanted to quit, when it seemed like we'd never get past the wall of silence protecting Hargrove and Dunning.

"It all came to a head when Dunning found me and took me to the boat where so many women were exploited. I thought I'd be dead." She sighed, and when she spoke, a tremble accompanied her voice for the first few words. "We talked about all this last episode, though. I'm sure you understand if I don't want to revisit it.

"Whenever I ponder packing it in, I think about the other cases out there. The other Darrell Wilsons. The other families still waiting for justice. And I know I can't stop."

Naomi did stop for a few seconds. No tunes filled the gap.

"I know there's been chatter about whether or not I would keep the podcast going. I'll tell you all for certain now. Yes, *Harbor Homicides* will continue. The format might go back to what you're used to before this year. We're already looking at several cases for next season. I can't promise they'll all have happy endings like this one . . . if you can call eight years of wrongful imprisonment and a young woman's murder a happy ending. But I can promise we'll keep asking questions. We'll keep pushing for truth.

"Before I wrap up, I want to acknowledge some people. First, those who never stopped fighting for justice in this case. C.T. Ferguson, who took on this case with his assistant T.J. and their intern Lexi." The two young women high-fived each other on the couch. "Attorney Liz Fleming, who fought tirelessly for Darrell's freedom." Liz raised her glass in my direction. "The Baltimore State's Attorney's office, particularly the Conviction Review Unit, who re-examined this case with open minds and integrity once presented with the evidence.

"And I want to acknowledge all of you, our listeners. Your tips, your support, your shares on social media . . . they matter. This case broke open partly because people were paying attention, because you made noise, because you refused to let this story disappear.

"I also want to say something about responsibility. True crime entertainment has exploded in recent years, and not all of it is ethical. Some podcasts sensationalize tragedy, exploit families, or present theories as facts. This season, working so closely with an active investigation, I've been more aware than ever of the weight of this responsibility.

"Alyssa Winters was a real person. She had dreams, fears, hopes for the future. She wasn't entertainment. She was someone's daughter, someone who died because she tried to do the right thing. Darrell Wilson isn't a character in a story. He's a real man who lost years of his life. Mayor Hargrove and Marcus Dunning aren't villains on a Saturday morning cartoon. They made choices, and people died. When we tell these stories, we have to remember that."

Music swirled to a crescendo, and another sound effect of paper rustling followed. All of us were leaning forward on the couches, our drinks forgotten.

"The civil lawsuit against the state and various officials will likely take months to resolve. Darrell Wilson deserves compensation for what was stolen from him, though no amount of money can give him back those years. The FBI is investigating Hargrove and Dunning for their so-called harbor parties. We did a lot, but the investigation isn't over. Official agencies will carry it forward. There may be more innocent people in prison, more families waiting for truth.

"The work continues. The questions continue. But today, I can say something I couldn't say when we started this season: Alyssa Winters' killers are behind bars. An innocent man is free. Justice . . . delayed and complicated as it was . . . has finally been served.

"The fall of a mayor and his chief of staff sends shockwaves through Maryland politics, but for me, the real victory is simpler: truth won over power. Evidence won over corruption. An innocent man walks free.

"From all of us at *Harbor Homicides*, thank you for taking this journey with us. Thank you for caring about the truth. Thank you for remembering that behind every case, there are real people whose lives have been forever changed by violence.

"Until next season, this is Naomi Chambers. Keep asking questions. Keep demanding answers. Keep fighting for justice." A musical outro swelled, this one with more guitar and rock than Naomi's other choices. It faded after about twenty seconds.

Gloria let out a long, slow breath as she stopped playback on her phone. "Wow. I can't believe you were involved in this."

"I wasn't alone," I said.

"You were in that old hotel," T.J. pointed out.

"All's well that ends well."

"Maybe we can avoid such big risks for a while," my wife said. She looked at T.J. and Lexi. "Can't you two keep him in check?"

They both snorted. "I am incorrigible," I said.

"I wish it weren't one of the reasons I love you, but it is."

END of Novel #18

Captain Sharpe's cold case squad is going to need some help . . . and he's going to bring a certain PI into the fold. When a cold case turns hot, however, everyone realizes a killer is still active. Preorder The Deep Freeze today! (Available Spring 2026)

THE END

Thanks for checking out this novel! I hope you enjoyed reading the book as much as I enjoyed writing it.

I write mysteries and thrillers with action, snark, and flawed heroes. If this sounds like something you like, you can check out my catalog below.

The C.T. Ferguson Crime Novels

1. The Reluctant Detective
2. The Unknown Devil
3. The Workers of Iniquity
4. Already Guilty
5. Daughters and Sons
6. A March from Innocence
7. Inside Cut
8. The Next Girl
9. In the Blood
10. Right as Rain
11. Dead Cat Bounce

12. Don't Say Her Name
13. Night Comes Down
14. Concrete Angels
15. Conduct Unbecoming
16. Bleeding into Winter
17. Unreasonable Doubt
18. Digging in the Dark
19. The Deep Freeze (2026)

The John Tyler Action Thrillers

1. The Mechanic
2. White Lines
3. Lost Highway
4. Four on the Floor
5. Forced Induction
6. The Low Road
7. Backfire
8. Redline
9. Collision Course
10. Steel Wheels (2026)

I release 3-4 new novels per year. For the most current list of books, please visit:

- https://tomfowlerbooks.com - Direct sales
- www.tomfowlerwrites.com
- https://books2read.com/tomfowler

(**Note**: C.T. Ferguson appears in *White Lines*. John Tyler appears in *Don't Say Her Name*.)

While the suggested reading sequences appear above, each novel is a standalone mystery or thriller, and the books can be enjoyed in whatever order you happen upon them.

Connect with me:

For the many ways of finding and reaching me online, please visit https://tomfowlerwrites.com/contact. I'm always happy to talk to readers.

This is a work of fiction. Characters and places are either fictitious or used in a fictitious manner.

"Self-publishing" is something of a misnomer. This book would not have been possible without the contributions of many people.

- The great cover design team at 100 Covers.
- My editor extraordinaire, Chase Nottingham.
- My wonderful advance reader team, the Fell Street Irregulars.

www.ingramcontent.com/pod-product-compliance
Lightning Source LLC
Chambersburg PA
CBHW061754190726
48289CB00007B/1952